Locked In

The Locked Series Book 2

By GP

To Dan

Hope this
Locks you in

First published in 2018 by Bloodhound Books

www.bloodhoundbooks.com

Print ISBN 978-1-912175-93-2

Also By GB Williams

Locked Up (The Locked Series Book 1)

Praise For GB Williams

Tense and claustrophobic, with a spine-chilling denouement!" ***Caro Ramsay, author of the Anderson and Costello series***

* * *

"A brilliant new and authentic voice in crime fiction - G B Williams knows how to tell a story and tell it well" **Katherine John, author of the Trevor Joseph series and "By Any Name"**

* * *

"A cut-throat, spine tingling, hair-raising and severely eye-opening novel; Locked Up is THE perfect book for losing yourself in - just as long as you can handle the pace. " **Kaisha Holloway - The Writing Garnet**

* * *

"I really enjoyed this story and even from just reading the book's blurb I knew it would be a book that is right up my street - I do love a good crime thriller!" **Donna Maguire - Donnas Book Blog**

* * *

"Highly enjoyable and exciting to read, I would recommend this to any thriller lover, looking for a book with a hero whose past puts him on the wrong side of the law!" **Susan Corcoran - Booksaremycwtches**

* * *

"The more complex this plot got, the deeper the conspiracy went, and the more my enjoyment levels rose." **Janel Harvey - Keeper Of Pages**

Chapter 1

The door banged open. Everyone inside jumped and turned towards the loud intrusion.

Ariadne Teddington looked round, heat washing out then back into her face. Well aware that she'd been stomping along the street, that her temper was foul, she still hadn't meant to use quite that much force on the door. She certainly hadn't wanted to draw the attention of everyone in the bank. She wasn't keen on being centre stage.

Murphy's Law.

If it could go wrong today, it had. At least the banking was the last thing on her to-do list; after this she could go home, stick on a film or three, put her feet up and drink the Viognier she had chilling in the fridge. Until her mother started nagging about wanting to watch the soaps. She rubbed the ball of her hand as she joined the end of the queue. Given the number of people ahead of her, this wasn't going to be the quick pop-in-and-out she'd hoped for on a dull Tuesday afternoon. Another day she might just walk out, leave it for a different time, but she had to get the accounts sorted, just in case the stealing wasn't over. One thing working with criminals had taught her was that there were more ways than she'd ever dreamed of to scam someone. Besides, she was on shift for the rest of the week and the last thing she wanted to do after eight hours with a bunch of convicts was deal with idiotic bureaucracy.

Adjust thinking to 'a film or two'.

There were four people in the line before her: a female customer at one of the two cashier positions, both of which were staffed, and another female sitting to the side in the waiting area.

Given the quality of the long red coat and the sleek blonde hair, Teddington suspected she might be waiting for the older man currently at the head of the queue. He looked well-established, his overcoat of heavy quality and only a little worn. His shoes—she shifted to check—yep, they were highly polished. Behind him was a mother and fidgeting daughter. For a moment, Teddington wondered why the girl wasn't in school, then the mother's murmur explained it.

'The dentist said it would be uncomfortable for a while, sweetie, but just think, soon you'll have lovely straight teeth.'

'Not zthoon enough,' the girl grumbled, her breath whistling through her new braces. Her hand went to her face.

'Lucy, don't do that.'

Lucy snapped her hand down and folded her arms in a huff.

Five years ago, Teddington had returned to the area and re-established her account here. Regular visits ensured she recognised both cashiers. Zanti was serving, her smile over-bright, slightly forced as she dealt with the customer at the window. Teddington was less sure about Samuel, who might have been serving, but for the fact that no one stood before him and that those in the queue weren't moving. Samuel shifted and looked towards her; his habitual smile wavered when he met her burning, accusatory glare. He turned his head away and looked more closely at whatever he was doing.

Feeling guilty for making him uncomfortable, Teddington sighed and tried to push away the tension in her shoulders and head. It didn't work. She rubbed harder on the swollen redness of her hand. The pressure hurt. She half expected to see a blister there, but it was only a compression injury, minor, and it really should have gone down by now. She placed her hand on the metal of the fixed rail separating the waiting customers from those doing business. The coldness eased the throb.

Maybe she should have got a locksmith in, as her mother suggested. That might have saved her the physical pain, but financially it would have cost her more than she had right now.

Besides, the pain would subside and she and her mother could breathe easy again knowing that only they had keys to the house, not some scumbag ex-lodger who'd already tried to rob them blind. So much for a female lodger being less trouble than a man.

Teddington was surprised to see the manager's office door opening. The branch manager, Mallory Presswick, was a big man dressed like he thought he was a bigger man. In status, at least. The double-breasted blue pinstripe suit did nothing to hide his protuberant belly, the result of his fat cat lifestyle. Teddington was sure he pulled the belly in as he looked at the seated blonde in the red coat.

'Miss Arden?'

He greeted the woman with the kind of smile that screamed 'smarm'. Teddington shuddered to watch it; she dreaded to think how the woman felt as she stood and took the hand offered to her. Teddington suppressed another judder, remembering how sweaty that palm had been when she'd had to shake it. The clasp was completed by Presswick putting his hand on Miss Arden's upper arm.

'Do come through.'

Teddington watched as he led her through to his office, never at any point removing his hand from the client's arm. She frowned at the action. *Aren't there laws against such things these days?* His attitudes were as out of date as the bank's decor.

The door behind her banged open again and she realised that it hadn't just been her excessive force at work earlier; the hinges had been oiled so that the door's weight moved more freely than people were used to. Turning, she saw a man she assumed to be youngish. He was of average height, lean, and there was a small wisp of sandy hair visible, though his face was largely covered by the peak of his baseball cap and the hoodie he wore over the top of it. Instinctively, she tensed again; it was a terrible stereotype, but stereotypes came about for a reason. The hoodie moved directly to the internet banking station, the Invicta Bank logo of a rearing Unicorn filled the screen. The installation had happened before she'd reopened her account, but the rest of the place hadn't been decorated in a lot longer. It was worn and just ever so slightly grubby. Teddington found it rather odd that any customer would come into the branch to do internet banking. That seemed to defy logic, but apparently people did it. The terminal the man went to was surrounded by pastel-pink happy bunnies with golden eggs; and smiles Teddington was in the mood to rip off. She hated the forced jollity of it all. An early Easter might be approaching, but it felt like someone had forgotten to tell Mother Nature it was time to let the sun come out to play. The weather continued to be murky and overcast, cold beyond anything a March day should be.

'What do you mean my driver's licence is "not valid"?'

Teddington shifted her attention back to the woman at the counter. Behind the glass, Zanti was looking lost. She glanced at Samuel, but whatever he was doing, he was doing it to ensure that he didn't have to deal with the problem customer.

'Next!' he called and the older man from the front of the queue stepped up to the counter.

An icy blast shot along Teddington's back, making her glad of the thick padded coat she wore. The bang was sharper, a retort; another followed in quick succession. Teddington's hackles rose as she turned to the noise. Screams from customers and the entry of armed men were lost in the distance as Teddington's world focused on the small black hole that loomed within arched blackness like a giant tunnel in her vision. The hole was steadier than she felt as she found herself staring down the barrel of a gun.

* * *

A handgun.

Teddington struggled to process it. As far as she knew, the only trouble that had ever happened at this bank was about twenty years ago when some graffiti was sprayed on the window, and to this day she was still ashamed of her part in that. This wasn't even an obvious target for a bank robbery. Yes, it was popular with lots of locals, but its practices were old-fashioned, the floor space limited, the staff small and there were six other banks within five minutes' walk, any of which would offer richer pickings. Come to think of it, they probably all had better security arrangements too, which would explain why this gang was here.

Murphy's Law.

There was a gun mere inches from her forehead. The fact that she'd been shot before and survived should give her hope. It didn't: it meant she'd beaten the odds once, but it also meant she knew exactly how painful a bullet wound was. She'd been shot in the shoulder and had a bad scar to prove it. A scar that throbbed like it was radioactive in this frozen moment, even though she knew it was just the memory of pain. That was then. This was now, now was different. This gun was different. For a start, she could see it; this guy wasn't some anonymous sniper looking to floor her from a distance, he was up close and personal. And he was aiming for her brain. No surviving a bullet to the brain. Well, she might survive it, but she'd be a vegetable at best. A lead lobotomy.

She didn't know what kind of gun it was, just mostly squared, rounded top, black and loaded. Her shoulder throbbed. What had she done to deserve this in life?

She shifted her gaze from the all-absorbing black to the man with the steady hand.

She noticed very dark hair in need of a cut over a heavy, Neanderthal forehead and a monobrow. His brown eyes met hers and for a second she registered his surprise. She guessed he hadn't expected to have to be this close to any of the bank's customers. His skin was swarthy. He was tall—significantly taller than her—and a little barrel-chested. As bulky as the thick sweater was, probably picked a couple of sizes too big so he could conceal the weapon, she was sure the man himself was bulky too. Fit. Strong. She didn't want to be hit by the man or a bullet. She could defend herself—her job as a prison officer had ensured that—but in the middle of what was already a hostage situation, that wasn't necessarily the best move to make.

Stay calm, observe and remember what you can.

The cries and sobs of others permeated her brain. People were scared and upset. One man held a gun to her head, but she was aware of others. Leading two other men, a skinhead in a blue suit stomped straight past her towards the cashiers, his two guns pointed at both Zanti and Samuel through the gaps in the glass. The screams intensified.

Another shot rang out, and one of the gunmen—this one in a black suit, white shirt and black tie—glared around the bank. 'Quiet!'

Teddington didn't dare look away from the Neanderthal, but couldn't help feeling the power coming from the man in the black suit. Even standing just on the edge of her vision, he had the look of a man of business. He was the Leader. The screams had died down, but the sounds of sobs and whimpers bounced off the walls.

'Be quiet!'

Every muscle tightened at the command from the Leader. Teddington felt her eyes slip in his direction, though she couldn't get a good look.

'Do as you're told and you won't get hurt.'

That wasn't as reassuring as it should have been.

'Over there with the rest,' the Neanderthal ordered her.

Teddington's focus snapped back to him. There was something about his voice that bothered her.

'Now!'

Even as she carefully stepped back, reaching her hand behind as a guide since she knew there were chairs somewhere back there, she was too focused on the gun to look where she was going. When she saw the little girl's feet, scuffed Mary Jane's, stuck out from her mother's lap as the two occupied the nearest of the customer seats, only then did Teddington stop moving and sink to the ground.

'Heads bowed,' the Neanderthal demanded. 'No looking at us.'

Sinking to sit cross-legged on the floor, Teddington supposed that was standard practice. She turned, putting her back more to the wall, now at ninety degrees from him, more part of the hostage group. Her head bowed, she wished her brain would kick into gear.

No looking at us.

Of course they didn't want the hostages looking at them; they didn't want them to be able to give good descriptions. It wasn't like any of them were covering their faces and it would be a long time before she forgot that overhanging brow. Though her head was bowed, she had good peripheral vision; she could see enough to know where everyone was.

A girly squeal came from Presswick's office. Instinctively, everyone looked in that direction. Teddington wasn't completely convinced that the scream had been female. The door opened and the blonde in red stumbled into the room. The gunman behind her, a man with a boxer's nose and a tan leather jacket above his jeans, pushed her towards the knot of other customers. The hoodie doing the internet banking had come up the counter side of the barrier. He had to catch Miss Arden as she tripped forward and helped her sit with him on the floor, since there were no chairs left for the two of them.

So, Hoodie isn't a part of this.

Boxer Nose had to reach back to grab Presswick, who gave another girly squeak as he was pushed towards the security-controlled door to the staff-only area at the back of the building and told to open it.

Presswick hesitated.

'You only need one finger to press out the code,' Boxer Nose said. 'Open the door or start losing the other nine.'

Presswick's swallow was cartoon-loud. Teddington had always considered him puffed up with his own pomposity. Now she had proof he was just a marshmallow man. His hands were obviously shaking as he pressed in the key code; it took two attempts. Then the door was opened and Boxer Nose and another of the robbers, this one a Pretty Boy carrying several bags, walked through behind the bank manager.

Two distinctly different clicks drew Teddington's attention back to the front door. The Neanderthal had switched off the lights at the front of the building and flicked the lock on the door. The guy turned, saw her looking up at him. As his pistol raised she looked down.

Her heart was thumping, but her curiosity was strong. She needed to know who the players were and what they were up to. Carefully, she lifted her head a little, glancing up like a teacher peering over her glasses at a classroom.

The Neanderthal was still near the front door, his pistol by his side but all too ready for use. The man in the black suit, the Leader, was next. Just behind the Leader, Two Guns stood in the ill-fitting blue suit, two guns still pointing at the two cashiers. Pretty Boy was behind the counter now, threatening Zanti as she stuffed money into a bag. She guessed Boxer Nose was in the safe room with Presswick.

Bringing her line of sight further down, Teddington found herself at the bottom tip of a crescent of customers. Mother and daughter were on the end of the run of three customer chairs. The smartly-dressed man was next, then the woman from the counter, who Zanti had been serving. Miss Arden was the first on the floor, then the hoodie at the other tip of the crescent, furthest from Teddington.

All of them had their heads down and their mouths shut. Good. If they kept this up they might just make it through. Though even Teddington had to admit she was getting a little bit sick of braces-girl crying. Every sob grated on her nerves.

She closed her eyes, internalised.

She monitored her own breathing. Smooth, regular, normal. In control without being controlled. Her heart rate was down; if not exactly to her normal resting heart rate, definitely within a few beats of it. She opened her eyes, saw the crushed pile of the hard-wearing commercial grey and blue carpet. It hadn't been cleaned in a while. She could see deep-grained stains, muddy footprints. It hadn't even been vacuumed recently—there was a small thread of white cotton two feet in front of her, perhaps from someone's shirt, the kind of loose thread that falls off at first wear.

Why are you thinking about cotton threads?

Because there are men with guns in the room and you need to ensure that you stay as calm as possible. Though that crying kid isn't doing much to help.

Taking a deep breath, she carefully extended her view. The guy in the blue suit was shifting from foot to foot. She could hear another woman sobbing gently, and looked slightly up. Zanti. She was crying, trying to control it, but her breathing stuttered as she transferred the cash from the tills into whatever bag she'd been given. Samuel was still in his elevated seat. He wasn't the tallest man ever. His hands were up near his shoulders, but slowly lowering.

Don't do it, Samuel, don't.

Pretty Boy looked like a boy band member in his sharp grey, though Teddington wasn't sure that she'd seen many boy bands wear suits this last decade. He did a double-check towards Samuel.

'Hands in the air,' he growled.

Samuel reached for the ceiling, his face grey. Pretty Boy concentrated on Zanti, telling her to move across to empty Samuel's till. There wasn't much room back there, and as Zanti reached for the furthest stash of cash, she pushed Sam, whose feet didn't touch the floor when he was sitting. He flailed, yelped, grabbed for the desk, and as he started to fall, Teddington hoped to God he didn't hit the silent alarm.

Chapter 2

'So, your intel was correct.'

'I never doubted it,' DCI Piper told Superintendent Broughton down the phone.

'I did.'

The other man disconnected. Piper sighed, suspecting Broughton was red-faced in annoyance and had only called in an attempt to gloat in case of failure. It had been made perfectly clear that if this operation proved to be an expensive waste of money because the informant was unreliable, heads would roll—and Piper's would be the first. Slipping his phone into his jacket pocket, Piper swallowed the dryness of his throat and thanked the Lord he hadn't been led astray.

'That didn't sound like a comfortable conversation.'

Piper turned to the man at his side in the nondescript Transit parked within viewing distance of the Invicta Bank. The surveillance van was big enough but there was so much in-built equipment that there wasn't much room left for the three workstations inside. Piper sat nearest the cab, nearest the bank; Tactical Adviser Jonah Andrews was nearest the back. He had one earphone to his ear, having taken it from Piper when the DCI's mobile rang. As Andrews was dressed all in black and sitting in the shadows, most of the detail of his uniform and bulletproof vest were lost and his black face the most visible part of the man. Piper knew Andrews was younger than him, but the guy had a face Piper doubted had ever smiled and a head that knew how to grow hair, but seemed too scared to do so.

'It wasn't,' Piper admitted.

'What did you expect, relying on information from Charlie Bell of all people?'

Piper had to force himself not to tense. He was sick of having to defend himself on that point. 'Charlie Bell was a damn good DS.'

'Yeah,' Andrews agreed lightly, 'right up to the second he crossed the line and killed a man. Dragging all of us and the station's name into the mud with him.'

That was an argument Piper had heard too often and only some of it was true. Charlie had killed a man, but he'd also served his sentence. Whatever Andrews said, Charlie's actions hadn't actually made that much difference to the standing of the police or the station in the local community. They were the police; any expectations of thanks or respect seemed to belong to a culture long past gone. Most locals just thought of them as pigs. People could live with the occasional bad cop being uncovered. One big headline, then tomorrow's chip paper. It was the police officers themselves that seemed to have the problem. Though thankfully not all of them. Even they got over the occasional negative headline. The problem with Charlie Bell was that he just kept on hitting the headlines.

Piper looked at Andrews, and considered Charlie's defence. What Charlie had done in killing Phillip Mansel-Jones was get a crook off the street who was too powerful for the police to stop. While the Force had rules, Mansel-Jones had force and no rules. What Charlie had done was save at least one little girl's life, a simple and important fact which had never come to light. Which never *could* come to light. Charlie had brought justice, albeit rough justice, where there was none to be had within the bounds of the law. Another thing only Piper knew was that if Charlie hadn't got there before him on that fateful night, *he* would have done exactly what Charlie had. He owed Charlie thanks for that at least; he wasn't sure he could have lived with himself as a murderer. He'd seen how hard that was for Charlie, too. The man wasn't broken, but it had been a close-run thing. And Rhys Mansel-Jones was still around to run the organisation his brother had left behind. Albeit not as effectively.

'Then last year,' Andrews went on, 'he breaks out of prison from his own son's funeral and digs all the dirt again.'

At least a lot of those headlines had been positive. The press had gone from vilifying Charlie for kidnapping a prison guard, to lauding him as a victim of attempted murder at his own son's funeral, and all but suggesting he was a hero for getting a wounded officer medical care until he could publicly surrender himself back into judicial care. It was a typical journalistic about-face. It opened old wounds within the station and rubbed a sea's-worth of salt in.

'He did not break out,' Piper said with deceptive calm. 'He attended his son's funeral and got shot at. As was the prison officer he was handcuffed to. The officer was, in fact, shot. Bell had no choice but to run. And he gave himself up voluntarily.'

'That's not how most of the boys see it.'

'Well, the boys need to open their bloody eyes. I know Bell a damn sight better than any of you. He was my DS. I was in charge of him. I arrested him. I gathered the evidence that built the case against him. I was in charge of the hunt for him. I received him back into custody. And in case I have to remind you, *I'm* in charge of this operation—an operation based on the information supplied by a registered informant. If CHIS can accept his information, and I can, you'd better learn to and fast, because the raid we were told about is in progress and our suspects are going to be running out any second. As your lads are in place and primed, and we've got cars standing by to follow and trap the getaway, with a little cooperation and trust, this op should be sweet as a nut. And that will be in large part down to Charlie Bell.'

His jaw was clamped shut as he turned to look out through the front windscreen. 'What the—?'

Two marked police cars came to a sudden halt either side of the Invicta Bank; Piper was moving from the van, shrugging his jacket into a more comfortable position, even as the first uniformed officer was stepping from the car. The ageing man was thickening around the middle and greying on top. Piper didn't need to flash his badge at a man he'd known for over twenty years.

'Sir!' The constable stopped short, surprised to see him.

'What's going on, Lawson?'

'Silent alarm from the Invicta Bank.'

Piper swore, making Lawson back up in surprise. 'And none of you bothered to listen to this morning's brief? The one telling you this was expected and not to act?' Even as he said this, uniformed officers were stopping traffic and holding pedestrians back. Piper knew recriminations would come later. There would be an in-depth review of every man's action and as senior officer on this operation, he would be first under particular scrutiny.

He pushed his hand through his hair. This was supposed to be straight forward. From Bell's information the plan was five men in and out quick, Piper's plan was Andrew's men would shoot out the tyres and move in, Piper would bungle and let Bell get away. Quick and easy. Ish.

Right now, though, he had to get hold of the situation and minimise the damage. Thankfully he'd had a backup plan in case this happened: he had to make it look like the only response was standard operating procedure. The van was currently far enough back that it wouldn't be immediately obvious from the bank, but he'd move it closer at some point to make it look newly arrived. He swiftly told Lawson what to do, move the squad cars back, block the roads, two-layer cordon. The man was dependable and reliable, acting quickly and well. As a PC, Lawson had more respect and leadership skills than many of his more senior officers. Lawson moved away to direct the other responding teams with Piper's total confidence.

Piper headed back to the van. His tie suddenly felt too tight. Andrews was still listening to the sound feed.

'What's happening inside?' Piper asked.

'Crowd control. They're grouping the customers and staff into one area near the rear of the branch.' Andrews was leaning towards the console. 'I'll pull my men closer.'

'Wait!' Piper ordered. 'An armed response unit arriving too quick could tip the gang off to the fact that we were already here. It'll compromise our man inside. Redeploy by all means, but give it a minimum ten-minute delay.'

Andrews gave him a sour look. 'Thanks, I've never done this before.'

Piper looked away. He deserved that sarcasm. He waited till Andrews had finished his instructions before he spoke again. 'Can we get video feed from your men?'

'No,' said Andrews. 'We were equipped for backup only. My men have individual video for review only, no transmission capability.'

Piper leaned into the van and pulled open one of the storage bays beneath the workstations. He dragged out a box of audio-visual equipment. When he straightened, he looked around to see people from shops filing past, being herded out of the exclusion zone that uniform were erecting around the intersection of Glenister Street and Arthur Road. PC Lawson was walking towards him, instructing two other uniformed officers.

'How are we doing, Lawson?'

The man trotted over, the thick stab vest adding more bulk than the years had.

'Cordons are in place at all three road points, neighbouring shops are being emptied. I've called Traffic to get diversions set up and minimise the disruption.'

Thankfully Tuesday afternoons weren't terribly busy, but give it half an hour and there would be complaints about loss of business coming through.

'I need this set up.' Piper passed over the equipment. 'Close but not obvious. Channel A.'

Lawson nodded, took the box and turned away from the van. 'Regan!' he called as he moved to the rear of the car he'd arrived in. A very young-looking man answered the call. 'I've got a job for our resident tech-spert.'

'How long to set that up?' Andrews asked, now standing next to Piper.

Piper shrugged. 'Couple of minutes, maybe. Sorry for—'

'Forget about it.' Andrews waved away the apology. 'I shouldn't have had a go either.' He drew in a big breath. 'Right, since this is now a hostage situation, who's our nearest negotiator?'

Mantrap open.

'I am.'

Foot straight in.

Andrews' look was assessing. 'Is that a good idea?'

'Only one I've got right now.' He sighed, all too aware of the potential for trouble as he looked at the Invicta Bank. 'What the hell went wrong?'

Chapter 3

As Teddington watched, wide-eyed, she saw Samuel had barely got to his feet before Pretty Boy punched him so hard he was on the floor again.

'Mr Orange!' The snap came from the black suited man who had fired and shouted on entry.

'He hit the alarm.'

God damn it.

'I don't hear anything.'

None of them did, but they wouldn't if it was a silent alarm that linked directly to the police station.

Teddington risked looking up at the men. So, Pretty Boy was Mr Orange, which was clearly just a code name. Chances were, the others would be colour-coded too, though it wouldn't be linked to anything any of them were wearing.

Oh no, the Reservoir Dogs are doing their Dog Day Afternoon.

The Neanderthal was by the door. Two Guns was just beyond the front edge of the counter. From where Teddington sat, he was surrounded by happy bunnies, their jollity throwing his crew-cut agitation into stark relief. The man in black, the Leader, stood casually, centre stage. Teddington wondered what people outside would be able to see.

The windows were full height but the bottom half was frosted; the public would only see anyone who was standing up. The customers—hostages—wouldn't be visible. The gunmen would be, but they were keeping their weapons low. Someone would have to really look to see them now. The lights at the front of the building were off, so most people wouldn't be able to see anything.

Except perhaps the overgrown Neanderthal by the door. While the door was recessed into the bank, and she was pretty sure she'd heard him throw the latch, he was relatively easy pickings if the police brought in a sniper. Was that likely? She had no idea.

The Neanderthal was watching Mr Orange push Sam and Zanti into the main space of the bank. His eyes moved down to Teddington. She felt like she'd been slapped so she looked away. A glance back up showed the man was now looking at the still sobbing girl.

Mr Orange pushed the two cashiers into the group; Teddington noticed that as he paused in the doorway of the cashiers' area, he did something to the latch so it wouldn't catch. As Zanti and Sam half sat, half fell to the floor, they set the little girl, Lucy, sobbing even harder. Teddington wondered how Lucy hadn't run out of tears yet.

Two Guns was shifting again, stepping back and forth.

Best way to stop a disturbance—don't let it start.

The words of a long-ago trainer whispered into Teddington's ears. The advice had served her well in work, hopefully it would serve them all well today.

Teddington turned slightly to look at the mother and child. Lucy was snuggled up to her mother. They were clamped tight together, both staring wide-eyed at Two Guns.

'What's your name, kid?' Teddington asked the girl. She already knew it was Lucy, but she needed to engage the child.

Lucy just tried to burrow deeper into her mother's shoulder.

'Lucy,' the mother whimpered. 'Her name's Lucy and I'm Megan.'

Teddington nodded but focused on the girl. 'Hi Lucy, I'm Ari.'

Though Lucy finally focused on her and nodded, the sobbing didn't stop.

'Shut her up.'

Teddington turned to face Two Guns.

'Mr Pink,' the Neanderthal grated. 'Ignore the kid, stick to the script.'

Two Guns, Mr Pink, huffed and turned back to his job. As far as Teddington was concerned, the only problem was Lucy was now sobbing even harder.

Teddington focused on Lucy. 'I know you're scared, Lucy, we all are.'

'Yous not.'

'Oh kid, I can assure you I am scared.' The weight of the knots in her belly proved that to herself, if no one else. 'But I need you to try to be calm for me okay, Lucy? It's okay to be scared—only a nitwit wouldn't be scared right now. You're not a nitwit, are you?'

The girl shook her head.

'You've just had a new brace fitted today, haven't you?' Teddington moved closer, her voice little more than a whisper. 'So I know you're a brave little girl. I need you to be brave again now. Take some deep breaths and control your tears okay?'

Lucy nodded and she was starting to take some deep breaths, controlling herself, but the sobs weren't done with her yet.

Sharply, Mr Pink turned to face the customers. His gun pointed directly at the girl.

'If you don't shut it—'

Instinctively Teddington put herself between Lucy and Mr Pink's guns.

'—I'm goin' t—'

'Mr Pink!' the man at the door warned as the girl's wailing ramped up.

'She can't help it,' Teddington said. 'She's scared and you threatening her is just going to make her cry more.'

Now on her knees, between Lucy and Mr Pink, Teddington was looking directly down the barrel of another gun. Round and silvery this time, but just as deadly. This one shook more than the last one. *Amend that to way more deadly.*

Lucy could have no idea how scared Teddington was at this point. Teddington was hard pushed to define it, except for another time when she was tied to the plumbing in the middle of a riot and being beaten with her own belt, and threatened with… well, she wasn't going to dwell on that. She had troubles enough this second, she couldn't take the weight of past troubles too.

She looked up at the man, Mr Pink. He was sweating. She was sweating. They were both breathing hard. His eyes were wide and full of anger. Her eyes felt just as wide and full of fear.

A hand, large and heavy, clamped on her head.

'You.' Her head was forced forward and down till she was crouched on the floor again. 'Head down and be quiet.' The gravelly voice told her this was the Neanderthal. 'You keep your kid quiet.' He must be talking to Megan. 'And you—' this to Mr Pink, 'calm down and back off.'

'And you, Mr Brown.' That calm tone had to be the Leader. 'Back to your post.'

There was a pause. The whole bank held its breath, even Lucy. Though her head was down, Teddington was aware that the Neanderthal, Mr Brown, hadn't moved. Mr Pink slowly lowered his gun.

'Of course, Mr White,' Mr Brown said, as he returned to his previous post.

As Teddington shifted to sit cross-legged again, she couldn't help wondering what it meant, the exchange she'd just witnessed. Not daring to look up, she pondered the sight of Mr Brown's shoes beneath his jeans. Salomon trainers, the khaki and brown nearly identical colours. Keeping her eyes down, she could look across the floor a little. Mr White, the leader, was in penny loafers. That nearly made her laugh. Penny loafers were her uncle's favourite. Mr Pink was wearing slip-ons of some kind. With a turn of the eye, she looked to Mr Orange—worn dress shoes.

Whatever plans these men had for getting away, only one of them had thought of running.

A four-letter imprecation sliced across the bank like a whip. Everyone looked up.

'Mr Pink?' Mr White demanded.

'The fucking pigs have turned up.' He moved slightly closer to the window and almost immediately moved back. 'There's three cars, one in each street.'

'That was quick.' Mr White moved forward, looked out, swore.

Teddington was aware that she wasn't the only one head up and watching, not that she could see much through the frosting. It was quick, but then again, the alarm had been hit, and the station wasn't far away. So maybe, for once, things had just worked as they were supposed to.

The suspended moment broke as Mr White turned.

'Mr Orange, fetch Mr Blue.'

Mr Orange nodded once and headed out to the back of the bank, and Mr White turned to the man by the door. 'Mr Brown.'

'Mr White?'

Mr White moved towards the recessed door and the two of them started to whisper. Teddington strained to hear, aware that the man in the quality overcoat was now the one trying to talk Lucy into being calm. She caught his name, Hickson, but tuned them out, struggling to hear Mr White and Mr Brown.

'… can we expect now?'

She watched them. Mr White had his back to her, Mr Brown side on, glancing at Mr White, but watching the street. 'Tactical Firearms'll be here in anything from ten to thirty minutes, depending where they're currently deployed.'

Teddington frowned over the word. Deployed? That was a military word. Did that mean Mr Brown was a military man? Could be. She'd dealt with a fair few ex-army men in her time. Army guys went through a lot and they couldn't always cope with civilian life, but the skills the army had taught them could be used to efficient criminal effect. When they got sent down, many made good prisoners: they were used to hard conditions, restricted freedom, generally—but not always—had a healthy respect for people in uniform with rank. But when they blew… they blew big time. It wasn't a pretty sight to behold. If the

Neanderthal Mr Brown snapped, she was afraid of what he could do.

'What's going on?' The fifth man, Mr Blue, he of the boxer nose and tan leather jacket, came back into the main section of the bank, pushing Presswick before him. Mr Blue pushed the manager towards the others. Presswick sat heavily, clearly not happy on the floor. Mr Blue placed two full holdalls by the counter, and Mr Orange put a third on top.

'The police,' Mr White said, then gestured the bags. 'Did you get it all?'

'Not quite.'

'This is her fault.' The surprise denouncement came from Mr Pink. As he came forward, attention moved to Zanti, who cowered back. Sam put his arm around her shoulders, shielded her. Teddington didn't know how much help he could be, given the split lip and already bruising chin.

'Argh!' Teddington's shout was unavoidable as she fell to her left, her right thigh screaming with pain where Mr Pink's foot had slammed into it.

Lucy screamed and cried.

Pain rung in Teddington's ears. It was all so far away, but she saw Mr Pink move closer, saw Mr Brown shove him back. Now on her side on the floor, she looked over her head, saw the hostages at the other end of the group, saw the horror on Zanti and Sam's faces, not to mention Carlisle's. She clamped her jaw on the shout of surprise.

Carlisle? Carlisle!

A lump lodged in her throat. She couldn't be sure if she was hot or cold or both. Her heart rattled against her ribs—it wanted to run screaming out of here as much as her damaged leg wouldn't let her.

'Do you know who that is?' Mr Pink demanded of Mr Brown. 'That bitch is one of the screws that locked us up.'

'Shut up.' Mr Brown's voice was controlled, his temper clear, nonetheless.

Stunned, she glanced at the gunmen, then looked at the hostage again. Yep. Under that baseball cap and the hoodie was Carlisle.

Not wanting to give herself away, she closed her eyes a second and tried to assimilate what she was seeing. Carlisle. She didn't even know his first name. She just knew him as Detective Sergeant Carlisle. A serving police officer!

Oh, dear Lord! Even off-duty he was a danger, not only to himself, but to everyone here. *If they recognise him…*

As long as he kept his head down, and she kept the focus of their anger on her, this was still salvageable. She hoped. She focused on what the men were saying.

'She humiliated me!' Mr Pink was saying. 'Did a strip search!'

Mr Pink moved closer, Mr Brown was there, his gun to Mr Pink's head. 'Shut up!'

Everything and everyone stopped, even Lucy. Tension radiated from the two men, filled the room.

'Why,' Mr Pink's voice was tight, 'are you protecting her?'

'He's not,' Teddington said carefully, keeping her voice soft, non-confrontational, trying not to wince as she sat up. 'He's protecting you. The more you say, the more it narrows down who you could be, the more likely I am able to identify you. So please don't say anything more, for all our sakes.'

Chapter 4

'We've got video feed,' Andrews confirmed as he joined Piper with PC Lawson on the street. 'It's not great. Could do with getting a higher vantage point.'

'Your men have already got all the decent ones,' Piper pointed out.

'True.' Andrews' smile was slightly on the smug side. 'Problem is, we can still see a problem.'

Andrews tipped his head and headed back into the van. Piper frowned, excused himself from Lawson and followed.

'Jesus!'

Piper looked up, Andrews hadn't reached the van, but the exclamation had definitely come from there, and it sounded female.

'Who's that?' he demanded of Andrews.

'PC Wymark,' Andrews said as he stepped up. 'What's up?'

Piper reached the open side door and stepped inside, using his body to block the light and better focus on the screen. Wymark was a slim-built Asian-looking woman in uniform, earphones over her head, quickly writing. Piper assumed Andrews had just plucked her out of the large crowd of uniforms now in the area. Wymark pointed to the screen. What Piper could see was five men. A tall man in an army surplus sweater was pointing a gun at a skinhead in a suit, a third suited man stood close, and the two figures further into the bank were little more than shadows. They really weren't going to get any usable evidence from this.

It was probably just as well. Bell was their informant, but for taking part in an armed raid, even one where the bullets were blanks, he would be tried along with the others. He might get a more lenient sentence for turning Queen's evidence, but he'd serve time. Again.

'He…' Wymark pointed to the skinhead. 'Attacked a hostage. He tried to stop him.' This time she pointed to the taller man. 'Hold on.'

Wymark went back to writing. Clearly something was being said.

'When you say attacked?'

Wymark shrugged as she continued to write. 'Couldn't see what happened, it was masked by the frosting on the window.'

'Well, at least he didn't shoot her.' Andrews turned to Piper. 'See the problem yet?'

No, Piper didn't. He looked again at the screen, at the two men facing off. He didn't recognise either of them. Now he saw the problem. 'Shit.'

Wymark passed him the sheet of paper she'd been writing so furiously on. Piper was rather surprised by the neat penmanship considering the speed of the writing.

'…bitch is one of the screws that locked us up.'

The words virtually jumped off the page at him. 'Shit.'

'So you said, Chief Inspector.' Andrews took the page from him. Scanned it. 'So at least two of them have been in prison. Which fits with what we know.' He looked at the screens. 'But those faces don't.'

'No.' Piper looked at the screen. 'But there are two at the back we can't see. Maybe…'

'Maybe what?' Andrews demanded. 'According to your informant, only two of the gang have done time. Charlie Bell and Lester Grimshaw. Neither of which are the two men in front of us.'

Piper swallowed as he continued to watch the scene. He remembered Superintendent Broughton's words when he'd first suggested Charlie Bell be taken on as an informant. *His fuck-up is your fuck-up.* It was hard to see how this could possibly get any more fucked up. *One of the screws.* He turned to Andrews.

'Did you get much of a look of that last woman to go into the bank?'

Andrews shrugged. 'Tall but wearing heels, so maybe not that tall. Long brown hair and a thick padded jacket, wearing leggings under boots. Nice legs. Her head was down, I didn't see her face. Why?'

'Doesn't matter,' Piper lied. It mattered a hell of a lot if his instant suspicion was correct and not just the result of a fevered imagination. Unfortunately, Andrews' description ruled nothing out. Having Ariadne Teddington in that bank was a nightmare he didn't want to have. When it came to things getting worse, that was one sure way he could see this getting worse. He pulled his phone from his pocket, grabbing the suspect clipboard from the hook on the side, and stepped out of the van as crouching was pulling on his back. When he had the Dispatcher's attention he read out five names and addresses. 'Yes, check all of them. And now. Call me back as soon as you can, report on them individually if necessary.'

'What are you thinking?'

Piper took a calming breath and turned to Andrews. 'My information was for five specific men. And while there are five men in that gang.' Piper pointed to the bank. 'At least three of them aren't the men we were expecting, so I need to know where the hell these five are.' He so wanted to throw something. Instead he stretched into the van and carefully returned the board to its hook.

Piper stepped back, ran his fingers through his hair and scratched his scalp as he looked to his right. He had direct line of sight to the bank, which meant that they had direct line of sight to him. To his left was the cordon, civilians rubbernecking. Behind him was a police car and Lawson controlling his men.

Damage control.

Piper stepped over to Lawson and the young PC with him. He vaguely recognised her from around the station, but he had no idea who she was. Her light brown skin and naturally black hair suggested some Middle Eastern heritage. 'Lawson,' he greeted, looking questioningly at the female officer.

'Siddig, sir,' she supplied.

'Siddig.' He turned back to Lawson. 'I need a base of operations out of sight of the bank. That hairdresser's should do.' He looked across the street in indication. 'Clear it with the owners. We'll set up there and I'll do a briefing in ten, okay?' He turned to Siddig. 'I'd like to see a Press Liaison Officer down here, too. They won't be any help, but it'll be chore off my back. You okay sorting that?' Siddig confirmed she was. 'Good, give Lawson a hand setting up once it's done.'

With a smart, 'Yes sir' from both, Lawson and Siddig headed for the hairdresser's. Siddig was already on the radio to Dispatch asking to be put through to the Press Office.

Piper turned back to the van to find Andrews watching him, arms folded, face inscrutable.

'You want us to move in there?'

'Hell no.' Piper kept his voice down and indicated that Andrews should go into the van. Only when they were both within its confines did he speak again. 'We'll move closer, but the three of us will remain working in here, and use the hairdresser's as a muster point to keep people out of our hair as much as possible. What's happening inside?'

'Not much.'

Piper turned to Wymark in hopes of a more illuminating response.

She pointed to the screen, to the sound trace that would visually announce if there was any noise. At the moment it didn't even look like there was much movement, so he assumed Carlisle was sitting still. 'The conversation I passed to was the last thing I heard.'

'Well, we've got eyes and ears,' Piper said. 'All we need now is two-way communication.'

'True, but—'

Hearing the reluctance in Andrews' voice, Piper raised his hand. 'Objection noted,' Piper assured. 'It will be noted in my report as well, but there's already been an attack on one hostage. We can't stand around twiddling our thumbs and allow another to happen, and we don't have the time to wait for—let alone brief—another negotiator.'

Chapter 5

Charlie understood the pain in his chest all too well—his heart was thumping. He could taste fear. His lungs were on fire.

This wasn't how today was supposed to be. Hell, nothing in his life was the way it was 'supposed' to be. He dragged in a breath and reached for a calm he was too far from feeling. For now, his hands were tied and all he could do was wait.

For now.

Wait and figure out how to get out of this mess.

Chapter 6

Locked us up. Strip search. Vicious little shit.

Teddington didn't look up at Mr Pink, but she ran everything she knew about him through her mind. He knew her, so she had to know him. Short—no. He only looked short against the overgrown Neanderthal, so maybe five-eight, possibly five-nine. Skinhead, not muscular, but obviously had some strength behind him. She rubbed her bruised leg. A football player maybe. *Football hooligan, more like.*

None of which really narrowed anything down. *Strip search.* She slowly exhaled. Conducting strip searches was a part of the job. Not a pleasant part, and not exactly routine, but if it had to be done it had to be done. There were men that got a kick out of the searches, some who got erections: she'd even had a couple who had peed on her just to make a point, but most endured—some loudly. Teddington figured that Mr Pink would be a moaner, one that complained about a beating from a mere touch. That didn't exactly make him unique. She risked another quick look up, nothing in the face to jog a memory.

But lifting her head revealed that Mr Brown was watching her. Nothing in that face jogged a memory either, though the intensity of his look twisted something in her gut. It wasn't an entirely unpleasant sensation.

Oh, get a life, Ari.

Hanging her head again, Teddington thought about Mr Brown. That brow was distinctive, but not revealing. His height, which was significantly over six foot, should tell her something too. The problem was that when she thought of tall inmates, she always thought of Charlie Bell. *Like he's ever far from your mind.* Annoying but true. She did spend too much of her time thinking about Charlie Bell. Just because he'd saved her life, twice, it didn't change the fact that he was a convicted killer who she should avoid at all costs. It also didn't change the fact that the right look from him could melt her bones, not to mention a quick kiss—*no, don't go there.* And nothing could change the fact that she hadn't seen him in the six months since she'd let him out of the jail. The date she'd tried to make and got stood up for didn't count and she couldn't even hate him for that. *There's something very wrong with you, girl.*

Closing her eyes, she forced blond, blue-eyed Charlie from her mind. The dark-haired, monobrow Neanderthal wasn't Charlie.

There had been other men tall men in the prison at various times, but again, none of them matched the overhanging brow. She sighed. Or maybe she'd just wiped them from her memory; there were over 150 men housed at any one time on the wing she worked alone. It was impossible to remember all who came and went.

The ramping volume of a telephone ringing drew attention to Presswick's office. Mr White stepped towards the room, his head turned to Presswick on the floor, the gun levelled at the man's head.

'You expecting a call?'

Presswick focused on the gun and shook his head. 'I am the manager. Of course, people want to talk to me.'

Teddington stared at the man and wondered how he managed to look both scared and so puffed up with his own importance all at once. The way Mr White's eyes tightened suggested he was no more impressed than she was.

'Mr White.'

There was something about the way Mr Brown spoke that tugged at Teddington's memory. The accent was kind of northern. Maybe he was a Geordie who'd spent too long in the south east? It wasn't only locals who ended up locked behind HMP

Blackmarch's walls. She closed her eyes to see if her hearing would tell her what her sight could not.

'It could be the police calling,' Mr Brown explained.

'Why would the pigs call?'

Teddington's eyes sprung open as Mr Pink stepped closer with his demand. The guy was on the edge, his voice high-pitched. She could see the two guns in his hands held too tightly, quivering slightly, the extensions emphasising the tension thrumming through the man's body.

'They—' Mr Brown paused to clear his throat. 'They need to establish a channel of communication.'

When Mr Brown spoke, it was to Mr White, who had yet to lower his gun. Mr Brown's own gun was in his right hand, the one on the far side from her, and remained at his side. His left hand was slightly raised, heading towards Mr White's firearm. Teddington frowned. Clearly Mr Brown was both comfortable with guns and reluctant to use them. A peacekeeper. *Deployed.* Mr Brown had to be ex-military. He just had to be.

'Why?' Pink demanded.

'Mr Pink,' Mr White ordered calmly, his eyes on Mr Brown, 'back to your station.' The ringing stopped. 'Apparently,' Mr White said, 'they aren't that keen.'

'They'll call back,' Mr Brown stated, 'and if they don't get an answer, they'll get their answers some other way.'

In the pause that stretched, Teddington watched Mr White. He was clearly the man in charge, but he didn't seem to be the one most prepared for the situation. The way he looked at Mr Brown was calculated, calculating. *Interesting dynamic.*

'Mr Orange,' White said over his shoulder, his voice measured and paced. 'Go to the back of the building, see what's happening. Let me know if you see any police.'

The man who had hit Sam pulled up the sawn-off which he'd dangled in one hand and gripped it in both palms as he turned and went through to the back.

The phone started ringing again.

'We need to answer that,' Mr Brown stated.

Mr White considered. 'Diluting the team through the building is a risk.'

Mr Pink was moving around, pacing. He was grinding his teeth now, glaring at Lucy as she cowered against her mother. *At least the sobbing's finished,* Teddington thought. *Everyone cries themselves dry eventually.*

'If we don't respond,' Mr Brown said quietly, 'there's a bigger risk that the police will take a more aggressive stance.'

'Aggressive stance?'

Teddington thought that whispered question came from the woman on the seat, the one who'd complained about her driver's licence being unaccepted.

'Storm in, guns blazing.' The low response was from Hickson, the well-dressed man. 'If that happens, hit the deck, hands behind your hea—'

'Shut up,' Mr White growled, now pointing the gun at Hickson. 'Go,' he told Mr Brown, nodding towards to the manager's office.

Mr Brown's long legs carried him swiftly past Mr White and over to the office.

'Keep it short and get back here.'

Mr Brown nodded in acknowledgement, the office door swinging shut behind him. Teddington watched as Mr White looked around the hostages, the gun moving across them in silent underlining threat.

'Next one of you who speaks, gets shot. Understand?'

There was a lot of fast, silent nodding.

Teddington looked towards the office door, but her attention was caught by the man who'd gone to the back of the bank, Mr Blue. He was leaning against the counter, the loot by his feet. He was calmest of them all, his joints soft, his muscles relaxed, his gun held loosely. But still held. At the ready. His eyes moved and suddenly Teddington was in his sights. He was looking directly at her and all she could do was look back. She read amusement in his eyes. He was actually enjoying this. Then his face broke into a grin, an I'm-having-fun-waiting-to-kill-you kind of grin. He pointed his gun at her. Ice washed through her nervous system as he mimed the act of shooting and mouthed the word boom, his grin widening as he lowered the gun and looked back to the office.

Teddington swallowed, and tried to calm her drumming heart. Mr Pink was antsy, Mr White commanding, Mr Brown intelligent, Mr Orange quick-tempered, but Mr Blue? Mr Blue was what? Enjoying himself?

Her thoughts were cut off when Mr Brown reappeared from the office.

'Well?' Mr White demanded.

'Told him other means of communication have to be found.'

'What other means?' Mr Pink demanded.

In the ensuing silence, Teddington felt the desert fill her oesophagus as she raised her hand, hating that it was trembling as she did so. Mr White spotted her movement out of the corner of his eye and levelled his gun at her head again.

'Is that really necessary?' Mr Brown asked.

'I said the next one to speak gets shot.'

'She didn't speak,' Mr Brown pointed out. 'She raised her hand to seek permission to speak.'

Teddington watched Mr White's jaw line clenching. Then suddenly the gun went down.

'What were you going to say?' Mr Brown asked at last.

Teddington looked up at him and while those brown eyes meant nothing to her, she felt there was a connection. She just wished she could define it. She swallowed. 'Mobile phones.' She turned to Mr White who was watching her intently, took a worried breath and went on. 'Look, you don't want your men diluted through the building, that makes sense, but the only phones in this room are the ones the customers are carrying. So, you give a mobile number to the police, and you can take the call in here.'

'What about that phone?' Mr Blue asked, pointing to the one next to the internet banking stand marked for telephone banking.

Presswick tutted and rolled his eyes, 'That onl—'

Mr Blue stormed forward and put his gun muzzle against the man's forehead. 'No one gave you permission to speak.'

Judging by the smell, Presswick must have peed a little at that point. Mr Blue sneered, then pulled back a little, looked at Teddington. 'You.'

She shrugged. 'Guessing it's for telephone banking only, probably a dedicated line.'

'Are you offering your phone?'

Swallowing her nerves, Teddington nodded. 'Okay.' Her voice squeaked uncomfortably.

'Why?'

She cleared her throat and swallowed before she could speak again. 'Your mate over there already pointed out that I'm a prison officer. Which means that I'm the tall poppy here, the last one you'll let go. Logically that means the more use I am to you, the better my chances of survival.'

'Or…' Mr Blue smiled, pure snake oil. 'I take your phone and kill you anyway.'

Cold washed through her. 'That's um…' She wouldn't have put it past the man to kill her in cold blood. 'That's certainly an option.'

'Mr Blue.' Mr Brown's voice was nearer a growl. 'Back off.'

Mr Blue's eyes gathered steel, his lip curling as he turned to the taller man. 'Why are you protecting her?'

'I'm protecting me,' Mr Brown corrected, his barrel chest moving as he took a deep breath. 'If we go down for this, we'll go down a damn sight longer if a hostage gets hurt. I want to avoid that. This is damage limitation only.'

'Both of you get back to your spots,' Mr White ordered.

Now turning to Mr White, Teddington wondered about him. He wasn't as calm as he'd like to think, as she'd like him to be when in command of an armed raid.

Mr Blue huffed, shrugged and sauntered back to the counter, virtually lounging there. Mr Brown still looked stiff, expressionless, as he returned to the door. In the silence that followed, Teddington thought about the difference between Mr Pink and Mr Brown. Mr Pink, a skinhead in an ill-fitted blue suit. Mr Brown in need of a haircut, wearing jeans and an army surplus jumper, that might even be his own former uniform.

The phone in Presswick's office rang again. This time Mr White looked to Mr Blue. Mr Blue pushed away from the counter and went to the office. They heard the ringing stop, then Mr Blue's gruff voice calmly pronounce, 'Phone 'ere again and I'll pull the phone from the fucking wall.' The handset went down hard. Mr Blue returned to his indolent slouch at the counter.

For a moment Mr White contemplated the situation.

Teddington cleared her throat. The way he looked at her suggested he was giving her permission to speak. She hoped that was what it meant, anyway. 'Mr White, you said you didn't want to hurt anyone, so prove that. Demonstrate good faith by letting a hostage go. The released hostage can take my number to the police.'

His eyes narrowed as he looked at her. 'I suppose you're going to tell me who I should send, too?'

She knew who she'd send, but all her hostage training told her she'd pushed the boundaries already. She swallowed. 'Wouldn't dream of it, you're the one in control.'

His look was tight; he didn't trust her any more than she trusted him. Then he moved to the divider between queue and counter, found a slip that had nothing on the back, and with a vicious yank pulled the pen chain from the base. He moved over to pass them to Teddington. 'Write your number on there.'

Teddington did so, leaning on the floor, then sat back up and passed the note to White.

Holding the note between his thumb and index finger knuckle, he held his hand out. 'Pen, too.'

Bugger. She'd been hoping to keep hold of that. With enough force, it could be a useful stabbing tool. She handed it back.

Now Mr White surveyed the hostages.

'Send the kid and her mother.'

Teddington was relieved to hear the suggestion from Mr Brown. Mr White didn't respond. His eyes narrowed as he looked to Megan and Lucy.

'Look,' Mr Brown continued when Mr White said nothing, 'the damn kid's annoying the lot of us, and she ain't letting go of her mother, so get the pair of them out of here. There are plenty of other hostages.'

'You're right,' Mr White said, 'there are.' He raised his arm and pointed the gun. Several hostages gasped and leant away from his aim. Megan hugged Lucy closer, the girl gripping her mummy for dear life, burying her face and sobbing again. The gun, however, was pointed directly to the well-dressed man at Megan's side. Mr White's gaze was also concentrated on Hickson. 'You. Get up.'

Polished shoes shifted and Teddington moved to her right to give the man room. The high gloss of his shoes, the precision of the crease in his trousers and the way he stood very erect, not cowering from the gun pointed directly at his chest, all added together in Teddington's mind. No wonder Mr White wanted to get rid of him. Hickson had military bearing; he'd shown some familiarity with hostage situations in what he'd advised the others to do earlier. This guy was a potential problem for the gang—his presence could foil their plans. Slowly and carefully, Hickson stepped around Teddington. Raising his hands away from his body, Hickson took the note only when it was offered and headed for the front door only when he was told. He stopped a clear metre from the door, facing Mr Brown. All the time his hands were kept carefully in view.

Mr Brown looked to Mr White, then carefully moved to the door, clicking off the latch and opening it slightly. He moved his head closer to the slight gap and shouted, 'We're sending a hostage out!' Then he turned back to Hickson. 'Put your hands higher and slightly in front of you, make sure that the police see you aren't carrying a weapon. The guy on the phone called himself Piper. He's probably in charge.'

Piper! Teddington held herself as still as she could. She didn't want to be seen reacting to that name.

Then the door was opened and the man walked out, hands high and open.

Carefully, Teddington eased herself back, surprised to realise that there was a space to her left. A quick glance told her Presswick had moved to the vacated seat. She couldn't entirely avoid rolling her eyes as she turned her head forward and down.

Lucy was crying again.

Chapter 7

Piper's stomach was in knots. His wife might be right, perhaps he should see his doctor and check this wasn't an ulcer. He wanted to throw something, preferably break something.

It had been clear that he'd spoken to two different men on the phone. He thought the first one might have been Charlie disguising his voice, but he couldn't be sure. He had no idea who the second man was. He eased the knot of his tie and remembered all those months ago when this started.

He'd met Charlie by accident. Carlisle sometimes got better results on his own and the DS needed to grow into the job to move to the next level, so Piper had let him go do his thing and waited in the nearby pub. Then Charlie had walked in. He'd never seen the younger man so lost or defeated. Everything about Charlie screamed 'beaten' from the lack of cleanliness and the body odour to the unwashed clothes and the obvious weight gain. When he'd told Piper he couldn't get a job but thought he'd been offered a place on a blag, Piper's ears had pricked up. The way forward was obvious to Piper. He hadn't said anything to Charlie, just told him to shape up—other things needed to be done first. Other things he wasn't going to forget doing in a hurry.

He had gone to Detective Chief Superintendent Broughton's office. They'd met as colleagues with mutual respect, possibly even friendship, but Piper had known that there was a strong likelihood that would change by the time the meeting was concluded.

'What's the problem, Matthew?' Broughton asked, indicating Piper should take one of the visitor chairs as he took his place behind the big dark wood desk.

Piper took a deep breath. 'I want to register a new informant, sir.'

Broughton looked rather amused and smiled. 'I'm not CHIS, you don't need to talk to me to do that.'

'No, sir, not usually, but this is a little different.'

Broughton was still smiling. A good sign: he was in a good mood. 'Why?'

'It's the er… it's the informant, sir.'

'Who is it?'

'Charlie Bell.'

Broughton's smile slid off his face like an avalanche from the Matterhorn. 'You are fucking kidding me?'

Piper had expected a reaction from Broughton, but hadn't expected quite so much venom in the tone. 'No, sir, I'm not kidding. That's why I wanted to run it by you first.'

'We, and the prison service, are still reeling from the consequences of the last time that man set foot in this station. And don't think I don't know what happened in cell four.'

'Nothing happened in cell four.'

'We only have their word for that.'

'And we only have our own dirty little minds to say anything to the contrary.'

An uncomfortable pause allowed that truth to fester in the open until by mute and mutual consent, it was swept back under the carpet.

'Why,' Broughton said with careful deliberation, 'would I allow this? Why on earth would you even suggest it?'

Piper went carefully through his thought processes, the position he thought Bell could work his way into, along with the potential implications of that. Broughton didn't look wholly convinced.

'He was a good officer,' Piper said. 'You once even said he reminded you of you at that age.'

Broughton scowled at the memory. 'I never killed a man.'

'No, sir.'

'I never appointed myself as judge, jury and executioner.'

'No, sir.'

The DCS was rather red-faced and angry as he looked across the desk. In a sudden move that nearly made Piper jump, Broughton was on his feet. He marched the short distance to the window, where he stood looking out, his back to the junior officer. For a moment Piper wasn't sure what to do.

'You're sure about the Mansel-Jones connection?' Broughton snapped.

He wasn't at all sure, but every instinct was twitching. 'It's impossible to be wholly sure, but it's a distinct possibility, sir.'

Broughton contemplated the point.

Piper waited. He knew if he pushed Broughton he'd lose out. He had to let the man come to his own decision.

'Then do what you believe is right.'

'Thank you, sir.' Piper rose.

'Not so fast.' Broughton turned to face Piper. 'If you do this, you're his handler. His fuck-up is your fuck-up. Understood?'

Of course he'd understood, he still understood even as he carefully placed the phone back on the van shelf. It was wired in to ensure that the conversation was recorded. He took a deep breath.

His fuck-up is your fuck-up.

Piper could only pray that this didn't get any more fucked up.

'Now what?' Andrews asked.

Piper turned to the man by his side, fully in the moment again. Unfortunately, the moment wasn't looking any better now than it had when the phone had slammed down.

His first answer was a shrug. 'Obviously they don't want to talk by phone.' He sighed and stepped out of the van, pulling up short as he found himself facing DCS Broughton. He was like a formidable black mountain. The sun glinted coldly off polished insignias. It wasn't as cold as his eyes. 'Sir, I wasn't expecting you on site.'

Broughton was scowling. 'Seems there's a fair amount neither of us was expecting.' He looked at the man behind Piper. Broughton took a moment to look the other man up and down.

'Andrews,' he recalled the name. Then he turned back to his DCI. 'What's the situation?'

Piper gave a quick rundown.

'And we don't know who the hostages are yet?'

'Only the three employees. Mallory Presswick, Samuel Frankfort, and Zanti Bashir are confirmed as on duty today.'

Broughton glowered at Piper in a way that told Piper there was thin ice ahead.

'Sir!'

Piper, Andrews and Broughton looked to Wymark as she leaned out of the van.

'Sounds like they might let a hostage out.'

As she said it, the door of the bank cracked open. Piper saw and heard the instant of high alert among the armed and uniformed police, and instinctively moved towards the cordon. Andrews stepped back into the van, advising his men to hold their fire.

'We're sending a hostage out!' a voice called.

The oddity of the gangster's shout coming after Wymark's statement sharpened the way Piper felt his superior's censure.

'Sounds?' Broughton hissed, close on Piper's heels. 'You've got ears in there?'

Piper swallowed, answered in a whisper. 'DS Carlisle's in there, he's wearing a mike and he's under strict instructions not to intervene unless there's an actual threat to life.'

'That was not part of the plan I approved.'

'No, sir, last-minute addition. Carlisle's idea.'

'That boy's too gung-ho, trying to prove himself.'

Piper had to agree with the gruff denouncement. Carlisle had potential, but there was something about him that meant he was never going to be a great officer. He was a touch too hotheaded; not over the top, but enough to bubble to the surface just when Piper didn't need it to. He missed Bell's level-headedness at his side. Not that Charlie had ever been one for sticking rigidly to the rules, but Piper had always known what he was up to, to the point where he had privately warned Charlie not to do something, knowing full well that he was still going to do it anyway. Like going to Phillip Mansel-Jones at night to rescue a little girl.

Piper stepped forward to get a better view as the bank door opened. The first thing they saw clearly were the man's hands, open and up—assuring the viewing world he was unarmed—a scrap of paper held safely between his fingers. A smart-looking man stepped into the light. His hair was greying, his face and poise exuding an air of intelligence and strength.

'Get on the ground!'

Piper wasn't entirely sure who had shouted that order, but the released man stopped as he stepped off the wide pavement and into the road. His expression suggested he couldn't quite believe what he was hearing. Piper understood that, too.

'Now!'

'Oh for God's sake!'

This voice Piper recognised as Lawson's, the respected voice of reason throughout the station.

'He's a hostage, for crying out loud! Don't treat him like a suspect.' As the PC spoke, he pushed his way through the others and stepped into the no-man's-land of the cordoned-off area. He stopped roughly a metre in front of the man from the bank. 'Sir,' Lawson said loudly, 'I'm sorry to have to ask this, but I need to do a quick pat-down to make sure you aren't armed in any way.'

The man gave a single nod. 'Of course.'

Piper suspected that the man was used to command situations. He also suspected he was used to being in command and in business rather than the military. He stretched out his arms and moved his legs to a wider stance, standing still and patient as Lawson did the necessary checks. The PC paused only once to take something clearly heavy from the inside pocket of the man's overcoat. Lawson asked, the man answered, but their exchange was too muted to carry. Lawson returned the item to the pocket and then turned, guiding the hostage through the lines of police and towards Piper and Broughton.

'Are you Piper?' the man asked Broughton, who stood erect and vaguely menacing in his uniform—the obvious figure of superiority.

'I'm DCI Piper,' Piper explained, 'this is Superintendent Broughton. And you are?'

'Brandon Hickson,' the man replied and held out the paper to Piper. 'This is for you.'

Piper took the paper, but didn't immediately look at it. 'Come this way please, sir.'

He pointed towards the temporary incident room inside the hairdresser's. As they went in, Piper glanced at the two women at the rear of the shop. Apparently, they weren't leaving. Piper would have to get that dealt with, but for now, he looked at the note. Obviously, it was a mobile phone number. He had the oddest feeling he recognised it. Chances were, it belonged to Teddington. Sitting together in a corner, Hickson proved clear and concise as he was debriefed, every fact matching what they knew so far and with welcome additional detail.

'The woman who gave that number,' Hickson said, 'called herself Ari. One of the gunman recognised her as prison warden.'

Piper felt the death ray glance from Broughton fall upon him and he tried not to react. He also held back on advising Hickson that despite what the general public seemed to think, a prison warden was an American equivalent to 'governor' and it was more likely that the woman in question was simply a prison officer. Definitely was if his suspicions were correct and that was Ariadne Teddington. Had to be, really.

'What do you know of her?' Broughton asked.

Hickson turned to the older man. 'Only what I've seen. She's intelligent, courageous, and she's prepared to put herself between the innocent and a loaded gun.'

Broughton was frowning. 'Or is that an act? Is she working with them?'

'No!' Hickson was suddenly on his feet, equalling the height of DCS. 'She's trying to calm the situation, she's trying to keep the people—the hostages—in there alive, but she's in just as much danger as the rest of them, possibly more.'

For a moment, tense silence smothered the air as the two men glared at one another.

As a throat was cleared near the door, Piper turned to Siddig. 'Yes?'

'Sorry to interrupt, but I thought you'd like to know that the Press Liaison Officer has arrived. As have several TV crews, and the Police and Crime Commissioner.'

Chapter 8

Teddington was overly aware of two things; the pain in her leg, and the one growing in everyone's necks. Lucy was crying again. Her inescapable upset was in turn upsetting others. As irritating as Lucy was, it was Presswick's tutting that was getting to Teddington.

Man's an arse.

Mr Pink was pacing again, the two guns rattling at his side. His identity was no clearer in her head, but whatever his past, his present was the problem. His tension, like Lucy's, was ratcheting her own tension. She didn't need that. None of them did.

Teddington looked round. Her fellow hostages all looked pale, misery cast over every feature. Despite the cold, she could smell the sweat, the fear. She felt it too. But they had been here a while now—though she had no idea how long, having forgotten to put her watch on after changing the locks—and the fear level was declining. Silence was a suffocating shroud over them all. Teddington shifted, hung her head, felt her spine bowing under the weight. The waiting was a burden she didn't want.

She heard a tut and a snap like a pinged rubber band. Looking up, she saw Brown was removing a latex glove to scratch heavily at his palm.

'Mr Brown?' White barked.

Mr Brown responded by removing the other glove and showing his hands. They were blotchy and looked a little swollen. *Latex allergy.* She looked at the others. They were, as far as she could tell, wearing latex gloves.

'Make sure you don't touch anything.'

The look in Mr Brown's eyes suggested that he wasn't that stupid. Even as he scratched, he turned back to the view outside.

Latex allergy. That made Teddington frown. Allergies were noted in prisoner files. That should narrow things down for her, but it didn't. They tended only to take note of food and medicine allergies. A latex allergy wouldn't be that big a deal, other than for cavity searches, in which case the prisoner would be asked at the time of the search anyway. Of course, latex condoms did make it into the facility. There might be rules against inmate sex, but it was stupid to imagine that it didn't happen, and some of them needed a prophylactic to avoid the spread of infection.

'What's taking them so long?' Mr Pink muttered.

Teddington switched her attention and found Mr Blue's eyes upon her. He still seemed chilled out, relaxed. Smiling right at her, he reached into his pocket. She froze as his hand bunched inside, his fingers moving inside the brown leather.

Does he have another weapon?

Her heart was thumping, her mouth slack, as his hand slowly withdrew. His fingers shifted, a stick of gum appeared and he popped it straight into his mouth. His grin broke as he started to chew.

Bastard.

She glared at his cold amusement before she turned back to the front of the building, deliberately ignoring Mr Blue's faint chuckle.

'Mr Brown?'

Mr Brown turned his head slightly at Mr White's call, but he continued to watch the road as he answered. 'They'll be asking the guy questions. How many? Who? Where? Getting a general sit-rep so they can make plans before calling.'

'Plans?' Mr Pink picked up. 'What plans?' He stopped pacing and stood glaring up at Mr Brown.

Mr Brown drew in a big breath as he turned to Mr Pink. 'No idea.'

Mr Blue stepped forward, and whispered something to Mr White.

Again, the painful lull. A strained silence fell. Teddington controlled her breathing and heart rate. There was nothing worse than waiting.

A guitar stroke shook the air.

The opening riff of *Highway to Hell* with drum accompaniment powered across the room, making everyone jump.

Teddington shifted to take her phone from her coat pocket, flipped the phone case open, swore and refused the call.

Pain exploded through her side, air rushed from her lungs. Her torso slapped to the floor. She was twitching in pain, sprawled and unable to speak or control her body.

'What'd ya do that for, you stupid bitch?'

Tears blurred her vision. She heard movement. Holding her side, she struggled to catch her breath. Hands were moving around her. Strong but careful, their grip sending spears of pain through every muscle as whoever it was helped her to sit. Thankfully the tight boning of the corset hidden beneath the bulky coat helped keep her body from misaligning too much, acting almost like a cast. The phone remained clutched tightly in her hand as she realised that Carlisle was helping her. He manoeuvred himself to sit behind her, letting her lean against him. Though every movement hurt like Mr Pink was kicking her all over again, she took shallow breaths and looked up, blinking her eyes dry. She focused on Mr White.

'It was my mother,' she gasped. Her breathing was ragged, and despite her efforts, tears were starting down her cheeks. When she tried to shift, her breath caught and she sagged, leaned completely against Carlisle, unable to support her own weight.

A collective breath went around the room as other mobiles started to ring.

'Hand them over,' Mr White ordered the close-gathered knot of hostages.

Mr Blue stepped forward. 'Phones and wallets,' he demanded. Teddington trembled as she turned her mother's ring tone to vibrate only.

'Yours?' Mr Blue demanded, putting a gun to Samuel's head.

'We… we're not allowed them.' The man's voice quivered in fear like the rest of his body. His lip was split and his chin swollen, starting to bruise.

'We have to leave them in our lockers,' Zanti explained as Samuel sobbed.

'You?' This time Mr Blue was focusing on Carlisle.

Carlisle passed the man a couple of folded bills from his back pocket.

'Where's your phone?'

'Left it in the car.'

Teddington pulled out her purse. There wasn't much cash inside, but there was one thing she couldn't afford to lose. She opened the purse.

'Leave the cards, they can't save you.'

She didn't care what Mr Blue said, it didn't change her actions. 'You can have all of that. They won't do you much good anyway.' She pulled the picture out and held the purse up to Mr Blue.

'What is that?'

She glanced at the baby picture, longing to see that face again. 'My daughter.'

'Give it to me.'

'No.'

A ripple of wordless disbelief ran though the bank.

'Hand it over. You can take another.'

'No, I can't.' Teddington unzipped the top three inches of her coat. 'Sasha died two days after this was taken.' She slipped the small image down her skin inside her top. 'You can take my money, but you take this picture over my dead body.' She underlined her statement by ramming her zip back up at, the last second pulling it forward so the zip didn't bite her neck.

His gun moved closer. 'Maybe I will.'

She dragged a breath in. With his gun pointed at her, she noticed that unlike Messers White, Pink and Brown, Mr Blue wasn't wearing gloves. It was odd. 'Maybe. But not right now. I'm still too valuable to you.'

'Don't expect that to last.'

She didn't, but he was backing off and she wasn't stupid enough to goad him further. She had the picture of her little girl. That was enough.

Mr Blue turned away and started taking batteries from handsets. He left everything in a pile on the counter. With the various metal casings, fingerprints were likely, but that wasn't her problem. If anything, it was a bonus. She frowned as she saw him pull another wallet from his pocket, brown leather and anonymous. That was added to the pile.

That makes no sense.

With Mr Blue back in place, Mr Brown leant down slightly to speak in Mr Pink's ear. Teddington strained to hear it.

'The more damage you do to her, the more you do to us. Leave her alone.'

Chapter 9

Piper followed in Broughton's wake, heading towards the commissioner as she stepped from her car. He was aware of Andrews following them, standing to the rear.

Paula Sheldrake was a solid woman. Her hair might once have been naturally blonde, but it wasn't now. If she'd been a man, Piper would have likened her to a prop forward. As a woman, the most terrifying nanny ever written into a Victorian gothic horror.

'Commissioner.' Broughton didn't offer a salute to the elected post holder, so Piper didn't either.

'Chief Superintendent.' She nodded towards Broughton, and her glance sliced coldly across Piper. 'Chief Inspector Piper?'

They hadn't met before and he wasn't wearing uniform to give her any clues. He wasn't pleased she knew, or had guessed, who he was. Top brass knowing your name was usually indicative of one of two things: either you were a rising star, or you were in serious trouble.

He knew he wasn't a rising star. 'Miss Sheldrake.'

'It's Mrs, but just use my surname.' She turned back to Broughton.

'We've set up a field office this way.' Broughton led the way, Sheldrake by his side, Piper and Andrews following. 'All calls are being routed to a central incident room at the station.'

Inside, she greeted Leigh Young, the Press Officer. The briefing was swift and accurate while politically minded.

Sheldrake turned to Andrews. 'Men in position?'

Andrews nodded. 'Ready and waiting.'

'Good, but it seems the press are too.' She looked to Young, who was already tapping something into the tablet she carried, nodded in satisfaction that all was ready. Sheldrake turned to Piper. 'This contact name we have, Ari. What do we know of the woman? Sounds Arabic.'

'According to Hickson,' Young answered, 'her accent's pure English.'

'So was Jihadi John's, did it make him any less dangerous?'

'No, ma'am, but—'

Sheldrake turned to Piper. 'What makes you sure that she's a customer and not a member of the gang?'

Piper chose his words carefully. 'There's nothing to indicate a connection.'

Sheldrake watched him with a cool regard. He figured she should've been a police officer: she'd have been fantastic in the interview room with glares like that. Suddenly she turned. 'Excuse me, gentlemen.' As she headed out, Young scurried behind.

Piper only withheld the groan long enough for Sheldrake's determined stride to take her out of earshot.

'Whatever you may think of her,' Broughton half-whispered as he, Piper and Andrews moved outside and stood together watching the interview set up and start, 'she's very good at all this public relations stuff.'

'True.' She'd done a fine job controlling the media after the HMP Blackmarch riot.

'Excuse me,' Andrews said and headed back to the surveillance van.

'Knows bugger all about policing though.'

Piper's lips twitched but he controlled the smile. 'I couldn't possibly comment.'

Broughton's chuckle was low and short-lived. 'Finally learning to play politics, Piper?'

'Sir.'

'She did have one very good question though.'

Piper held his silence but he knew what was coming. It would have come earlier if they had been alone. Politics. He wove his fingers together behind his back, holding his tension there as Broughton folded his arms.

'Ari.'

It sounded more like a statement than a question.

'Please tell me we're not talking about Ariadne Teddington.'

No avoiding it now. 'I've no proof, but I believe so.'

'So…' Broughton rose on his toes then rocked back on his heels. Piper knew this was not a good sign. This was Broughton unconsciously acknowledging his annoyance. 'Bell informs of a bank raid, and it *just happens* to be the branch where his girlfriend banks, and she *just happens* to be in there when the raid takes place?'

Swallowing the lump in his throat, Piper tried to frame an answer. 'Awkward, I agree, but a couple of points. One—It's a popular bank around here. I'm with Invicta, lots of people are. This is my branch. Even the Mansel-Jones family banks here. Two—Charlie didn't plan it, Simon Lincoln did. Charlie didn't know what bank or when until this morning. Three—'

'Three? You said a couple, that's two.'

And that level of pedantry belongs in the school yard. Piper had learnt enough politics not to voice that particular sentiment. Or maybe he just didn't want to piss off the boss.

'Three—Teddington is not Bell's girlfriend. They haven't been in contact since his release from prison. In fact, as far as I can tell, the only contact they've had since the riot is when she opened the prison door to let him out.'

'He told you that, did he?'

'No,' Piper said easily, 'she did.'

'When?'

'Last week in the court, while we were both waiting to give evidence against Len Robbins and Peter Jones.'

As Broughton considered that, they watched Sheldrake being interviewed.

'…secured the release of one hostage already.'

'Yeah,' Piper grumbled, 'she did that all on her own.'

'Politics, Piper,' Broughton growled at his side. 'It's not your head they'll want on the chopping block if this goes wrong.'

'No, but you'll want my balls, and it's not her head that's got a gun pointed at it right now either.'

The deep rumble from Broughton's throat was some sort of agreement. 'What's the uncertainty about Ari's identity?'

'We haven't seen her.'

'But everything else suggests it's her.'

'Yes sir.'

'How's she holding up?'

Piper considered. 'Better than most. We think she's been injured, but we can't be sure.'

Broughton frowned at him. 'Hickson said she'd been kicked, so why can't we be sure?'

'Hickson said she was kicked before he was released, but she might have been hurt again after. The video feed isn't clear, poor lighting and the window frosting on the bank are making it difficult to tell. However, the sound feed strongly suggests a second attack.' Piper looked around. Siddig was talking into her radio mike, turning to frown at Piper as she did so. When she signed off, she headed towards him. 'Something wrong, Siddig?'

'I hope not, sir,' she answered as she stopped before him and Broughton. 'I just got a call from a DS Unwin. He said five of five empty, he also said you'd understand.'

'I do. Thanks.' Piper nodded. 'Oh, Siddig!' He called the young woman back as she turned away. 'Lawson tells me you were instrumental in securing use of the hairdresser's. Well done.'

'Thank you, sir.'

Then he spoke more quietly, to ask what had been bothering him. 'What did you say to the manager to secure her agreement?'

Her olive complexion turned slightly rosier as she glanced at Broughton. Her gaze slid momentarily away, but only momentarily. When she looked back at Piper, he wondered if she was even aware how tense she suddenly appeared. 'I said that if she helped, I'd give her a week before I mentioned the greenhouse in the basement.'

Piper blinked, then realisation hit and his brows lifted. 'You smelt that over the chemicals in there?'

She swallowed again and gave a slight head shake. 'No, sir. But it's not exactly warm right now, and I noticed all the staff were barefoot. Even my feet were warming through these soles.'

Automatically Piper glanced down at the thick soled shoes she wore. He had noticed it was warm in the shop, but he'd assumed it was just lack of wind chill. 'Okay, one week, no notes on today. Thank you, Siddig.'

The tension washing from her, she nodded her thanks and went back to her position on the cordon.

'That girl will go far,' Piper commented.

'Hmm,' Broughton sort of agreed. 'And talking of women who go far…' He nodded over at Sheldrake's approach. After a cursory greeting, Broughton invited Sheldrake to the field office. As Sheldrake was offered tea and a chair, of which she accepted only the latter, Piper noticed that the manageress was still sitting guard by the door to the back room. An Asian-looking hairdresser stood behind the manageress, tightly plaiting a cornrow. Neither woman wore a smile or anything approaching a welcoming, happy expression. It took him a moment, but he realised they were guarding the way to the basement. Apparently, they didn't quite trust the grace they'd been offered.

He turned his attention to his superior officers. Neither of them could fairly be described as happy either.

Acknowledging him, Sheldrake spoke. 'I suppose we have at least established open dialogue?'

'Not exactly,' Piper admitted.

'Why not?'

Piper wasn't sure how to name his reaction, but he tamped it down. Sheldrake wasn't impressed and Piper couldn't blame her. He hadn't done anything impressive yet. 'We only got the contact details just before you arrived.'

Her look was cold. 'Then you'd best get to it, don't you think, Chief Inspector?'

Piper's spine stiffened. 'Yes, ma'am.' The urge to goose-step away was quite strong but he resisted.

Chapter 10

Strictly speaking, Teddington no longer needed to lean on Carlisle.

The initial pain had passed, and the lingering pull when she shifted, breathed or otherwise moved had calmed to a dull ache. Yet she couldn't deny that the human contact was the most comforting thing about the situation. She hardly knew Carlisle, and they had a history of arguing—well, she had a history of wanting to slap him—but here and now none of that mattered. She knew him, and that was as close to trust as she could get in these moments. She wanted so much to ask him the million and one questions that rang through her head, but his manner of dress was clearly for hiding: he was undercover, on an operation. She knew why, and he would have much more information than she did. Right now, knowledge was power; but also right now, questions could prove deadly. So, she rested against Carlisle, aware that his hands on her deltoids weren't for comfort, but in preparation of having to shove her out the way if he needed to move.

'It's your fault I'm stuck in here.'

Surprised by the complaint, Teddington looked around, saw the woman from the counter glaring at Zanti. Zanti looked up at Teddington with big brown eyes. It was an odd moment to notice how beautiful the smudged kohl eye make-up was, but Teddington acknowledged the thought that jumped momentarily into her head before it was chased away by greater urgency.

'What was the problem with the licence?' Teddington asked, keeping her voice low and hoping that the others would follow that lead. This brief interlude with the freedom to speak could be good for all of them. 'Sorry, what was your name?'

'Judith Montgomery, Judy, and they require two forms of ID.' The woman nodded towards the bank staff. 'One has to be a utility bill for proof of address and the other either a passport or a driver's licence.'

'Fairly standard,' Teddington acknowledged.

'Only they won't accept my driver's licence.'

'It's not a photo license,' Zanti said.

'So what?'

'We need photo ID,' Presswick stated.

'Your literature doesn't say that,' Teddington pointed out, having opened a new account a few months ago for receipt of rent, and trying to ignore the odd looks from Mr Blue as they spoke. 'The new account literature only says driver's licence, it doesn't specify you need the photo card section.'

'All licences are issued with photo sections,' Presswick said snootily.

Teddington gave him a cool look. 'Only if they've been issued or renewed since 1998.'

'Which mine hasn't.'

'Then it's not legal. All licences have to be renewed every ten years.'

'Only photo-based ones,' Carlisle put forward, 'and the old paper licences *are* still legal.'

'Those new photo card driver's licences are just ID cards by stealth,' Judy complained.

There was a general murmur of agreement. Teddington noticed Mr White was glaring at them, so she shook her head towards Judy, who looked about to speak again, and hung her head. Peripheral vision was sufficient to tell Teddington the others had done the same.

Except Presswick. 'Regardless of your personal opin—'

'Shut up.' The order was deceptively calm as Mr Blue pointed his gun at Presswick.

Presswick's chest puffed up again, but at least this time he had the sense to keep his mouth shut.

Teddington kept her head low, and went back to her silent search for Mr Pink's identity. To strip searches, she added petty crimes, vicious, and ran the combination through her memory. Ten names came to mind. Not much use really, but it filled the vital seconds until Mr Blue lowered the gun and Mr Pink started pacing again.

The phone rang again and she flinched. Teddington wasn't sure which wanted out of her most, her heart or lungs. The number was withheld. And never had the music seemed more appropriate—she was definitely on the Highway to Hell.

'Here you go.' She held the mobile out to Mr White.

'You answer it.'

Swallowing hard, she drew her arm back and answered, switching it immediately to loudspeaker.

'Hello?'

'Hello, this is DCI Matthew Piper.'

She started at the voice and name, though why, she wasn't sure. The Neanderthal, Mr Brown, had mentioned Piper, so it was only logical that must have been Piper who'd phoned, especially with Carlisle in the bank.

'Who am I talking to?'

Teddington took a breath, realising that she had a very delicate line to walk here. 'I'm one of the customers caught up in this action, officer Ariadne Teddington of Her Majesty's Prison Service.'

There was a pause. She imagined Piper frowning.

'Don't worry, Chief Inspector, they already knew.'

'Thank you, Miss, Mrs—'

'Teddington will do.' She appreciated the fact that Piper was effectively denying their prior acquaintance.

'May I speak with the man in charge there?'

Teddington looked to Mr White, who simply shook his head.

'You're on loudspeaker, Chief Inspector, so, effectively, you are speaking to him. Mr White just shook his head in response to your request.'

'It's my job to resolve this situation as quickly and calmly as possible. Can you advise what Mr White requires to bring this to a successful resolution?'

A bullet to the head?

Of course, now was not the time for sarcasm. She looked to Mr White. 'No response has been made thus far, Chief Inspector.'

'Call me Matt.'

Teddington would rather keep with Chief Inspector, but she understood the negotiator's need for humanisation. 'In that case, call me Ari.'

'Thank you, Ari,' the voice said. 'Is Mr White in charge?'

'He is.'

'Can you tell me what's going on in there?'

Again she had to fight down the sarcasm. Again she looked at Mr White and got no response.

'All's calm,' she said carefully. 'There are nine remaining hostages, including me.' She chose her words carefully, used a measured tone, paused between sentences and watched Mr White for any indication that she was going too far. 'Three male, six female. Three are staff, six are customers.' Not knowing what else to say, she stopped.

'Can you give me names?' The voice came back once she'd paused long enough.

Mr White shook his head.

She swallowed. 'I'm sorry, Matt, I'm being given a negative indication. Then again, I don't know most of them anyway.'

'Can you confirm that you are all well?'

'We're fine.' She was a long way from fine. She was in a great deal of pain. 'If you want confirmation of what the man released would have told you, yes, one of the men, Mr Orange I think, did punch Samuel Frankford.'

Suddenly Mr Pink was there in front on her, his gun at her head. 'How'd you know his name? I don't know his name.' His voice was too high and too fast. Too far from normal control. 'How do you?'

Teddington stared up at the gun; no one else dared to move. Eventually, she took a breath, though her voice shook as she replied. 'I—I've banked here for years. Until a few months ago, the bank name badges had both first and surname. Which is why I know Samuel Frankford and Mallory Presswick, but haven't the foggiest what Zanti's surname is. She's newer.'

Mr White pointed his gun at her head. 'I said,' his voice was low and she wasn't sure that it would carry to the phone, 'no names.'

She switched from looking at Mr Pink to looking at Mr White. She took a careful breath, keeping her voice as neutral as she could. 'The names I gave are of the staff here. The police probably already have those from the bank's HQ. I haven't told them anything they couldn't have found out for themselves.'

His eyes narrowed at her, his lips straight, but his gun lowered and he stepped away.

'What do you want?' she asked again.

'A van.' Mr Pink pointed through the window. 'That van.'

'What van?' Teddington asked. 'I can't see from here.'

'It's a white Transit type,' Mr Brown said, looking through the door.

Teddington looked up, Mr Brown looked back. He was rather expressionless, yet his eyes looked questioning. Which made Teddington question. 'Is it inside the police cordon?'

'So what?' Mr Pink snarled back.

'So, when did it get there?' Mr White was almost whispering.

Mr Pink shrugged. 'I think it pulled up a few minutes ago.'

'Then you won't get that van,' Teddington said.

'Why not?' Mr Pink demanded pointing both guns at Teddington. 'If we want that van—'

'You won't get that one,' Teddington told him flatly. 'Inside the cordon, arrived only a few minutes ago means it's a police vehicle. You don't want that one, it'll be trackable. Matt?' This last was said louder as she picked up the phone and spoke directly too it. 'You still there?'

'Still here, Ari.' His voice was steady, the kind of calm assurance that comforted her.

'A van,' she said. 'They want a van. Unmarked, Transit type.'

'I see.'

The way he said that made her wonder how much of their conversation he'd heard. Mr White was giving her orders under his breath. She had to listen closely.

'Did you hear that, Matt?'

'There was nothing to hear.'

Teddington took a deep audible breath and huffed it out. 'They're saying that the van must be unmarked and have a full tank of fuel.'

'Okay.'

She imagined him nodding, not that that would do much good over the phone.

'That'll take us a little time.'

'Of course, Matt, but please make it as little time as possible.' She hated the nervousness that she heard in her own voice.

'I'll do what I can, but you know how this works. We'll give them something if they give us something.'

Teddington looked up, Mr White just looked back. He neither said nor did anything that gave her direction.

Damn.

'They did give you something,' she said carefully. 'The man that had my number.'

'I'll do what I can.'

'Call back when you have news. And, Matt?'

'Yeah?'

'Soon. Please.'

Chapter 11

Piper found his heart was thumping as he ended the call. Hearing that voice, even before she had clearly identified herself, was both a blessing and a curse. Ari would keep her head in a bad situation and that should be a calming factor; on the other hand, he knew her, and that ramped up his stress levels. Add in the Charlie factor and this could get explosive.

Which was all before he added in the Sheldrake factor. *Oh God, make that 'this could go nuclear.'*

Broughton, he could handle, he could be reasoned with, but Sheldrake? Part of her election campaign had been to make it clear that no man was above the law, and the example she'd used on more than one occasion was Charlie Bell. And now he had to go and face her, with no further excuses for putting that off.

When he returned to the field office, Sheldrake and Broughton were heads together looking at Hickson's sketch of the men who were inside the bank, which he'd managed to cobble together with his fountain pen and a roll of white paper towel from the hairdresser's. The ink had blotted on the absorbent material, but blurred was still better than nothing. Hickson himself had gone, taken to the station for an official statement.

The senior officers turned to Piper as he entered.

'What have you learned?' Broughton asked.

Surprised by his lack of gruffness, Piper took a steadying breath. 'They want an unmarked van with a full tank.'

'They don't get one,' Sheldrake said. 'Did you get any details on the conditions inside the bank?'

'Not a lot, ma'am.'

Sheldrake was watching him. 'What aren't you telling me?'

Piper swallowed. He hadn't considered himself that transparent. But the calm detachment of his training and experience had deserted him today. 'Our contact, Ari, confirmed what Hickson told us, but failed to mention that she'd been hurt.'

'How are you sure she was hurt?'

'We have partial sight from the cameras and sound from our man inside, DS Carlisle.'

'Are you still sure that this "Ari" isn't working with the group?'

'Positive. It was one of the few things that he was sure of.'

'How?'

Time to come clean. 'Because I know her.'

Sheldrake regarded him calmly. 'This is the county town, so it's not beyond believability that you'd know a victim, I suppose. Who is she?'

Piper had to lick his lips before he could reply. 'Ariadne Teddington.'

Sheldrake frowned at the name, her lips pursed. 'You mean the prison officer that was linked to Lucas Bell last year?'

'He goes by his middle name of Charlie, but yes.'

Sheldrake now turned to Broughton. 'Who exactly did you say the informant for this operation was?'

Piper turned to Broughton, whose eye line slipped momentarily and accusingly to him. But there was no getting away from it now.

'Charlie Bell,' Piper admitted in a low voice.

'You trust *that* man?'

'His information put us in the right place at the right time, ma'am,' Broughton stated.

Piper felt pinned by her gaze, a moth stuck to card like a specimen. 'I trust Charlie Bell.'

For a moment the only movement from Sheldrake was the switch of her eyes between Broughton and Piper. It was obvious that she'd been in teaching at some point. He felt as chastised as a naughty school boy. Then she pinned Broughton with a hard stare.

'You're sure Teddington's not part of this?'

'Yes ma'am.'

She turned to Piper, 'And you?'

'Positive.' The moment hung about him like the manacles of a condemned man.

'Fine.' She nodded at last at Broughton. 'I'll trust your judgement on this. For the time being.'

The manacles fell unexpectedly away. Though he doubted that would last long. It rarely did.

'So, walk me through who should be in that bank,' Sheldrake requested.

'Let me get the file from the van.' As Piper stepped from the hairdresser's, he gulped in a chest full of air. *How much of this is going to come back to haunt me?* He collected the clipboard from the van without a word to Andrews or Wymark.

'This,' he stated, passing the first picture across to Sheldrake, who was now sitting rather primly in one of the hairdresser's chairs, 'is Simon Lincoln.' The picture was of a middle-aged man with greying hair and a deep natural tan. 'Officially he imports furniture from the Far East, unofficially he imports rather more. He's the one who organised this heist.'

Piper passed across a second photograph that had been collected during the surveillance of the group in the run up to today's events. The man it showed had boyish good looks, the kind that wouldn't be out of place in a boy band.

'He looks a little Like Enrique Iglesias,' Sheldrake suggested, to Piper's surprise.

'If you say so, ma'am.' Piper wasn't entirely sure who Enrique Iglesias was—Julio's son, possibly—but now wasn't the time to show his disinterest in popular music. 'His name is Martin Stubbs. Originally a locksmith, but he apparently found picking locks more lucrative than replacing them. He was implicated in a safe crack a couple of years ago, but there was insufficient evidence for CPS to take the prosecution forward. If he's in, it's a backup in case the staff won't open up. This one is Lester Grimshaw.' Piper passed over a mug shot of a man in his late twenties who looked closer to his forties. The blond hair was thinning, the complexion sallow and the eyes and cheeks sunken. Even allowing for the always-awful outcome of mug shots, the guy did not look good. 'Grimshaw has form, was inside HMP Blackmarch for eight weeks for shoplifting. He seems to see doing time as an occupational hazard. From what I can tell of his home life, he probably lives better inside than out. He was the one that approached Bell to join this blag.' Finally, Piper passed her over the last eight by ten image. 'This man goes by the name of Andrew Beamish.'

'Goes by?' Sheldrake asked.

'We know it's an alias, but don't have his real name yet. We haven't been able to trace who he really is, not even from some prints Bell managed to lift. He's not in the database, has no known previous.'

He watched as Sheldrake frowned over this last mystery man. That sense of irritated curiosity was one Piper understood far too well.

Sheldrake's lips were compressed as she finally shuffled the images together and handed the photographs back to Piper. 'There's no image of Bell in there.'

Piper turned his clipboard around and showed her the last picture, one of Charlie looking rather serious in his service photograph. 'Didn't think you'd need to see that one.' He lowered the clipboard and put all the images back together.

'What did Bell have to do to prove himself to this gang?'

'Nothing.'

Sheldrake looked up at him, her head still slightly tilted forward, her eyes hooded. Still the look was sharp, pointed. 'Really?'

'He did time with Grimshaw. He's a convicted murderer. Maybe that was enough.' Piper hoped his voice didn't share the quiver of his gut. He didn't like lying to superior officers.

'Piper if I find out you're lying to me, what do you think the consequences will be?'

Guts for garters. Incarceration. Unemployment. It all flashed through his head as acid burned his stomach.

'So,' she asked with only the thinnest veneer of patience, 'what did Bell have to do to prove himself?'

The noose was around his neck, only the truth could free him. Though more likely the truth was the difference between long lingering strangulation and a quick neck snap. 'Not what we made it look like he did. Ma'am, I understand the interest in this topic, but at the moment it's irrelevant. We can deal with it later.'

Her brows rose, her head tipped slightly in question. 'Along with your insubordination?' She didn't wait for a response before she turned her attention back to the clipboard.

His fuck-up is your fuck-up.

Piper's eyes rose over Sheldrake's bowed head and clashed with the glare from Broughton. Would he make it out of this with his career intact?

'I was led to believe,' Sheldrake said as she looked up, 'that none of those men are actually in the bank?'

Piper's gut movement escalated from quiver to quake. 'The video feed isn't as clear as we would like, but the images we're getting don't match, and the descriptions from Mr Hickson were significantly different. I spoke with Walsh in the station, asked him to pick about thirty images to show Hickson, including the five we're expecting to see, see if he recognises anyone.'

'And?'

'And he's probably still looking. I don't expect an answer for at least another half hour.'

Chapter 12

Registering as an informant was probably the stupidest thing Charlie Bell had ever done in his life. He had always known life was a game of consequences, and he had to face his. He was already sick of the price.

He lived in a shitty little flat, one hardly big enough to be worthy of the name. It was only just bigger than his prison cell. The only job he'd been able to get was manual handling at a paper mill warehouse, strictly leave-your-brain-at-the-door stuff. Skulking in a pub hadn't done him any good either. That was the stupidity that had led him to bumping into another ex-prisoner, who'd led him down the slippery slope to meeting Simon Lincoln.

Driven in a big black town car, Lincoln pulled up beside Charlie as he walked from work to home and made him a cut-in offer, following a gesture of 'good faith'. To be carried out immediately. Charlie got in the car.

The demand to prove himself could hardly be ignored. If he was to inform, he had to have something to inform about, and he'd only have that if Lincoln let him in. He had to control his disgust when he heard what he had to do to prove himself. But he still did it.

Lincoln's driver, a big man with yellow-toned skin and black hair, pulled over. They were in the better part of town, near the railway station. The people wore suits, carried briefcases or laptop rucksacks, and they had money. Money he was expected to liberate.

Without a word, Charlie stepped from the car. His throat was dry and his heart pumping. He'd never robbed anyone before. Could he do this?

Moving into the crowd, he kept his head down. These men all moved with purpose: it was surprising that more didn't bump into one another. Without warning, Charlie stopped, and a man whose concentration was clearly on his mobile walked straight into him. They staggered and straightened themselves out. The mid-five-foot, designer stubble moron who couldn't tie his tie properly hurled a barrage of abuse about how Charlie had deficient eyesight and no father.

Offering the office idiot a one-fingered salute, Charlie sauntered on. He took the long way around the back of the station, walking in a wide arc as he returned to the car. Once he was back inside, the driver pulled away and merged with the steady flow of traffic.

Lincoln didn't look happy. 'I didn't see a mugging.'

'Good,' Charlie retorted, 'then neither did any of the five CCTV cameras focused on the station. Besides—' He threw the thick wallet into Lincoln's lap '—you said you wanted a wallet, not a mugging.'

Again there was that minuscule flicker of surprise, then Lincoln picked up the wallet by the edges, opened it and looked through. Charlie watched, showing no emotion as he saw the self-portraits the man had carried. Any man that much in love with himself deserved a loss every now and then. The wallet was padded with credit, debit and store cards. When Lincoln pulled out the cash, there was easily two hundred there.

Lincoln kept the brown leather wallet, but offered the money to Charlie. For a moment he just looked at the wad. His persona was strapped for cash and struggling to make ends meet. Hell, that wasn't just a persona. He took the money.

'The Don would approve.'

That was the phrase that had finally secured him, trapped him. The Don was a figure of shade in a world full of shadows. The Don, allegedly, was a safety barrier that couldn't be breached, the figure keeping a lot of the organised crime in the area going.

No one knew who The Don was. If Lincoln did, then Charlie needed to work his way in and find out.

That money was still sitting in a drawer in the flat. He hadn't touched it, he probably wouldn't. Right now he wasn't sure he'd ever get the chance.

* * *

'How you doing?' Carlisle whispered in her ear.

Teddington turned her head slightly. The intimacy of the moment surprised her. She was still leaning against him, her shoulder blades to his chest. His hands were on her upper arms, no longer holding her, resting there ready to support or shove her if he needed to. Her head was on his shoulder, so in turning, her face was now barely an inch from his. It was all but a lover's embrace. For a split second, the memory of her last kiss flashed in her mind. Charlie Bell. *Damn the man.* She felt her face wash with blood.

'I'm fine.' She offered a small smile. 'As long as I don't do anything stupid. Like move, or breathe.' Her laugh was a bitter huff. 'I'll survive though.'

Carlisle smiled at her. 'You do tend to.'

As she shifted to face forward again, she clashed with the dark look from Mr Brown by the door. His fists—well, the one she could see—were tight, his lips a compressed line. Apparently talking didn't meet with his approval. Fear shivered through her, and clashed with the vibration of her phone. Her mother, again. *Christ.* She refused the call.

The chord was softer now she'd turned the phone down, but *Highway to Hell* rang the second the first call was refused. *Shit.* She looked up. 'Mr White?' Once she had his attention, only then did she answer. 'Hello, Matt.'

'Ari. Is Mr White listening?'

She looked up at him, he nodded once. 'You are on speakerphone and you have his attention, yes.'

Which made it odd that Piper didn't immediately speak again. When he did, Teddington was no more pleased than Mr White looked.

'I'd like to meet you, Mr White.'

Teddington tried not to show her surprise. Why would Piper want a meeting? Judging by the scowl on Mr White's face, he didn't understand it either. When he didn't speak, she raised her eyebrows, mutely asking for his response. Nothing was forthcoming.

'Ari?'

She swallowed, licked suddenly dry lips. 'I'm not getting any response from Mr White, Matt.'

'But he is still listening?'

Her eye line hadn't shifted so she knew Mr White was watching her, not the phone. 'Yes.'

'Mr White, if I might speak to you, one-to-one, then we will have a better chance of successfully resolving this situation to everyone's satisfaction.'

Mr White said nothing.

'They've already told you what they want, Matt.'

'Which I'm working on,' the disembodied voice told her, 'but these things take time. While waiting, a face-to-face will assist our mutual understanding and expedite the resolution.'

Has he been on a training course to learn this corporate bullshit?

'Mr White, it really would be useful for us to speak face-to-face.'

The silence smothered them like a duvet. A 500-tog duvet, heavy and stifling.

Ari swallowed again. 'Matt, I think Mr White needs time to consider his response,' she tried at last. 'Perhaps you could text me your number and once he's figured out what he wants to do, I can call you back.'

She hoped she sounded more reasonable than desperate. Her nerves were shredding, her hand on the phone trembling.

'Okay.'

She nearly dropped the phone with relief. 'Thank you, Matt. And I'm sorry to ask this, but can you contact my mother and ask her not to phone me? I don't want to risk missing a call from you because she's on the line. You can get her contact details from Blackmarch.'

'Will do.'

'Cheers, Matt.' She signed off. Then she looked at Mr White. 'You'll have to figure out what you're going to tell him.'

As Mr White looked at her she felt pinned, instinctively backing away. Carlisle's hands gripped her arms tighter as she pressed against him.

'Don't tell me what to do.'

The words were ground out through clenched teeth. At least he didn't point the gun at her. All Teddington dared do was mutter a tiny apology and bow her head, lower her eyes. Only after Mr White turned away did Carlisle's hands relax on her arms again. Taking a shaky breath, one restricted by the bruising and the corset beneath her winter jacket, she was grateful for Carlisle's presence.

Like a lot of Marchs over the last few years, they'd had great weather, but in the last two days the cold had washed back in. Though today was dry, it was chilly, hence the thick jacket. At home she'd been wearing a thick cardigan, her favourite cardigan. It had lost all pretence of shape or style years ago. The seams were more her mending stitches than the original, and her mother groaned every time she saw it. Her mother said she should throw it away, and she should—she had others. But she couldn't. She wouldn't be seen dead in it, which was why she'd taken it off to come out, but she loved it all the same. That cardigan was like an old friend. In fact, she had only one actual friend she'd known longer and that relationship had cooled somewhat of late. Which was her fault. She'd been a pig-headed fool to take such offence at the truth Enzo had told her. So, the cardigan stayed home, because putting it on was the closest thing she had to having someone to hug her. She wished Charlie was here.

'He wouldn't do you any good,' Carlisle whispered in her ear.

She hadn't realised she'd said it out loud, and huffed a small laugh. 'He never did. Carlisle, can you do me a favour?'

'If I can.'

Their voices were little more than tiny breaths. The wind whispered louder.

'If I don't make it, can you tell Enzo Sanchez that I know I'm the one who got it wrong, and I'm sorry.'

This time Carlisle's hands pulled her back against him, his right arm sliding across her left shoulder. He held her tight, though careful not to touch her bruised ribs. 'You'll make it.'

Resting against him, she turned her head away from the other hostages, blinking to hold back tears she couldn't afford to shed. Now was not the time to be sorry for herself. Mr Brown was watching her again. Again she felt that pull in her gut. What was it about those eyes that called to her? Why didn't she remember such a distinctive-looking man, if he'd been under her care in the prison?

A double trill shook the phone in her hand. A text message. She opened it up.

'That from them?' Mr Pink demanded.

'No,' she said as she closed the message. 'Apparently Pizza Plaza think I don't order enough. They're offering a 10% midweek discount.'

Evidently, the Plaza's persistent advertising was annoying a lot of locals, given the small groans and gripes that rippled around the occupants of the room. Some of the weight of the silence lifted with this unexpected shared experience. *Oh, the joys of modern technology.*

'You know we all have families.'

Teddington looked to her right, to Judy. 'What?'

The older woman scowled at her, like she was mentally deficient or something. 'I said we all have families. Don't you think I might like someone to let *my* mother know that I'm stuck in here?'

Something about Judy, the hardness in her eyes—or maybe it was just a lack of warmth—gave Teddington pause. 'Would you want your mother informed?'

The woman reared slightly. 'Well I do have a husband and children, they'll be worried.'

'If they knew, of course they would, and I'm sorry that there's nothing I can do for you or them. But they're not the ones constantly calling on a phone that needs to be kept free.'

'I haven't heard your phone ring *constantly.*' Judy moved a heavily liver-spotted hand to her heart, pressing it over the Hermès silk scarf looped around her neck.

Teddington couldn't help noticing that the hands seemed far older than the rest of the lady's appearance. She tuned back into the conversation. 'That's because I turned her ring tone to vibrate so it annoys no one but me. Your family isn't causing an immediate problem.'

'Doesn't mean they won't be worried.'

Teddington sighed. 'Anyone with friends or relatives who use this bank—or who work here—will be worried, just in case. Right now, yes, your family will be worried, wondering where you are and hoping that at any moment you'll walk back into the house. The second that they actually find out that you *are* a hostage, that hope flies out the window and all they'll have left is gut-wrenching fear. Would you wish that on them?'

Judy sat back, pale. It seemed the message had got through. Looking at Judy meant seeing the hostages. They were all afraid, cowed. But of all of them, Miss Arden was the one that worried Teddington. The blonde's silence told her nothing and too much. In triage, the walking, talking ones were on the road to recovery; it was the still and silent sufferers that were the problem. This was a similar situation, she could judge how they were coping by their responsiveness. None of them could walk, but everyone could talk. And had. With the exception of Miss Arden. Was she so far into fear she was numb? There was no way to tell right now, and nothing Teddington could do for the woman anyway. Sighing, Teddington relaxed against Carlisle again.

'You're saying releasing your identities will cause more concern outside?' Mr Blue asked.

It wasn't exactly what she was saying, but as these guys didn't seem to like having things explained to them, she kept quiet.

'Then maybe we should release all their names.'

Her eyes snapped to Mr White. She suspected her skin went that shade, too.

Chapter 13

Charlie was worried. Worried about things he couldn't do anything about. That felt like a waste of time, so he pushed it away. He needed to distract himself for a few minutes at least. *Remember why you're here.*

When he'd bumped into Piper in that pub, his old boss had, quite rightly, kicked his arse for being a self-pitying layabout. The words that had cut him with the keenness of a samurai sword were simple, 'you can't be a cop, but that doesn't stop you investigating.'

Simple and true.

If he could bust Rhys Mansel-Jones' organisation from the inside, he was still busting it. So, joining an ex-con on a blag was his way in. The nebulous idea of The Don just cemented his interest.

They'd started hearing rumours about The Don around six, maybe seven years ago. But that was all they got—rumours. Linguistically mafioso, and connected with organised crime. Everything about The Don was whisper and shadow, smoke and mirrors. Nothing concrete. Nothing that linked directly to any individual. Nothing he could even link to Mansel-Jones. No matter how much he listened, what he looked into, The Don remained a ghost.

If he could find The Don before the police, it would be… sod 'feather in his cap', it'd be a one-finger salute to all the bastards who'd turned on him, spat on him, told him he was worthless. He hated the way they made him feel, because he believed them. He had to prove to himself that he was worth something again.

He'd failed his family. He'd failed his son. God, he hadn't been back to the grave yet; that was just one more birch twig to beat himself with. And he'd failed the only person whose good opinion he cared about.

His eyes slipped over to Teddington. What would she do when she found out? Not that he was here; there was a good chance she'd already figured that out, or would soon. What would she do when she found out what he had done to get here? He felt sick just remembering it.

* * *

Charlie felt sick. The copper taste of adrenalin coated his throat. The bad beer wasn't making it any better. He leaned on the sticky bar and figured if this was their best, he did not want to taste their worst.

The interior of the pub, The Prosser Arms, was even shabbier than he remembered from his pre-incarceration days. The only thing the place had managed to maintain was the reason it was alternatively known as The Prozzie Arms. Charlie was about as welcome as a fart in a lift.

Being in here was risk enough; which was doubtless the reason why Lincoln had selected the place. Far too many people knew him from his old life—most knew him as their arresting officer. There again, that was part of the point.

Stealing a wallet was next to nothing, a minor test. It wasn't enough to secure his place in Lincoln's trust, not after all he'd done. Lincoln had suspected links to Mansel-Jones and The Don. He'd know of Charlie's part in the downfall of Peter 'Leo' Jones. If Charlie was going to gain Lincoln's trust, it had to be something major.

As major crimes go, murder was pretty much at the top of the list. The weight of knowing what had to be done was a ten-tonne anchor against the turbulent sea he navigated.

Lincoln had it all worked out. The bar. A random pick up. The alley with CCTV he could hack into. He wanted to watch, wanted to be sure Charlie did what he was told—wanted to gather his evidence.

Charlie had opened the block of flats front door that morning to see Lincoln's car parked on the road side. The big Asian driver opened the rear door and, without a word, Charlie got in. He hadn't responded when Lincoln had told him what was required. Then he let him out the car. Charlie had had to jog the route to work to avoid being late. All the time his head screaming that he couldn't—he wouldn't—kill again. There was one incontrovertible truth. He had to gain Lincoln's trust, and one last stipulation: it had to be done by midnight tonight.

Charlie checked his watch. 10:02 p.m. There wasn't much time left. Looking around the room he recognised several faces. Several glares were sharpened in his direction, most he understood. Then one face caught his attention.

The man was a stranger to Charlie, but he was watching him intently. There was something unnerving about the man's hooded eyes. Maybe it was the lack of blinking. If the guy had been a girl, Charlie would have wondered if it was a come-on. One the other hand, after three and a half years in prison, he'd learned gender had less to do with advertising for sex than he'd realised before. Only he wasn't that way inclined. Deciding not to care one way or the other, Charlie looked away. Charlie didn't recognise the man, but figured if he did start something, he, Charlie, would be able to finish it.

Taking another unpleasant sip, Charlie wondered how much longer he'd have to nurse this horror. He prayed his contact wouldn't let him down. Arrangements had, by necessity, been hastily made that morning, but he needed them to be carried through. He couldn't actually just pick a woman, working girl or not, at random and kill. He wasn't that kind of man. He wasn't that kind of killer.

The door opened and a young girl, slightly tubby and a bit stooped, which given the size of her breasts was hardly a surprise, walked in. The size of the soles on her heels might have had something to do with the terrible posture and inability to walk straight, though, at this time of night, there were other probable reasons for that.

She wobbled haphazardly up to the bar and asked for a zing and topic.

The barman just looked at her.

"Oh get her a gin and tonic," Charlie told the man, "on me."

That was all it took; the price of a single drink and she was all over him. Which wasn't unusual in here. The fact that it was prearranged didn't mean that they didn't have to make it look real. She even haggled over the price, raising him by a tenner and wanting the money up front.

Ten minutes later, he took her hand and led her out of the pub.

The alley was twenty yards down the road. It ran between the off-licence and the betting shop. It used to lead to a school, but the school had been pulled down ready for redevelopment and the alleyway blocked off. There hadn't been any development for twelve years, just a blocked alley that led nowhere. Crucially for Lincoln, there was a CCTV camera on the opposite side of the road that could be hacked into. Charlie knew where it was and was careful not to show his face to it.

The girl, Lexi, was all over him. Her hands everywhere. Apparently, she was determined to have a bit of a good time at his expense. Another time that might have been exciting, but right now it did nothing for him. Lexi worked at the morgue and had been surprisingly eager to help when he'd explained the problem. They'd always got on; he knew she was slightly twisted in her choice of lifestyle, but he wouldn't judge her for it, only use her for it. The turn-off might also come from knowing her buff boyfriend, Pip, and his roid-head mates who would happily beat seven bells out of Charlie if anything actually happened to Lexi. It also didn't help that he knew the enlarged breasts were fakes prepared by her boyfriend, a surprisingly talented special effects enthusiast. He was an event organiser who did most of the work for the local zombocalypse attraction.

Without going too far into the alley, just enough so they were only half in shadow, Charlie pressed Lexi to the wall. Leaning down he pressed his mouth to her, surprised when she deepened the kiss, even more surprised when he discovered she had a tongue stud. Careful to avoid the breasts, just in case he showed up their fakeness, he raised his hand to her throat.

'Squeeze harder,' she whispered when he broke their kiss to take in air.

'I'll hurt you.'

'Good.'

Suddenly her hands were in his hair, it needed a cut and she grabbed a handful to pull his head back. His grip tightened, hers did too. For a moment he read increased pleasure in her eyes. He was worried about the girl, not because he'd hurt her, but the idea of getting pleasure from being strangled just seemed odd to him. He shook her a little and she changed her fake sex action for fake fight action. Thankfully he'd got her pinned against the wall, he suspected she might have kneed him in the nuts otherwise, he was certain to have bruises on his calves from the way her heels cut into him.

'Ease up, Lexi,' he learned forward to whisper in her ear, 'I've still got to walk away from this remember. And make sure you look at that camera.'

Soon enough her struggles diminished, stopped, and she sagged against him. Once he was certain she was ready to play dead, he leaned slightly back, gathered her against him before starting to lay her on her back. Her feet were to towards the entrance of the alley, her torso and head in shadow. Charlie used his body to block the camera's view of Lexi as much as possible. He figured Lincoln would still see enough, but not enough to know what Charlie was really up to.

Lexi lay prone on the cold, filthy and frankly stinking alley floor as he pulled a bag from his pocket. He lay the bag to one side, pulled out some items ready for use. The first was a scalpel, one Lexi herself had given him earlier. He pulled the safety cap off.

'Be gentle with me, Tiger,' she whispered, her lips barely moving.

'Hush now, or I won't let Pip spank you later.'

'Spoilsport.'

First thing, Charlie pushed up her faux-leather jacket and cut away the T-shirt exposing what to the naked eye was clearly plastic, but would look real enough on black and white CCTV. With precision and care he pushed the scalpel into the plastic above her clavicle. The spurt of blood that shot into his eye was a surprise. He tried to blink it away, but had to reach instead for a wet wipe to clear the gloop. As he did so, a dark pool spread from Lexi's shoulder. Thank God it wasn't real blood, or at least not hers.

Returning to his work, he made a full slit across her shoulder. Lexi had said that there were only two ways to get the heart out: break open the chest or delve into the ribcage from above or below. Below and up was easier, above and down was easier to fake. 'Blood' pouring over the floor, Charlie quickly rolled his sleeve up, and forced his hand into the slit in her shoulder. There wasn't any real resistance, but he had to make it look good. He had to hurry too. The CCTV could be hacked, but it was still monitored, he wasn't sure how long he would have before the first responding officer got here.

He walked his hand down, able to feel the swell of her real breast under his palm, and the feel of something that felt like hard kidney slipping over his hand. That had to be the heart. He twisted his hand, took hold of it and pulled his hand back.

He pushed down the nausea of knowing he had an actual human heart in his hand, one that looked ripped from a body rather than cut, as there was a hole where an artery would have gone in.

'Did you actually tear this out?' He placed the thing on Lexi's chest and wiped his hand.

'Authenticity.'

'Warmth?' The sound of opening up a plastic bag covered his word.

'Sat it on a hot water bottle for an hour before I come ou'.' Her accent was slurred as she avoided moving her lips.

Turning the bag inside out, he grabbed the heart and tipped it into the bag. Concurrently wiping blood off the outside as he ziplocked it, he put it into the large pocket of his jacket. He took a moment to wipe the last off his hand and bung the soiled wipes into a second bag along with the re-capped scalpel. That bundle went into the other pocket.

'They'll be here soon.'

Pushing himself away, forcing himself not to look back, Charlie rushed away from the area. Already he could hear sirens of approaching emergency vehicles. He prayed it was the crew he'd put on standby. If it was another crew, their discovery that Lexi was very much alive would not go down well and might even give him away before he got to Lincoln.

Two minutes later he met with Lincoln and passed the prize across.

"It's still warm."

"What did you expect?"

* * *

Lexi.

Charlie thought about her. Alexandra Galfario.

So far they'd kept the wraps on that, but it couldn't last forever. It was going to come out at some point and God alone knew what would happen when it did.

Pulling away from the all too familiar downward spiral, Charlie shook the memories from his head to concentrate on the here and now.

Chapter 14

Piper scrubbed his hands over his face and stepped from the van. Andrews had gone ahead to advise Broughton what had happened while he stayed in the van to call Family Liaison. Strictly speaking, he should have made the call from the meeting point, but he didn't need extra scrutiny from Sheldrake. The constable who answered his call simply accepted the address and the direction to get Family Liaison out there to be with Mrs Whittaker. As Piper walked along the street, a mere five steps, he ignored the calls from the TV journalist across the way. He vaguely recognised her face from the local news, but couldn't be bothered to remember her name. He disappeared into the field office without a word.

'I've spoken to the Family Liaison,' Piper said in answer to Sheldrake's question as he joined the knot of officers in the front corner of the hairdresser's, 'they're going to send someone over to see Mrs Teddington's mother.'

'Do they have a contact at the prison to get the details?'

Piper regarded Sheldrake for a moment, trying not to react to the fact that yet again she'd asked the very question he didn't want to answer. 'I've a good memory. I know Teddington's address from previous dealings, and I know she lives with her mother. There's no need to make a delay by contacting the prison.'

'According to Andrews here, that's what Teddington told you to do. Why would she ask that, if your personal relationship with her means you're already aware of her address?'

Piper controlled his reaction to her tone, but his jaw was tight as he spoke, 'I do not have a personal relationship with Mrs Teddington. I have been to her home twice.' That was a small lie, but the third visit, chronologically the second, was one that had never made it to any official report. He wasn't going to report that now. 'First time in connection with Bell's running after the funeral, second time in connection with the riot. Ari's not to know that I've a good memory for names and addresses. She probably thought she was being helpful, and if I were anyone else, I *would* need to go to the prison for the contact details. Don't forget that she's already the target for hate from the gunmen in there because she's been recognised as a prison officer. If she made it clear we already know each other, she'd only increase her present risk level.'

'Is it possible to increase her risk level?'

Piper swallowed as he looked over Sheldrake's head to consider the point. What he saw when he contemplated the worst-case scenarios wasn't pretty. He looked back to the commissioner. 'Probably not, but pissing off gunmen is always best avoided.' *Pissing off the Police and Crime Commissioner and your commanding officer isn't recommended either, and it looks like that's where I'm going.*

'And yet you're still convinced that she's not in on this operation?'

'Yes,' Broughton insisted.

Piper was glad he and Broughton were in agreement on something for once.

'Hhmm.' Sheldrake took a deep breath, glancing between them. Piper felt the urge to squirm but controlled it. Finally, she pinned him with the kind of hard stare Peruvian bears would be proud of. 'Why do you think it was a good idea to register Bell as an informant?'

Piper was getting sick of having to defend his decision. 'Charlie Bell was one of the best officers I ever worked with. He's intelligent, capable and honest.'

'He's a murderer and apparently a bank robber,' Sheldrake threw back.

'He's a good man!'

'Yeah, sure, amazing someone hasn't proposed him for canonisation.'

A ragged clearing of a throat sliced the air between them and they turned to Young, the Press Officer, who made a small movement of her eyes and head to indicate behind her. Piper saw in the mirrors behind Sheldrake that they were being watched with intense interest by other plainclothes officers and various uniforms. The owners had been cleared out. Piper's eyes flicked back to Sheldrake. This wasn't the time or, more importantly, the place for this discussion. He flexed his shoulders and dragged in a deep breath, releasing it slowly.

At last Piper had to say something. He didn't usually get the urge to fill silences, but felt it was important here. 'We know who we were expecting to be here, but clearly they aren't. Why things changed, we don't know. I requested a check on the mens' addresses. None of them are at home, but that really isn't confirmation of anything. Right now I'm treating this as I would any other robbery, as if I have no idea of who is in there or why.'

'Which is pretty much the truth right now, isn't it, Inspector?'

'Yes,' the word was forced out through nearly clenched teeth, 'and it's Chief Inspector.' *And that crashing silence is the death knell of my career. Still, may as well be hanged for a sheep as a lamb.* 'What they want, just to remind you, is a van.'

'No.'

Sod the sheep, let's go for the flock. 'No? That's a really bad idea.'

'All the time they're in the bank, *Chief* Inspector, they're contained. It's bad enough we've endangered the lives of the nine civilians in that building; I won't allow the endangerment of any more by giving mad men with guns free rein to roam. While we have them contained, they stay contained. Clear?'

Piper clenched his jaw to avoid grinding his teeth.

* * *

Teddington looked at her palm. It wasn't sore any more. Or maybe she just couldn't feel it because of all the newer aches and pains.

Today was her rota day off, but she'd been offered overtime to help with one of the inmate training courses. She'd said no so she could change all the house locks. If she hadn't, she'd be safe at work, in prison, and knowing she'd be going home safe in about… she checked the time on her phone… ten minutes. One more bloody thing to hate that thieving scumbag bitch of a lodger for. That particular problem was in the past, though. For now, she had this problem to deal with.

Would they really release the hostages' names? She wasn't sure how she felt about that. Her mother knowing was a necessary evil; but how would the families of the others feel?

'You.' At the indiscriminate call, all the hostages looked up to Mr White. 'Is that a monitor or a TV?' He pointed to the 32-inch screen near the counters, the one surrounded by annoying, ubiquitous clusters of Easter eggs and overly happy bunnies.

When no one answered his question, Mr White stepped up and pushed the muzzle of his gun into Samuel's temple. 'I asked you a question.'

'T-t-t-TV.'

'Then get up and get it on a news channel.'

Samuel was clearly wobbly as he did so. He was also clearly too short; he stood on tiptoes and reached up. Barely able to touch the buttons on the side of the screen, he just about stretched enough to make a few stabs and channel changes, and the 24-hour news channel appeared.

'What about sound?'

'Can't reach those buttons, they're even higher up.'

'Useless boy,' Presswick muttered.

Teddington's head snapped around and glared. The bank manager didn't even bother to notice the censure.

'Get the sound on!' Mr Pink put his oar, and one of his guns, in.

'I ca-ca-can't.' Samuel was near tears.

Mr Pink was clearly out of patience. For a second Teddington thought Mr Pink would shoot the cashier. Mr White reached out, jolted Samuel's head forward, smacking it into the wall below the TV.

'Back to your seat, short arse. You…' Mr White glowered in Mr Pink's direction. 'Back to your post.'

As Samuel stumbled back to his place on the floor and Mr Pink went to the front of the building, Mr White reached up and found the volume control himself. Teddington could see a lump rising from Samuel's forehead, but the skin wasn't broken, it hadn't been that hard a blow. Thankfully. A concussion was the last thing any of them needed.

Zanti reached out and took Samuel's face in both hands to examine his forehead. 'Bruised, but you'll live.'

As Teddington watched, Samuel's face went from white to pink. Was he a bit soft on his colleague? Given the skin colours, Zanti's head scarf and the stereotypical Jewish-motherishness of Samuel's mum, Teddington doubted that relationship was worth the effort of pursing. She remembered the day she'd seen Mrs Frankfort in the branch. Poor Samuel had been so awkward, she'd grown embarrassed just watching.

'Pathetic.'

The word stunned several of the gathered hostages, and almost all turned to Presswick. Presswick was sneering down at Samuel.

'You can't do anything right can you?'

Samuel had been tentatively touching the growing lump on his forehead, but now he looked up at his boss, his top lip drew back, and he let every ounce of personal loathing show. 'What would you know? You just don't do anything. You're all high and mighty like you're king of the world, expect the rest of us to bow and scrape, while you sit on your fat backside doing bugger all. Trombenik!'

Never having expected Samuel to have such fight in him, Teddington was rather impressed, though she'd rather Samuel had followed his obviously usual route of just taking the punishment.

'How dare you!' Presswick shot to his feet. 'You lazy good for—'

'Sit down!' The roar came from Mr Blue, who was again pointing his gun at Presswick.

The big man deflated and sat back down. His chair groaned, thrumming through the strained air like a jumping bean on a kettle drum.

Mr Blue went back to his lounging.

'You'll be sorry for what you just said,' Presswick hissed the words at Samuel.

Seeing him drag air into his lungs, Teddington feared the smaller man's response, but then she saw Samuel's eyes move. His attention had shifted to Lucy, who was sobbing again. Teddington watched as Samuel took one last evil look at Presswick before he shifted to sit cross-legged, his head bowed. Others might think him a coward, but Teddington internally thanked the cashier for having the sense not to escalate the situation. He really was the bigger man after all.

Another weighty silence descended. Waiting was all they could do, and it was dragging at them all. Teddington wasn't the only one who jumped when her phone beeped. She checked the text. 'This one is from the police. I have their number, whenever you want to contact them.' As she spoke, she started programming the number into her phone for easy use later.

'Three five,' Carlisle whispered in her ear.

She moved between the phone and the text screens, checked again, realised she'd transposed the numbers. She changed the five and three, added the last seven and saved the combination.

The TV, which was now loud enough to hear, but not too loud, seemed to have drawn everyone's attention. Mr Blue wasn't bothered by it; the position he was in, he'd struggle to see the screen. On the other side of the room, Mr Brown was still watching what was happening outside, but again as Teddington watched him, he shifted, returned her regard. That indefinable connection jumped in her gut again. She swallowed.

A noise behind, and the way Mr Brown looked over her head, made her turn. Mr Blue was going into the manager's office. He reappeared a moment later with a pad and pen in hand. He thrust them towards Samuel Frankfort, who was now the furthest from Teddington. 'Write your name and pass it on.'

Leaving him to get on with it, Mr Blue moved over to whisper with Mr White. As he turned, he caught her watching him and held her gaze. Finishing his conversation, he raised his gun towards her, mimed shooting her, mouthing the boom of the bullet. His mouth turned up in a vicious smile. She imagined blood-sucking fangs extending—

Oh, get a grip.

'Mr Blue,' Mr White said, 'don't you have a job to complete?'

Mr Blue disappeared into the back of the bank. The staff-only area.

The pad appeared at her side. Carlisle was writing on it. She was surprised that he wrote his own name, though she hadn't known his first name was Dominic. He pushed the pad towards her, but she saw no reason to add her own name. The police already had it. She looked down the list, willing to bet that most, if not all, of these people normally had better handwriting. She wasn't entirely convinced by the blonde's name, Beth Arden, but fans did all sorts of weird things. Changing a name by deed poll was relatively minor. But what did it say about a woman to be that hung up on her make-up brands?

She sighed, looked up and saw Mr White striding over to Mr Pink, who was shifting his weight from foot to foot to a beat that certainly didn't match the rhythm of the questions on the TV's mid-afternoon movie review slot. Mr White put his hand on Mr Pink's shoulder with a grip that looked really quite hard. Mr Pink stopped swaying, but it was only a heartbeat or two before his foot started bouncing. She remembered a similar nervous tic on her ex-husband, Edward, and the constant movement of his feet in her peripheral vision. It wound her up like a top. It was quite possibly Ward's most annoying habit. Well, that and turning his back on her when she'd needed him most. Still, another of yesterday's problems.

The worrying thing, of course, was that Mr Pink was brimming over with nervous energy—a bad thing in a man carrying two guns. A very bad thing.

Mr White had a short exchange with Mr Brown, then spotted the pad beside Teddington. 'That the list of names?'

'It is.'

Mr White looked down the list, though it was upside down to him. 'It's one short.'

'They already have my name.'

Mr White's gaze was scrutinising, assessing, as he decided whether he would react or not.

The silence weighed too heavily. The urge to break it was inescapable. 'You really want to do this?'

'Why not?' He shrugged. 'Maybe if the police have names, they'll start seeing you lot as humans. They might even get their arses in gear to get the van, so we don't have to start hurting people.'

If that was meant to scare her, it did. But more worryingly, it made Lucy whimper. The last thing she wanted or needed was for the kid to kick off again.

'Okay. If that's what you want, I'll call Matt and read him the list.' She brought up the phone.

'No, not you,' Mr White said. 'Get the kid to read it.'

Teddington was hardly surprised when Lucy wailed a 'no' and gripped tighter to her mother. Presswick's tut earned him a dirty look.

'If you've got a problem with the kid,' Sam snapped, 'why don't you move away and let Zanti or your visitor…' He indicated to Miss Arden. 'Have your seat?'

Teddington thought everyone in the room was stunned by Sam's outburst, but no one looked overly surprised that Presswick just drew in a breath, tipped his chin up and looked away to the front windows. Of course, all of this and all of them were so far beneath him.

Looking up at Lucy, Teddington shifted, the pain in her side making her fall back. Thankfully Carlisle caught her.

'Cheers.'

'What do you think you're doing?' Mr White demanded.

'Help me sit forward.' Teddington gritted her teeth as Carlisle pushed her gently. She shifted her legs to the side, leaning on one arm, and holding her ribs with the other. The phone was on the floor. She looked up at Mr White, flicking her head to get the hair from her face. 'If you want Lucy to give the names to the police, she'll need to be a little calmer than she is right now. I was turning to talk to her, but the pain in my side stopped me.'

'Mr White,' Mr Brown called.

The man switched his attention.

'We could move the other three chairs back for their use.'

Mr White glanced to where Mr Brown had indicated. At the front of the bank, before the window, were three tubular seats. Five of them were still sitting on the floor, but she suspected Carlisle and Samuel, gentlemen that they both were, would probably be okay with staying there. For herself, she would very much appreciate being able to sit upright. It would ease her breathing tremendously.

'Fine,' Mr White agreed.

'I ain't moving them,' Mr Pink snapped.

'You.' Mr White pointed his gun at Carlisle, then Samuel. 'And you. Stand up.'

Carefully, slowly, and with his hands clear from his body, Carlisle stood. Watching him, Teddington noticed that he was still keeping his head down, using the peak of his cap to shield his face. Samuel hadn't shifted. His wide eyes darted from the gun to the others. All eyes were on Samuel as he sought either reassurance or protection. It seemed unlikely he found either; Teddington saw none. Peer pressure was a wonderful thing. Looking ready to cry, Samuel swallowed, then in shaky imitation of Carlisle, rose to his feet.

Mr White looked to Carlisle and tipped his head towards the seats. Carlisle took one step away from the group, waiting to make sure that Sam did the same, then led the way.

'You take one, I'll get the other two,' Carlisle told Sam, who nodded, but nearly dropped the one chair he picked up because his hands were so sweaty. They carried them back to the group. Beth took the first seat, Sam helped Zanti into the second, before sitting back on the floor, cross-legged. Carlisle leaned down to help Teddington to her feet. She winced at the move, taking a moment once on her feet to catch her breath before stepping over, gripping the wooden arm rests and carefully lowering herself down. As Carlisle knelt beside her, she saw the concern in his face, grateful for the hand he placed on her knee.

'You sure you're okay?'

She nodded, laying her hand over his. 'Bruised but not broken. I'm fine.' As she sat down fully, she was glad he didn't move his hand away. The human contact was oddly reassuring. He wasn't the man she wanted, but he was the man here. She knew it was stupid to be so needy, but right now she was. She patted his hand and placed both of her own in her lap, watching the phone screen for a moment. Her mother was no longer trying to contact her, so Piper had been good to his word. As worried as she was by the constant calls, their absence left her bereft, like she was finally severed from her family.

Drawing in a shaky breath, she knew it was time to put her own personal problems aside. Family was important, and right now there was another family she needed to think about. Trying not to let the pain of reaching across show too much, she placed her hand on Lucy's shoulder. The girl flinched under her touch.

'Lucy, sweetheart,' she said softly, 'it's okay, baby, can you just turn to look at me?'

The girl tensed up, her face buried in her mother's neck. Time to try another tack.

'Do you enjoy school, Lucy?'

The odd question obviously caught the kid's attention. Though she didn't look round, or say anything, Lucy did go suddenly very still. Teddington found she was almost holding her breath, waiting for Lucy to come back to her. Finally, there was a small shrug.

'I used to love school when I was your age. Didn't have many friends, except those I read about in books. Most of the girls were more interested in who had the latest fashions, who'd gone on the most expensive holidays, who led the most exciting life.'

The girl shifted, turned her head and looked at her from beneath her mother's chin. She was all red eyes and just a touch of snot on her top lip.

'You get that too, huh?'

A small nod.

'And if the girls in your school are anything like the girls in mine, they'll be relentless when they see your braces.' Teddington could hear Mr Pink stomping around and muttering, though she couldn't hear what he was saying, and she wasn't interested in his opinions anyway. 'But you know, you'll have the last laugh.'

Lucy looked up at her. The question in her eyes convinced Teddington she had the girl's attention and interest.

'Because you'll be the one with perfect teeth, and the one with the most exciting story that none of them are ever going to be able to beat.'

Lucy blinked. There was even the faintest ghost of a smile.

'If you want to make the most of that excitement, I need you to do what you've been asked to do, alright? I'll call Matt, you read the names on the list. That okay?'

Lucy was looking at her. Teddington knew that look, she knew that feeling. Wanting to do something, but terrified of doing it. Last time she'd felt that way she'd been signalling to the man she wanted to date. Fat lot of good finding her courage had done her. Sitting for an hour in a pub she didn't much care for, feeling like a prize idiot. The hour had been enough, but she'd thanked the barman as she left. Somehow, she'd even managed to get home and to her bedroom before she sat down and let the tears go. Sitting there and silently crying, like a stupid love-sick teenager. For the first time since her husband's defection, she'd dared to reach out to a man, to risk trusting. And he'd stamped all over her heart. *Bloody man. Damn Charlie Bell and his bone-melting eyes.*

'I can't.'

'You could try,' she said. 'Remember, you'll be talking to a policeman. His name's Matt, you've heard him. He's a good guy, he'll listen to you, he'll be nice. You can talk to a nice guy, can't you?'

Lucy sat up a little to look at her mother.

Megan nodded. 'It's okay, Cwtchy, you can do it.'

Cwtchy? Teddington didn't know where that came from, and kind of hoped never to find out. But for now, she turned to Mr White. 'Shall I call Matt?'

Mr White nodded. Teddington returned the nod, just once. She found the number and the phone dialled as she put the handset to her ear. It rang on.

Mr White's attention focused darkly on her.

It wasn't a good sign that Piper wasn't instantly answering. *What the hell is he busy with?* The idea of him being caught short during such an important call would normally have made her laugh, but current threats put that response on mute. Thinking fast, she took the phone from her ear, disconnecting as she did so. 'Apparently I forget to press to connect,' she lied, and started dialling again. It barely rang before she heard Piper answer.

'Ari?'

He was short of breath, just enough to tell her he'd run to answer.

'Hi Matt.' She felt her hand grip the phone, her knuckles so tight it actually hurt.

'This call sounds different,' Matt said, 'are we on speakerphone?'

'No. I've been asked to call you. Mr White wants you to know something.'

'What's that, Ari?'

'Our names.' She paused deliberately.

'Do you know any of the gang holding you?'

He spoke quietly, his voice going no further than her ear. She ran her hand over her forehead. There was so much she wanted to tell Piper, but she didn't dare. She apparently did know two of them, but she didn't know who they were. 'No,' she whispered, hoping Piper heard her. She looked up at White. 'I have a list, but I'm not allowed to read it to you. Don't worry,' she assured at the odd noise of confusion he made, 'I'm going to hand you over to Lucy, the little girl you will have heard about. She's scared, so be nice.' She held out the phone to Lucy. The girl looked nervous, but reached out and took it.

'Hello?'

She could imagine what Piper was like on the phone to the kid. Lucy's voice shook, tears were close to the surface, but she made it through the list, and as she revealed each name, Teddington looked at the person belonging to each one.

Sam Frankfort. Cashier, sweet guy who didn't like conflict and wasn't coping as well as he might.

Zanti Bashir—Megan had to tell Lucy how to say that—clearly nervous, but coping. Something told Teddington this wasn't the first time men had threatened Zanti.

Beth Arden. The woman in red.

Judith Montgomery. The woman who thought photo driver's licences were ID cards by stealth.

Mallory Presswick. Bank manager and prick *extraordinaire*.

Megan Burton. Mum.

Lucy Burton. Kid.

Dominic Carlisle. At least Lucy couldn't say that he was a Detective Sergeant.

As Lucy quivered over the last name, tears burst forth again. She let go of the phone and Megan had to catch it before it fell to the floor.

Chapter 15

Piper heard the girl crying, an odd noise, a movement or two, then the line went dead. He looked at the list he'd scrawled. Wymark had the same list in a much neater hand. Carefully, he put the phone down and re-wrote the names, before he turned to face the open door. Sheldrake and Broughton had followed him out to the van, and Andrews was sitting by his side, silent as normal. Piper tore the second copy off the pad and passed it to Broughton. The older man nodded and disappeared from sight.

'Why,' Sheldrake asked softly, 'would they give us the hostages' names?'

Piper shrugged. 'I suspect that they want us to see the hostages as humans, not just collateral. To make it harder for us to forget that lives are at stake.'

'Humanisation,' Sheldrake murmured. 'They're using our own tactics against us.'

Again all Piper could do was wait.

'Is this Bell's doing?' Andrews asked.

'I don't know,' Piper admitted. 'It's possible, but that doesn't seem like the kind of thing Charlie would do.'

'And while vilifying Bell would be easy,' Sheldrake pointed out, 'we can't discount the intelligence of the other men in there. It may have been someone else's idea. We'll have to check Wymark's transcripts, see what was said.'

Piper looked at her, Sheldrake might know bugger all about policing, but, apparently, she knew enough about people. When she turned her eyes up to him, there was an accusation in them.

'After all, as far as we can tell, Bell isn't even in there.'

'Bell isn't in there,' Piper affirmed as Broughton reappeared. 'Ari stated she didn't know any of the gang.'

'Family Liaison are working on the list,' Broughton confirmed, looking at Piper. 'I don't think that there's any doubt Ariadne Teddington would know Bell if he was in there, even if they were wearing masks, she'd recognise his voice. And they're not wearing masks. Besides, Bell's height makes him rather distinctive, there's no disguise going to hide that.'

'There's one man in there who's tall,' Sheldrake pointed out. 'I believe Hickson said he was the one closest to the door.'

'Yeah,' Piper agreed, 'he's also the one we have the clearest image of, and the one closest to Teddington.'

'If that were Bell, she'd know,' Broughton reasoned.

Not necessarily. Piper thought about it. She won't have seen Charlie for months. She was under a lot of pressure and probably more concentrated on the guy that keeps attacking her. On the other hand, she was intelligent, capable and observant. Piper really didn't know what to make of it.

'What do you think that means for Bell?'

Piper considered Broughton's question. While Bell had to be recognised as their informant, there was no guarantee he wouldn't be tried along with the rest of the gang. However, right now, no one believed Charlie Bell was in that bank.

What if Charlie isn't in there?

Piper swallowed. 'All I know for certain right now is that information he supplied was good. We are at the right bank at the right time. Whatever's going on now wasn't known to our informant. As for Charlie, all I can tell you is that he's not at home, he's not at work and he's not answering his phone. As far as I know, he's not in there either.' He tilted his head towards the bank. 'In other words, it doesn't look good and I'm worried about him.' And that was what was making his heart thump and his stomach acid rise. 'Anyone got an indigestion tablet?' Somehow, he wasn't surprised when Andrews silently reached into one of the many pouches on his vest and passed across half a packet of Rennie.

'How "not good" do you think this could be for him?'

Piper looked up at Broughton, but he couldn't bring himself to say the words as he started to chew the tablet and passed the packet back to Andrews. The seriousness of the silence said everything Piper couldn't.

'But if he's not here, and he's not at any of the places that you've looked,' Sheldrake began quietly, 'let's assume he's alive, for now. Where would he be and what could he be up to?'

For a moment Piper met her regard and thought about it. It wasn't a happy prospect. He dragged in a breath. 'Right now, there's no way of knowing, but if he is alive,' Piper muttered through clenched teeth, 'next time I see him, I just might kill him. Excuse me.' The last was said as he moved from the van and headed for the hairdresser's.

Chapter 16

Lucy was crying again.

Teddington wondered if there was anything she could do. But she'd already told the kid she did well on the phone and she should be proud of herself. It hadn't done any good and now she was worried about doing something to make Lucy worse. She was overly aware of Mr Pink pacing again at the front of the bank, back and forth, back and forth. There was a new and unwelcome background noise—Mr Pink tapping his guns against his legs. Teddington suspected he'd be glaring if she looked up at him, so she relaxed her mandible and pushed out the sense of irritation. Hoping she'd reached some sense of calm, she glanced up at Lucy.

If that kid didn't stop grizzling soon, she could really cause some trouble. Teddington felt the frown forming on her forehead. She must have been watching for a while, as Megan looked up and saw her.

'She needs the loo,' Megan whispered as her daughter squirmed on her lap.

'She's not the only one,' Judy added.

'Tough,' Mr White snapped. 'You'll all have to wait until the police get us our van, and we get out of here.'

Teddington looked up at the man. Did he have any idea what the reality of the situation was? That prompted her to check out her own new reality. Now on a chair, she had a different perspective. She still couldn't see a thing outside, but at least the blurs were in a slightly different alignment. She could see various high-viz blobs. They would be the local police; any SWAT team members would be in black to reduce visibility. There was one big white block, presumably the Transit van Mr Pink had mentioned earlier. The probable police van.

Do you know any of the gang holding you?

Her head echoed the question. Why would Piper ask her that? It could be because she was a prison officer and bank robberies were rarely first offences. It was a logical progression and therefore a logical connection. Only it wasn't like she'd been in a position to have told him anything over the phone. There was also a good chance that these people were local, another reason she might know them. She was glad it was Piper out there. Knowing he was involved gave her some assurance. *It's Piper out there.* Her eye line moved down. *And Carlisle in here.*

'Shit.'

She hadn't meant to say anything out loud, but the whispered word caught Carlisle's attention. His head turned to her, tipping more than usual so he could see under his cap peak.

'What's wrong?'

Her heart was hammering again. Maybe her brain was misfiring.

'Ari?' He reached up and took her hand.

Couldn't be. Could it? 'Cliff Richard hit just ear wormed me.'

'What?' Carlisle looked truly confused.

'I like small speakers,' she said almost without moving her lips, 'I like tall—'

His wide eyes and tiny shake told her he got it. Told her she was right. He not only recognised a song that was probably older than them both—she only knew if because her mother had been a fan—he was almost definitely *Wired for Sound.*

Shit.

'Mr White?'

Teddington turned to the sound of the voice—everyone in the room did. Mr Brown glanced momentarily at her, but focused on Mr White. 'If the hostages are feeling the need to go to the toilet, maybe we should take them—one at a time of course—because we don't want it getting messy or smelly in here.'

'I don't want us spread too thin,' White grated in response.

'We could get Mr Blue or Mr Orange to come back through,' Mr Brown suggested.

'Treating us right,' Teddington risked, 'will go in your favour, not only now, but later, if by some chance any of you do face charges.'

Two guns came up, straight at her head, she'd forgotten how quickly Mr Pink could move if he needed to. She was squeezing Carlisle's hand now, too tight, she could see him grimacing, but she could only focus on the guns pointed at her.

'We are not going to get caught.'

'Okay.' She didn't like how her voice cracked, but she couldn't help it.

'We won't!'

The manic gleam in his over-bright weaselly eyes scared Teddington. He was a loose cannon, he could do anything.

Brown moved. 'I'll—'

'You'll stay put.' Mr White stopped Mr Brown with the aim of his gun.

Teddington watched Mr Brown rest back on his heels, though relaxed was about the last thing he looked. His body was tense, like elastic ready to snap at any moment. This wasn't good.

Lucy was still fidgeting.

Teddington jumped as Mr Blue slammed back into the room from the staff-only area. He obviously saw her reaction, as his smile was little short of lascivious. She felt her skin crawl and hugged her jacket around her. Mr Blue put another now full bag on the pile before he moved over to whisper with Mr White. She saw something exchange hands, but she couldn't make out what. Then Mr Blue was frowning, his volume increased.

'But—'

'I said now,' Mr White cut off whatever Mr Blue's objection was. 'Start with the kid.'

Teddington watched Mr Blue's lips compress, his scowl toward the girl was full of disgust. His footfalls were stompy as he rounded the rail and moved towards Lucy. When he leaned over and grabbed her, she screamed. Lucy's arms were so tight around her mother's neck, Megan was in danger of having her head pulled off as Mr Blue yanked her daughter away. She was dragged to her knees before the chair.

'Be gentle!'

Teddington got side-swiped. The near punch knocked her to one side as Mr Blue continued to pull at the girl. Suddenly it felt like the world stopped. Teddington turned her head back to see Mr Blue and Megan staring at each other, his gun at her temple.

'Lucy,' Teddington used that school ma'am tone she hated. 'Let go of your mother right now or she's going to die.'

Everyone in the bank was as stunned by her words as they were by Mr Blue's actions. Was the whole world holding its breath?

Trembling and quaking, Lucy let her arms slide from her mother and stood up. Even the sobbing was finally over, though Teddington saw big fat tears rolling down the girl's face. Megan sat back in slow motion, her face the aged reflection of her daughter's.

'Please don't hurt her.'

The whispered phrase was repeated over and over again as Mr Blue stood straighter. For a second he turned his gun to the daughter's head. Even Lucy didn't react this time. Then it felt like the pair just vanished. Teddington sat staring at the space where Mr Blue and Lucy had stood, it was empty now, but she didn't remember them moving. Megan was still pleading and all Teddington could register was the sting in her cheek where Mr Blue had hit her. Was she going to get out of here alive? Were any of them?

Carlisle was nudging her. Numbly she looked at him, not understanding as he indicated to her phone. Realisation was another slap in the face as her ears finally registered the ringing.

She answered the call. 'Hello?'

'Ari? You okay?'

'Loudspeaker.'

Teddington looked up at Mr White. She had to compute what he was saying. 'Oh.' She lowered the phone and switched it to loudspeaker.

'Ari?' The disembodied voice repeated. 'What's wrong, what's going on?'

Teddington dragged in a breath and blinked, desperately trying to find a spot of calm inside her. 'Matt, sorry. I… I…' she shook her head. 'I'm sorry Matt, what did you want?'

'I wanted to let you know that Family Liaison are dealing with the families of all the hostages you named.'

'Thank you.'

'Quid pro quo, Ari. I still want that face-to-face.'

Teddington looked up at Mr White. He shook his head. 'Mr White says no.'

She could hear Piper's deep breath even over the phone. 'Then let me make this clear. No face-to-face, no van.'

Still watching the unmoved and unmoving Mr White, Teddington felt the ache in her cheek and the unshed tears burning behind her eyes. 'Please Matt, don't do this to me.'

But Matt didn't answer, and Mr White wasn't about to agree. Afraid her fear was going to overtake her. Teddington spoke as quickly as she could.

'I'll get back to you.'

Chapter 17

Piper kept the disconnected phone to his ear. Teddington was in trouble. She was losing her grip, fear clearly eating away at her. How was he supposed to just stand here and do nothing when he knew as well as Teddington that the chances of her surviving this were rapidly slipping away?

'While they're in the bank, they're contained,' Sheldrake reiterated.

Ten minutes later and Piper was grinding his teeth, the acid in his stomach bubbling like a potion in a cauldron. He, Andrews, Broughton and Sheldrake were huddled together in the corner of the hairdresser's again. Other officers buzzed around, some taking a break, some working on the phones, running liaison.

'We've got two chase cars ready and waiting to follow a van that has a tracker on it,' Piper said. 'Effectively, they'll still be contained.'

'And don't forget my men are in place to stop them dead in their tracks,' Andrews added.

'No one dies on my watch.'

Piper was half surprised Andrews didn't curl up and die just from the withering look Sheldrake shot at him.

'We cannot,' she barked, sounding more like she was addressing a political rally than a cluster of seasoned police officers, 'risk the lives of more innocent civilians. We open fire and they'll open fire, and right now—as you keep reminding me—Ariadne Teddington is the one they have their guns pointed at. Or are you prepared to pull the trigger on her yourself?'

* * *

Mr Blue had returned with Lucy, the little girl looking sullen and pale. When she moved to race to her mother, Mr Blue pulled her up short. Literally. He grabbed her by the upper arm. Lifting her shoulder wasn't enough for him, she was stretched up, all at odd angles trying to keep away from him while virtually on her tiptoes. She was wide-eyed as she looked to her mother, but Mr Blue raised his arm and pointed his gun directly at Megan.

'You next.'

Teddington watched as Megan stood shakily. Mr Blue's gun sent Megan to his right. Only then did he shove Lucy roughly forward. The little girl veered, heading towards her mother. Surprising Teddington with his speed, Carlisle was on his feet, snatching Lucy, pulling her to him. The girl screamed. Megan looked round, terror in her eyes, but Mr Blue pushed her on. Carlisle was leaning over, holding Lucy to him, whispering, clearly soothing her. When Carlisle knelt, Lucy knelt with him. Holding him.

Watching from her seat, Teddington felt oddly jealous of the little girl. Everyone needed comfort. She remembered another time, when she'd been held captive, though it was more by the weight of Charlie Bell's arm around her than the handcuff attaching her to the bed. Turning her head away, she tried to push Charlie from her mind, but the images were caught in her head. Even without the images, there were the sounds, the smells, the feel. How many times had she woken in the night and imagined Charlie spooned behind her, his body hot against hers? She remembered the soft sound of his breathing, the occasional huff that wasn't quite a snore. The smell of his skin, warmth and musk—manly. That one night burned more strongly in her memory than the five years of her broken marriage. She shouldn't want any man this much, but as the rest of the hostages were taken one by one to the toilets, she fought to get her own emotions back under control.

Mr White had moved over toward Mr Brown. They were closer to her now than where Mr Brown usually stood. Mr White said nothing to start with, but passed something to Mr Brown.

Teddington caught just enough of a glimpse to realise it was a watch. Mr Brown displayed no emotion. He barely even glanced at it before slipping it into his jeans pocket.

'Why would they want to meet face-to-face?' Mr White asked at last.

She watched Mr Brown shrug.

'No idea. It's not standard operating procedure.'

'Can you speculate?'

Mr Brown filled his lungs and looked outside. 'Not really.' He turned back to Mr White, but his eye line was caught by the TV. 'Maybe it was her idea.' He indicated to the screen, which was showing a picture of the Police and Crime Commissioner. She looked very serious, but very calm, trustworthy. This was her campaign picture. 'I've no idea how she'd think.'

Mr White took a second to look behind him. He saw Teddington watching them, but other than give a small scowl he did nothing before turning back to Mr Brown. 'Do you think they're getting a van?'

Doubt it. Teddington kept her thoughts to herself, and continued to listen.

'Probably, but that will likely take time.'

'Why?'

'Paperwork and official sanction.'

'What will speed them up?'

Doing what they asked, you moron.

Apparently Mr Brown had to think about it. 'I don't really know,' he said, meeting Mr White's eye. 'Siege situations were never my province. Most negotiations are about humanising the whole situation. The authorities want you to see them as human, not the enemy. Same with the hostages. They want us to see them as real people rather than poker chips. Maybe that's what it is. Maybe that's what he wants, to be more than a voice on the phone. Maybe you should, you know, go face-to-face with this Matt bloke. Probably the best way to find out what he's up to.'

Siege situations were never my province. Teddington considered that statement. Mr Brown was looking more and more like a military man. *Or a policeman.* Afraid of what her expression might reveal, she bit her lip and stared at the floor, her brain doing double time for all it felt like she was thinking through treacle. *No.*

'Mr Pink.'

The call made more than Mr Pink jump. The room's attention focused on him, then Mr White. Mr Blue stepped back into the room with Samuel, who sank back to his place on the floor. Teddington realised Lucy was back with her mother.

'What's going on?' Mr Blue demanded.

'I'm sending Mr Pink out to do this damn face-to-face.'

'You ca—' Teddington strangled off her own objection.

'What was that, Ari?' Mr White demanded, stepping up to point his gun directly at her. 'What can't I do?'

Her breath caught in her throat. She realised it was only Carlisle's presence at her feet that kept that muzzle from being pressed against her flesh. Finally, she swallowed and found the words. 'You can do anything you want to.'

Mr White smiled. It wasn't warming. 'Yes. I can. But let's hear what you were thinking anyway.'

She didn't want to say anything, but she had to. She dragged in another breath, her hand automatically going to her side, pressing the kick site and holding herself together when she felt like she was closer than ever to falling apart. 'You should consider sending someone else. Someone who isn't your most volatile gang member. Send someone you trust to behave, who's not going to jeopardise your place here. Send him.' She pointed at Mr Blue.

'Stand up.'

'Please don't send me.' There were tears in her voice but not her eyes.

'How foolish of me. I thought I was sending someone non-volatile.' His cold look challenged her. 'Stand up.'

This time Teddington obeyed, her knees knocking. She felt sick, lowered her head and eyes to the floor. Her breathing wasn't normal and her sniff was too wet. She tapped Carlisle on the shoulder with her phone and passed it down. It was the only link they had to the police outside. She had to leave it with someone who could be trusted.

Mr White indicated she should head to the door. Apparently he'd decided to do the face-to-face himself. That was a relief. Teddington felt the trembling judder through her. She palms were sweaty, so she wiped them on her leggings. Moving to the door, she looked up at Mr Brown. There was no expression on his face. *It's not him, it can't be.*

'We want that van here, out the back, in thirty minutes,' Mr White was saying. 'If we don't get it, I'm going to start killing people.'

That meant he wasn't going to step out himself.

'Understand?'

Not sure that she did, Teddington turned, and found Mr White wasn't talking to her, he was concentrating on Mr Brown. Turning back, she decided Mr Brown didn't exactly look comfortable.

'Mr White?' he asked.

'You'll go out there, do the face-to-face. She's your shield. Anyone tries anything funny, one of the remaining hostages dies. Understand now?'

All too well. She saw Mr Brown nod, just once.

'Thirty minutes, out back.'

Since there was no other choice, Teddington stood quietly as Mr Brown shifted his gaze to her.

'Take off your coat.'

She looked down at the bulky, padded jacket she'd picked to protect her against wind chill. She didn't want to take it off. She knew what was below it.

'I said—' Mr Brown pressed his gun to her forehead, 'take your bloody coat off.'

Carefully, reluctantly, she drew down the zip and shrugged the coat off, letting the cumbersome garment drop to the floor, Brown kicked it out of the way, it stopped by the wall. She tried not to be affected by the way the gang and hostages stared. Her corset had over-shoulder straps which covered the scar on her right shoulder where she'd been shot, but it was otherwise fairly revealing. Mr Brown's eyes seemed to have fallen into the trap of her cleavage.

'The camera's going to love that,' Mr White commented.

'Lack of that bulk just makes my job easier,' Mr Brown declared.

Teddington stood tall and as still as her quaking body would allow as Mr Brown side-stepped. His gun was in his right hand, so it was the left that moved around her. She gasped both from the movement and the jolt to her ribs as he pulled her up against him. She could taste the fear in her throat, the copper-tinge of the fight-or-flight response. The worst of it was knowing she could do neither. Rumble or run, the result would be the same: someone else would pay for her mistake. She couldn't live with that.

She felt him move, his cheek now rested against her head, his mouth by her ear. His breath was warm over her skin. Memories of another time and place were inappropriate and tamped down. The gun came up to press against her neck, just below her ear. She swallowed and tried to breathe as normally as she could. It wasn't easy. He was moving her forward.

'Open the door.'

Automatically, she raised her left hand. It couldn't go far, trapped as it was beneath his arm. Instead she had to use her right hand, which for a leftie was rather awkward. For a moment she held the door open. Those inside the bank were silent; outside, the whole world seemed to be holding its breath. Though the door opened into a recess, the air was suddenly colder. Goosebumps jumped across her skin. Mr Brown stepped them into the doorway. The glass door fell shut behind them, the world lay in front. For a moment they were in their own space, a separate dimension from the bank and from the outside world. The man behind her shifted, bringing his cheek against her left temple.

'God, I've missed your apple scent.'

Teddington lost control of her knees. She'd have fallen if he hadn't had such a tight hold on her.

'Charlie?'

She didn't want to believe it. *Prosthetics.* That was why they weren't wearing masks—they'd changed their faces so they'd never be recognised. Charlie's hold slackened, became more of a caress. His head moved minutely, she felt his lips—

'Don't,' she warned.

Chapter 18

Don't. She was right, he shouldn't. Now wasn't the time or the place.

But damn it all he wanted to do was kiss her. This wasn't how things were supposed to happen. She should never have been here. How cruel could fate be to put the very woman he wanted right in his way at the worst possible moment?

'Nice corset.'

'At least it binds my ribs, otherwise your mate might have broken them.'

That put a new and unwelcome twist on it.

'I can't believe you're doing this,' she hissed the words between clenched teeth. 'I thought you were a better man.'

Ice washed through his veins. There was so much he wanted to tell her, no time or freedom to explain. He was as trapped as she was. And right now, he had a job to do.

Ahead he could see the police cordon, people crowding the limits to see what was happening. The camera crew—*crews*, he realised—were focusing on them, jostling each other to get the best position.

At last he saw Piper, moving through the ranks, ducking under cordon tape. The DCI looked rumpled in his customary suit. Piper came a few steps inside the exclusion zone before he stopped.

He's trying to draw us out.

Charlie took half a step forward, putting Teddington into the open beyond the shop front, while he remained in the recess. The black gun at her throat was the perfect counterpoint to the white of her porcelain skin. That should keep the cameras happy.

'Mr White?' Piper called.

Charlie pressed the gun harder to Teddington's throat. Her head moved up and to the left as he burrowed his face into her hair. No one was about to recognise him, but he wasn't going to give them the chance. She got the scared act just right.

'This isn't Mr White,' she called with a quake in her voice.

A glance down showed Charlie that she was breathing too shallowly and even with his grip nowhere near a pulse point, he could feel her heart racing. He spoke more out of hope than attention to the evidence, easing the muzzle pressure against her neck. 'This fear's an act, right?'

'No,' she squeaked back. 'Don't forget your accent.'

It was true—his hint of Geordie had slipped away. Thank God she'd reminded him. 'I won't hurt you,' he whispered his words through her hair, dragging the apple scent into his nostrils and lungs.

'You already did.'

Her words robbed him of his lungful.

Piper came forward; there was a murmur from the crowd. Every footfall echoed, an ominous toll. On the edge of the pavement, Piper stopped, settled into a casual stance. It was one Charlie remembered from his own negotiation training. To appear open and seemingly relaxed, stand with feet parted, knees unlocked, hands relaxed and open, away from the body and never in pockets. Piper might be uncomfortable but he was carefully doing everything by the book. With Sheldrake and the press on his back, he couldn't afford to do anything else.

'My name is Matt.'

Charlie had to think before he spoke. Had to keep the accent going. 'We want that van you promised. You've got thirty minutes or we start shooting hostages.' To emphasise his point, he pressed the gun harder into Teddington's throat. The move turned her face even more intimately against his. The thought of kissing her, unbidden and inappropriate, filled his head. As he pushed the image away, he was glad of the heavy prosthetics obscuring his face, his blushes. 'Get the van to the back of the building.'

'Wheels are in motion, but these things take time. Half an hour's not enough. I need an hour at least.'

'Mr White says half an hour or he starts shooting hostages.'

Piper looked strained. There was a tension around his eyes that Charlie recognised. Chances were Piper was between a rock and a hard place. Piper took a careful step forward. 'He can't.'

'He can,' Charlie said. 'It's a very *live* threat.'

'Yeah, just ask the ceiling, two very obvious bullet holes.' Teddington added.

'But he hasn't hurt anyone as yet, has he? I need to know that the hostages are alright.'

'They are,' Teddington answered when Charlie didn't.

'Really, Ari? You're looking rather pale.'

'I'm cold.'

Charlie felt the truth of that in her shivers, in the obvious goosebumps pulled up by the chill of the sunless afternoon.

Piper obviously wasn't convinced. 'You sure that's all?'

This time her voice was stronger, if not louder. 'Matt, I'm a prison officer being held by criminals. They're not happy with me. But thank God, I'm just a serving prison officer, imagine how they'd react to a serving police officer in there.'

The point was clearly rammed home to Piper. He swallowed and considered. 'Ari, be careful, this is starting to look like you're working with them.'

'Really?' She risked the sarcasm she hadn't dared earlier. 'What makes you think that? The gun at my head, maybe?'

The silence was awkward.

'They know who I am and what I do, Matt. The chances of me surviving this are small enough as it is. Cooperation is my only stalling tactic.'

For a moment, Piper closed his eyes. Charlie knew the feeling, but with at least half a dozen guns aimed at him, he couldn't afford to look away. Worryingly of course, Teddington was right.

She had the lowest chance of all of them of getting out of this alive. When Piper opened his eyes again, he was clearly back in control.

Piper turned to Charlie. 'We'll get you a van, but you know how this works: you have to give us something. Release one of the hostages.'

'No.' Charlie pulled Teddington closer. She winced.

Piper considered her. 'Just how badly hurt are you?'

She drew another breath, swallowed, easing some of the air back out before she answered. 'Bruised but not broken. They already gave you a hostage.'

'You'll get them all when we get the van,' Charlie growled. The need to play the role made this easier. 'And no more face-to-face. Phone contact only. You have twenty-five minutes left.'

'I'm trying.'

'Try harder.'

Chapter 19

Try harder.

Teddington's words echoed through Piper's soul as he walked back behind the line, where Sheldrake and Broughton were waiting for him. He felt the weight of every eye on him; he was overly aware of the young journalist pushing her way around the cordon. He ignored her and focused on Sheldrake, and the concise report he had to make.

'Nothing's changed,' Sheldrake was quick to pronounce, his report done.

Except that they're threatening to start shooting hostages. But there was no point reiterating that. Sheldrake had listened closely enough.

'They haven't shot anyone yet, Inspector.'

Apparently she was a mind reader. 'Yet,' Piper underlined in a tight growl as Sheldrake headed away.

'Inspector Piper!'

His already tense shoulders tightened further as he looked across to the keen young reporter. She was eager, and when he turned to her, she stilled, the neutral expression she wore for bad news stories wasn't quite so neutral now, but it reminded him who she was. 'That's Chief Inspector.'

'Chief Inspector.'

Her smile was too barracuda to be ingratiating. 'What can you tell us about the robbers' demands?'

Not a lot. 'A statement will be made in due course, Miss Dowling.' The rest of her questions he ignored as he and Broughton followed Sheldrake. Before they entered the hairdresser's, he turned back to see Dowling back with her cameraman, whispering urgently. Broughton sensed Piper's interest and stopped a step ahead. She was up to something. Whatever she was saying to the cameraman he looked interested too, and unusually, they both pushed through the crowd, this time away from the cordon. 'What are those two up to?'

'God knows.' Broughton managed to sneer the words with next to no facial movement.

Inside they joined Sheldrake. She didn't look happy when she regarded Broughton. 'Why exactly did you defy my orders and get a van ready to hand over?'

Piper was impressed not only that Broughton had defied orders, but he didn't turn a hair at being called on it.

'Eventually, ma'am, we may need to change our stance on that. I merely want to be ready if the time comes.'

'Unlikely,' she returned. 'According to your paperwork, your informant said that the bullets would be blanks.'

'Makes little difference,' Andrews put in as he joined them. 'Even a blank can do serious damage at close quarters. Fire a blank against someone's temple, you'll still kill them. And they've demonstrated a willingness to hurt. We know Samuel Frankford was punched and Ari has been attacked in some way. I think we have to err on the side of caution here and assume that the bullets aren't blanks, and that yes, they might kill someone.'

'The bullets aren't blanks,' Piper said as he pushed back his hair and ignored the pain in his gut. 'Teddington mentioned two bullet holes in the ceiling.'

'You don't,' Andrews stated, 'get those from blanks.'

The statement was met with dread silence.

'What's that?' Piper asked pointing to the paper in Andrews' hand.

'Oh, this is the best image we could get of the man who stepped out of the bank.'

Piper took it and realised that the toner in the van printer was nearly out. There was a strip not printing and the bottom was greyer than the top. The image itself was more interesting. Ariadne

Teddington was looking pale and scared. Who could blame her for that when a man was pushing a gun to her throat. Even if she knew the man, which she clearly did given their exchange, there was no way of telling that from the evidence in front of him.

'Well that's not Charlie Bell.'

Broughton's statement was part relief to Piper.

It was patently obvious to him that he'd been speaking to Charlie Bell, but if his colleagues couldn't identify the man, there was still a chance he could get out of this. For a moment Piper closed his eyes. Working in shades of grey was one thing, but he wondered how far he was going to have to wade into those murky waters.

'He doesn't match the descriptions of any of the men our informant said was involved,' Andrews continued, 'and he's not tall enough to be Bell. I've sent the image to Control. They're running a picture match, but with what's basically a third of a face, I doubt it'll do much good. Talking of which, Hickson couldn't identify any of our suspects and could only suggest that there were a couple of possibilities in the books, even those he wasn't sure about.'

Piper continued to stare at the image. Whoever did that work was a damn fine make-up artist. It was a hell of a cover-up. Was he going to be able to do so good a job? If he attempted and failed, he'd kiss his career and his pension goodbye.

'Piper.'

Piper pulled back and turned to Broughton. 'Sorry, sir?'

'I said this doesn't add up.'

'No, sir.' Piper rubbed his hands over his face, struggling to bring everything together.

'What have we missed?' Andrews asked.

'Nothing,' Piper stated, as he re-joined them. 'We've seen precisely what they wanted us to see.'

'Piper!' One of the DCs called his attention to the TV in the van. He glanced to Sheldrake, who dismissed him with a small inclination of her head. Piper stepped over to watch the TV. They were streaming a live broadcast and what he saw chilled him to the bone.

* * *

Teddington was unsure if her shivers were from the cold of the air, or from knowing that Charlie Bell was beneath the overhanging brow of Mr Brown. Her legs had barely held her as she returned to the chair. She was vaguely aware that Carlisle had had to guide her down, that he'd spoken to her when he'd put the phone back in her hand. She gripped it now like a lifeline.

Charlie Bell. *Here*. The man of her dreams taking a starring role in her current nightmare.

Obviously the other gang members knew who he was, but did they know of her connection to him? She thought about what Mr Pink had said. No. He couldn't know, or he'd have shot her by now. As long as they didn't know, she'd be okay. At least she could kid herself she'd be okay.

'…this reporter recognised Prison Officer Ariadne Teddington.'

The woman's voice penetrated Teddington's mind and she looked up to see a young woman doing a piece to camera just before her own picture flashed up, a hideous work photo of her in uniform, which made her look like something Frankenstein would have rejected for being too ugly.

'Officer Teddington made headlines last May when she was shot during the funeral of Oscar Bell and Baby Hamilton.'

The screen changed again. This time showing the footage of the funeral. Footage that, until that moment, Teddington had managed to avoid. Now she stared up, wide-eyed and slack-jawed. In the footage, Richardson and Sanchez were on the ground. She stood beside Charlie, handcuffed to him, looking stunned. Then she was down.

The rest of the world disappeared and she was there in that dreadful moment. She felt the force against her shoulder knock her off her feet. The rapid pulse of heat that radiated through her body, so quickly followed by Arctic cold. The pain as Bell unceremoniously pulled her up, extending the damage in her shoulder. Explosions at his feet showed he'd had no choice but to run, and with the handcuffs he'd had to take her with him.

Just the memory of it sent judders of pain down her arm. Her right hand felt unaccountably numb, and she was only distantly aware of the tears burning a path down her cheeks. The story moved on, their return, the prison riot, but Teddington was locked in her memories. It all crowded in on her.

The pain of being shot.

The pain of being manhandled.

The pain of the bullet being removed.

The nearly dying in hospital.

The pain of being pulled to her feet by the scalp.

That hadn't happened.

Reality snapped back. Teddington realised Mr White had the hair on the crown of her head in his fist. People around her were crying out, Mr White calling her a catalogue of names while she scrambled to find her feet as he dragged her from the chair.

* * *

'Fucking bitch!' Piper didn't even try to hold back his exclamation as he moved his attention from the live broadcast report to the camera feed from the bank. One of the men was grabbing Teddington by the hair, dragging her out of shot.

'Get that *reporter* over here now.'

Piper was surprised by the anger he heard in Sheldrake's voice as he saw another officer scurry off in search of Miss Dowling. Her eyes were still blazing as she turned back to him.

'Can we see anything?'

He shook his head. 'The man dragged her into the manager's office. We can't see through a closed door.'

'Windows?'

He shook his head, but said nothing as Lawson and the plain clothes officer brought the overly eager Miss Dowling to stand before the commissioner. Another woman followed. Young, the Press Liaison Officer.

'Miss Dowling.' Sheldrake was surprisingly controlled as she ignored the reporter's questions. 'While I appreciate that you are young and eager, you seem to have misunderstood the role of broadcast news. Are you proud of the release you just made regarding Mrs Teddington?'

Dowling straightened her back. 'Of course, it's my job to report the facts. You lot weren't releasing any names, and I recognised her. It's not my fault I got there before you did. It was quite a scoop.'

'It was breath-takingly stupid.' Sheldrake surprised the woman and the officers with her vehement retort. 'We knew she was in there, and unlike you, we appreciated the kind of danger that her job puts her in when she's surrounded by a bunch of armed men.' The emphasis on the last two words made an obvious impact on Dowling. She didn't move but she was starting to diminish. 'By announcing to the world that she's in there, you've announced to the robbers who she is. That increases the danger to her life. We have a very difficult job to do here, Miss Dowling. We release information as and when it is safe to do so, and we withhold information when necessary. When covering a live situation of this nature, you run all information and supposition through Police Liaison *before* you broadcast it, or not only do you risk breaching laws of prejudice, you risk—as you have today—other people's lives. Do you understand me?'

Dowling wasn't as cowed as she should have been. Piper figured her youth was blocking her sense.

'Hadn't you heard? This country has a free press.'

Sheldrake moved closer, her voice deceptively soft. 'Maybe you can remind me of that at Mrs Teddington's funeral. If she dies, you're the one who will have killed her. Now get out of my sight before I have you arrested for obstructing a police officer.'

Chapter 20

Teddington scrambled for balance, forced along by Mr White's grip on her hair. She was virtually dragged into Presswick's office.

Her hair was released but a vicious shove propelled her forward; she tripped, landing awkwardly against Presswick's desk, sending files and pens flying, the wireless keyboard smashing to the floor. Her own phone stopped just short of the edge.

Every breath pulled against her bruised ribs. The corset wasn't helping, but she suspected that without its steel boning, she'd have broken ribs right now. Taking shallow breaths, she turned to face Mr White. His blow was sudden and hard and she bounced against the wall, fell in a heap on the floor.

'Stay down.'

Too shocked not to, Teddington watched in horror as Mr White turned to face the man storming through the door after them. Charlie.

'One more step and you're a dead man.'

Teddington's brain wasn't functioning and she sat staring at the two men pointing guns at each other. In that frozen moment, the office door banged shut behind Charlie. Suddenly the world felt like a very small place. Teddington was struggling to breathe. Yet she had to. She had to stop this. She didn't want to see anyone die.

'Stop. Please.' Neither man reacted to her words. She had to break this up, but she didn't really want to get between two guns. 'Please, you didn't come here to kill anyone.'

Mr White offered a sneer of a laugh. 'Trying to save your lover?'

'I am not!' Teddington wasn't quite sure where the vehemence in that statement came from, but it obviously affected both men.

'You don't even know who he is.'

'I—' Teddington caught herself '—know who I've slept with, which is no one since my divorce.' Five years and she missed sex. She missed having someone to be close to. That sad thought was enough to put her back on track. 'Look, let's take the personal out of this. One shot gets fired in here and the SWAT team will descend on this place like a ton of bricks.'

'TAC team,' Charlie corrected, 'but otherwise she's right.'

'And how did they get here so quick?' Mr White demanded, still locked against Charlie.

'How the hell would I know?'

'We're not,' Teddington said carefully, 'all that far from the station, and probably there was no other shout on at the moment. Please, both of you, put the guns down.'

'What did you tell them?' Mr White demanded of Charlie, ignoring her. 'Did you grass us up? Is this a set-up? Did you betray me?'

'No.'

Teddington could hear Charlie's voice much more clearly now.

'I betrayed the Force. They'd never trust me again. Besides, you've got your own controls in place, remember?'

Mr White said nothing but his breathing was heavy and audible, his nostrils flaring and his eyes narrowing.

'I can't have told the police,' Charlie said with soft, calm reason. He opened his hands up, to show they were empty, other than the gun, which was now pointed away from Mr White. Mr White did not lower his own gun.

'You only gave us the name of the bank this morning and I'm not carrying anything by which I could be identified, including a phone. Look.' The hand that wasn't holding the gun pulled out the lining of his front left jeans pocket so it hung empty. He just had a small handful of change in his palm. He shoved the cash back into his pocket, turned carefully around and lifted the bottom edge of his jumper to display his back pockets. He pulled out a pair of latex gloves—no, two pairs, one purple, which struck Teddington as odd—and then the pockets were obviously empty over his glutes.

Nice butt. Teddington shook her head to clear it of the stray thought. Then she realised that he hadn't shown the contents of his right-hand front pocket. Not that she was going to call him on that.

'What about *her*?'

She didn't like the way Mr White sneered the word or nodded toward her.

'What about me?'

'Did you call the police?'

'How? The first I knew of any of this was when you walked in and started shooting.'

Mr White only moved his eyes, yet still she felt pinned. 'Not even for Charlie Bell?'

She kept her voice soft, not wanting to aggravate the situation, 'I haven't seen Charlie Bell since I released him from prison. If I'd known anything was going to go down here today, I wouldn't be within ten miles of the place. I'm done with being shot—' Her phone interrupted, nearly dancing off the desk on vibrate '—at.' Still on her knees, she grabbed the phone, took one look.

'It's the police.'

For a moment she just looked up at Mr White. His mouth was a thin tight line, his nostrils flared. He looked back to Charlie. His jaw moved. Charlie lowered the gun, Mr White lowered his too.

Mr White turned, grabbed her upper arm, almost dragging her to her feet. He nodded once. She accepted the call on speakerphone and leant against the desk for support.

'Matt?'

'Ari?' the voice came back cracklier now. 'Is everything okay?'

'Fine.' *That word really needs a new definition.*

'You sound odd.'

'It's a bad line. Was there something you wanted Mr White and his colleagues to know?'

'I had reports of a flurry of activity that coincided with a news segment.'

'Oh.' She didn't know what to say. As usual Mr White gave her no direction.

'There's an indication that you might have been able to see that report.'

Teddington supported the phone in both hands, afraid her shaking might make it fall.

'Ari?'

'We saw it.'

'That information was not released by us,' Piper stated, clearly not approving of the report.

Teddington breathed and swallowed, waiting for any indication from Mr White. 'I appreciate that, Matt, thank you. But frankly the damage was done when I was recognised and that wasn't anyone's fault.' She didn't like that her voice was trembling and that tears were forcing their way out. 'Please tell me the van is on its way.' The squeak in her voice was particularly pathetic and she hated herself for it.

'We're on it.'

Mr White moved up close. The gun pushed against her lips. She tasted cold steel and gun oil, some kind of carbide and hot salt. Her whimper was involuntary as she shut her eyes tight.

'Clock's ticking, Matt.' The name was sneered as Mr White reached down and ended the call.

The pressure against her lips moved, mashing the sensitive flesh against her teeth. She felt hot breath against her cheek. In the dark, her world was concentrated on sensation and sound. She was uncomfortably aware of Mr White pressed up against her, her own tight grip on her phone, the weakness of her knees and the stretching of her nerves. Now his breath filled her ears.

'Are you scared, Ari?'

All she dared do was murmur an unintelligible sound of agreement, a slight nod.

'Good.'

She felt inexplicably cold as he moved away.

'You have one minute.'

Then he was gone.

The door slammed.

She was alone and the need to collapse overtook her, only she didn't fall to the floor. She was being held, supported, and helped to sit back on the edge of the desk.

'It's okay.' Charlie's soft words weren't as soothing as his presence. 'You're okay.'

She leant her head against his unyielding chest. The bitter laugh escaped her and she tipped her head back to look up at him, her smile wavering. 'What the hell happened? He's known I work at Blackmarch for hours. Why lash out now?'

Charlie put his gun on the desk, using both hands to frame her face and stroke her hair back. 'Because he hadn't connected you with me until that report.'

Of course. Mr White hadn't dragged her in here just to threaten her, he'd done it in expectation that Charlie would follow. And he had. She wondered what Mr White would have done if Charlie hadn't followed. *Put a bullet in my brain probably.* Had Charlie saved her life simply by following her? Even if that was true, it didn't make him her hero.

'Sorry,' he murmured.

His tentative smile warmed her as much as his thumbs lightly brushing her tears away. Then a new heat flared behind those wrong-colour eyes and he pressed a kiss on her. It was hot and passionate and left her wanting more. 'God, I've missed you.'

For a moment she wasn't sure he'd said those words, they were such a clear echo of her own thoughts.

'Then why didn't you meet me? And what's wrong with your eyes?'

'Contacts.'

He moved closer and for a second she thought he was going to kiss her again. Her stomach tightened and her nipples hardened. Only he stopped, rearing back. Her need howled in disappointment. That brow seemed to overhang even more.

'What do you mean, why didn't I meet you? When? Where?'

She felt her jaw go slack. 'When you left Blackmarch. I invited you to meet me.'

For a second, he thought about it. Did he see that moment as clearly as she did? Him, with an archive box of possessions about halfway between the prison door and the gate, turning to look at her?

'You never gave any invitation, you just pointed to the gate and waved. Go and goodbye.'

She wasn't sure she believed it. Could he really be so dull? 'I pointed to the Lock Up pub, and indicated four o'clock.' She did so again by raising her hand, thumb across her palm and fingers slightly spread.

'It looked like a wave to me.'

'Who waves with their thumb across their palm?'

'Well you could have been a little less obscure.' He leaned close in order to keep his voice low and still sounded admonishing despite the smile.

'How?' she demanded in a similar half-whisper. 'Did you expect me to shout it across the forecourt? When my colleagues could hear? I still have to work with those guys.'

'You said you couldn't get involved with me. "Screws and cons and all that," you said.'

He was so close now and the anger was fading as hotter emotions rose.

'I also pointed out you were a free man, and therefore not subject to that rule any more.'

The small sound as he bowed his head could have been either frustration or amusement. 'Can't believe I've wasted six months.'

His half smile was a small warning before he closed the last gap to press his lips to hers. The temptation to surrender was so great, but now wasn't the time. She turned her head away to break the kiss and scowl at him.

'Hold your horses,' she told him, 'I'm not sure I forgive you for your part in all this yet. I didn't even know for sure it was you until we had to face Piper.'

'Yeah, well I nearly had a heart attack when I walked in and you turned around. Spotting Carlisle seconds later was no better. He wasn't part of the plan either.'

Teddington frowned up at Charlie, kept her voice low. 'He's wearing a wire, so Piper can hear what's going on.'

She got the impression from the stormy eyes that Charlie was frowning, it didn't show.

'That's a last-minute change. Which isn't good.'

'Why?'

'The operative in the cover situation, me, needs to have all the facts to avoid endangerment or miscalculation. Adding Carlisle and a wire without informing me puts both of us in greater jeopardy.'

'Maybe that's why they sent Carlisle, so you'd recognise him straight off. Which apparently you did, so they kind of did inform you. In a way.'

There was no covering up his smile this time. 'Trust you to see good intentions.' Again he swooped in for another kiss.

Again, she met him only for a moment. 'Hell, your make-up tastes worse than mine.'

His chuckle warmed her more than she wanted to admit.

'When we get out of this I'll waste no more time.'

'*If* we get out of this.'

He looked her in the eye, his eyes steely with determination. 'When.'

She dragged in a breath, but she wasn't going to be too soft yet. 'There's no guarantee of that.' She looked at the phone, it was shaking in her hand. She answered and put it to her ear.

'Chief Inspector?'

That put a pause in the response. 'Ari? What's different?'

'You're not on speakerphone. Why the call?'

'We have visual confirmation of one man returning to the front of the bank, but not you. What's going on?'

'Oh, just had my life threatened. Again.' She didn't feel quite as breezy as she sounded to her own ears. 'But I'm okay. Tell me you've got their van.'

'Sheldrake's holding it up.'

Teddington frowned. 'Who?'

'Police and Crime Commissioner,' Piper told her. 'She thinks we're all better off keeping you controlled where you are.'

Ari couldn't believe what she was hearing. Her emotions were boiling so she gave them the only available outlet, pouring all the heat into one bitten-out sentence. 'Well tell the bitch to get her arse in here and find out how controlled it feels to have a fucking gun pointed at *her* head.'

Chapter 21

Piper could hardly blame Teddington for her anger, but it was harder still not to laugh at the black humour he found in the fact that while she hadn't been using speakerphone, he had been at his end. And 'the bitch' was listening in.

He controlled his features as he sat at the rear of the van, and turned to the woman in question. Her pinched reaction was obvious, as was the barely controlled amusement of both Andrews and Wymark, both of whom were safely behind Sheldrake, and out of her line of sight.

'Apparently,' Sheldrake grated, 'the Prison Service needs to learn some respect.'

'Perhaps, ma'am.' Piper was suddenly less amused. Sheldrake's lack of empathy for the hostages was a serious concern. 'But it's not necessarily the lesson one learns when there's a gun pointed at one's head.' Sheldrake clearly wasn't open to the message so Piper ploughed on. 'The point is, we may seem to have the situation contained right now, but we're losing what little control we may have had. We have to give them the van.'

Sheldrake's eyes were cold dark spots. 'We have to get the hostages out.'

Piper barely controlled the clenching of his jaw. Open insubordination wasn't going to help the situation. 'The best way,' he said calmly, 'to get the hostages out is to let the robbers think they're getting away. We have a tracker in place on the van. We let them go, get the hostages back, follow the van discreetly and pounce once they stop.'

Sheldrake just looked back at him, utterly resistant. 'No.'

Locked in determined opposition, there didn't seem to be much either of them could do.

'Andrews, Wymark,' Sheldrake didn't look behind her as she spoke, 'get out.'

The two moved quietly from the van, Andrews carefully closing the sliding door after them. Piper felt ridiculously vulnerable. He understood the theory of elected commissioners, but with Sheldrake as the reality, the practice was less appealing. Less appealing again was the memory of seeing her at County Hall for a Chamber of Commerce evening drinks party with Rhys Mansel-Jones.

Sheldrake studied him like he was something unpleasant under a microscope. He supposed to her, he was. He looked back, attempting not to show the contempt he felt. He wasn't backing down but he knew he couldn't disobey a direct order from the commissioner.

'You don't like me do you, Detective Chief Inspector Piper?'

He didn't like the way she expanded his title with such chilling civility. Still, if that was the game she wanted to play, sod it. 'No.'

'Good.'

* * *

Their minute was easily up. Charlie went behind Teddington, his gun pointed at her back for appearance's sake. She hoped to reach the support of her chair, but the way was blocked by Mr Blue.

'So, you're the guard who got shot while handcuffed to a prisoner.'

Teddington kept her eyes on his chin; eye contact at this point was a potential tinderbox. 'Yes.'

'Where?'

She reached up with her left hand and pushed the strap of the corset as far aside as she could to show the scar. Mr Blue moved in close, too close. He also spotted the top of Sasha's picture, which he snatched out before Teddington could stop him.

'Give it back,' Charlie said.

Mr Blue looked at Charlie, and Teddington knew what he was going to do before he did it. Two hands rose—another shot out, pulled the picture clear from the threat of being ripped in two.

'Back off,' Charlie warned.

'Back to your post, Mr Brown.'

Teddington was quaking inside but she knew as well as Charlie would, he didn't really have any choice. There were too many heavy heartbeats before Charlie moved, but when he did he took Sasha's picture with him, slipping it into his back pocket. She decided Mr Blue had had more than enough time to see what needed to be seen. Her hand went back to hang at her side.

'If you're the woman Charlie Bell took on the run, then you lied to us.'

Teddington frowned, this time meeting Mr Blue's eyes. 'No I didn't.'

His slap stung across her face. The same cheek three times now. It was sore already and she was sick of being the beating post. Her head snapped back and this time she didn't even calculate the risk, she just glared at Mr Blue. 'What the fuck was that for?'

Suddenly the gun was back at her head. This time he had it pressed up into a nostril, forcing her to tip her head back.

'You know that negotiator,' Mr Blue sneered. 'You know DCI Piper.'

'What?' The demand was Mr White's.

This time Mr Blue slightly turned his head to talk to White. 'When Bell gave himself up, it was at a news conference held by DCI Matthew Piper.'

There was no denying it now. Teddington swallowed. 'Yes. Okay. I know Matt is DCI Piper. Yes, I've dealt with him before. But I never lied. Not one of you ever asked. What difference does it make anyway?'

'You went through a lot of hoops to make it seem like the two of you were strangers.'

'He's a copper, he must deal with masses of civilians. I wasn't to know if he remembered me straight off. Besides, Mr Pink over there had already recognised me, already kicked me. I didn't see any reason to make the connection known. You'd just have stuck a gun to my head and threatened me again.'

For a brief moment a smile flickered across Mr Blue's face. That scared Teddington.

'According to the report,' Mr Blue was too calm as he indicated to the TV, 'you were also caught up in the riot at Blackmarch. Says you were instrumental in the evidence trail. From what I hear…' He moved in, his lips uncomfortably close to her ear. 'You were wearing a wire.'

'Really?' It might be true, but had yet to come out publicly, which made her wonder who Mr Blue was, and what connections he had.

'You wearing a wire now?'

She frowned at him as she stood back. 'No.'

'Maybe I should check.' His fingers curled around the top of the corset.

'Blue!'

'Brown.'

Teddington's eyes jumped first to Charlie, then to Mr White as they issued their warnings, then she looked at Mr Blue, struggling to keep her voice under control as her phone started ringing again 'It's a corset. I've nothing on beneath it and I am not taking it off. There's plenty of steel boning which *could* hide a wire, but none of it is. Why would it? I had to be in that bloody riot, I had no choice. I didn't know this raid was going to happen. I didn't have to be here and I wouldn't have bloody well volunteered for it.' She pushed her head forward to snarl at him, not caring about the gun pressed viciously into her nose. 'Now either shoot me or let me answer this fucking phone!'

* * *

Piper blinked.

'Yes. I said "good", Matt.' Sheldrake gave him a strangely warm smile that looked out of place. 'May I call you Matt?'

He was too shocked to do anything but indicate agreement.

'Men like you shouldn't like me.'

Maybe the stress was finally getting to him. 'Men like me?'

'Yes, men like you. Good, capable, honest coppers.'

When did honest become a barb?

'Men who don't need anyone looking over their shoulders to do their job right,' Sheldrake went on. 'You should resent my existence. You should also be smart enough to know that plenty of your colleagues do need the likes of me looking over their shoulders. All the same, you should also be glad when someone like me is prepared to step up and be the public face of an op like this one, because if it goes wrong, it's my blood they'll be baying for.'

'Yes, ma'am.'

She actually smiled—slightly. 'When this is over, talk to Broughton. He doesn't like me either, but he plays the politics game much better than you do. But for now, we know we can only trust half of the information your informant passed on.'

'It seems he wasn't as high up the food chain as we thought.'

'Do we know where he is right now?'

Piper glanced away, shaking his head, then froze as his gaze fell on the video feed. 'Bollocks!' He was already hitting speed dial.

Chapter 22

Charlie was struggling to breathe. He was stuck out on the periphery of the action. Moving would risk Teddington's life, but she seemed determined to risk it anyway. She was visibly shaking with anger. She'd had the hostage training at work, he remembered her telling him that. Right now she should be calm and logical. She should be. But she wasn't. If she kept this up, she would be leaving this place in a body bag and there was bugger all he could to do to prevent it.

Mr Blue only lowered the gun and stepped away when Mr White ordered him to.

Only when he'd moved did Teddington accept the call, taking two steps towards the leader of the pack and holding the phone out to him.

'Hello?' Matt's disembodied voice seemed to echo in the bank.

Mr White said nothing, his features hard. Her look was just as fixed. Had they had pushed her to the point that she was no longer afraid? If they had, then a tense situation just became potentially explosive.

'Ari?' Matt sounded worried.

Charlie knew how the man felt. He was more worried seeing how belligerent both Teddington and Mr White looked.

'Mr White?'

'Oh for God's sake! One of you speak to him,' Mr Pink shouted.

Teddington huffed air through her nose. 'We can hear you, Matt,' she finally said.

'Is there a problem?'

For a moment, again, no one spoke.

'No.'

Charlie knew that 'no'. Spoken from between gritted teeth. It did not bode well.

This time the pause was Piper's. 'I'm not convinced by that, Ari. If there's a problem, I need to know about it.'

Again with the heavy silence.

'Okay,' said Piper, 'if that's the way you want to play it, fine, but here's the result. I've a van on its way as requested, but you don't get it until I get another hostage out here.'

Teddington didn't move, didn't speak. Neither did Mr White. It seemed like forever until Mr White slowly shook his head.

The room was holding its breath. Finally, Teddington inflated her lungs, then she did the stupidest thing Charlie had ever seen.

She stepped forward, grabbed Mr White's free hand and slapped her phone into it. She turned on her heel, heading for the only vacant chair as Mr White put the phone closer to his mouth.

'You want a hostage?' White barked. 'You can have a dead one.'

Charlie moved, but Carlisle was faster. He surged up from the floor, grabbed Teddington around the waist. Teddington yelped in surprise as Carlisle dragged her down, covering her body with his. Her head hit the arm of the chair as they tumbled to the floor.

Mr White fired.

Carlisle grunted, just audible through the sounds of the hostages screaming.

Teddington landed with an awkward heavy thump, Carlisle landing on top of her.

Charlie was rooted to the spot, focused on the fact that neither Teddington nor Carlisle were moving. So much for blank ammo. Teddington's hand rose to her forehead. When she moved it away her fingertips were red. Carlisle groaned.

Teddington looked over her shoulder, swore and twisted. Carefully, she eased Carlisle to the floor. He was sweating and pale, his eyes were scrunched, his teeth clenched behind drawn-back lips.

Coming to her knees, Teddington ignored the gushing gash on her forehead and turned Carlisle on his side. Numbly, Charlie took a couple of steps forward. Once upon a time he and Carlisle had been good friends. He still cared. His gut twisted to see Teddington pulling up Carlisle's hoodie, jumper and t-shirt, exposing a bullet hole in his upper back. If anyone noticed the slim black wire that also got exposed, no one commented. Carlisle coughed, spitting blood.

'Oh my God! Oh my God!' Zanti cried.

Samuel pulled her to him, cradling her as she sobbed.

Lucy was all-out screaming. Charlie wanted to scream right along with her, but found himself rooted to the spot.

Teddington looked up at Judith. 'Give me your scarf.'

'It's Hermès.'

This time Teddington just grabbed the printed silk. 'It's not worth more than a man's life!' She yanked the scarf, bundling it into a wodge and pressing it against Carlisle's back. 'We have to get him to an ambulance!'

Charlie stepped forward, galvanised at last. 'You—' He pointed to Samuel. 'And you.' This time at Judith. 'Get up.'

'What do you think you're doing?' Mr White demanded as Charlie knelt to help Teddington help Carlisle to his feet.

'Not getting put away for murder!' Charlie draped one of Carlisle's arms around Samuel's shoulders.

'You can't do this!'

'Keep the pressure there,' Teddington told Judith as the two swapped hold of the already soaked pad. Charlie helped on the awkward trip to the door as Teddington rounded on Mr White. 'He can do this, and what's more, he has to do this.' As he checked they were safe, he looked up to see Teddington glance behind her, making sure that Samuel, Carlisle and Judy were already out on the pavement. To her clear relief, and to Charlie's, men in yellow jackets and green boiler suits were already rushing to help. Teddington glared at Mr White, Charlie shut the hostages outside. 'Clearly no one else in this building knows, but that man you just shot… he's an off-duty police officer, you moron. Let him die and you'll never see freedom again!'

White's expression was torn between hate and surprise. Charlie knew he should intervene but he couldn't see a single route that wasn't going to make things worse.

'You still have six hostages, that's enough,' she snarled, then she lunged at Mr White.

Charlie's stomach turned to lead.

She was going to tackle Mr White?

No, she just grabbed the phone.

'Are you still there, Matt?'

'I am.'

'Good, pin back your ears and listen. That news report also told these men that I know you, and they are not happy bunnies. Not with me or you. If you want any hope of getting five more hostages out of here alive, then you get that van here and you do it now.'

'It's on its way,' the voice came back. 'Wait! A second ago, you said six hostages.'

Teddington took a breath before she answered, 'I said you'd get five back alive.'

* * *

Piper swore, already climbing from the van as Teddington hung up. This had all gone badly tits up. He looked at Andrews.

'Get that van here now.' Piper hardly cared that he was throwing orders over his shoulder to the commissioner and he wasn't pleased that he heard her getting it arranged—he was relieved.

As Piper pushed through his colleagues to the cordon, Carlisle was already on a trolley, the paramedics rushing him into an ambulance reeling off a list of stats that did not sound good or even hopeful. Piper grabbed the nearest uniform, having no idea who the guy was. 'You go with him, and you keep me informed.'

He pushed the man towards Carlisle as he moved on to the other hostages, both of whom were being wrapped in blankets and taken to other medical vehicles, being checked for shock.

'Are you Matt?' Samuel asked.

'DCI Piper,' he confirmed with a nod.

'That woman, Ari. She's been so strong, but I think she's losing it.'

Piper frowned, not liking the fact that he had to agree with... Piper looked at the Invicta Bank uniform and ran the list in his head. 'Samuel Frankfort?'

'Yeah.'

As they moved closer to another ambulance, where the female hostage sat, Piper asked him what he had seen.

'All that quiet self—' Sam fumbled for an apt description.

'Assurance?'

'Yeah, that'll do. It's cracking. Whatever they did to her in Presswick's office, it got to her. I think I heard her calling Mr White a moron as we left. That can't be a good sign.'

It wasn't. When Broughton found out, the air would turn blue. He dreaded to think what Sheldrake would make of the exchange. Delaying that dreaded moment, he turned to the woman sitting at the end of the ambulance.

'Ma'am, are you Miss Arden or Miss Montgomery?'

'Montgomery, Judith,' she supplied. 'It's Mrs. Is that man going to be okay?'

'I don't know.' Piper hoped so, but he doubted it. Still, he had to push down his own concerns and get on with his job. 'And I'm sorry to be brusque, but I need to know what's going on in there.'

In a succession of quick questions and rapid answers, most from Samuel, who'd been surprisingly observant, Piper learnt where each of the men had been stationed and where the hostages were.

'Okay, thanks for your help. Is there anything else you think we should know?'

Samuel shook his head.

Judith was frowning.

Piper watched as she turned away. 'Judith?'

She was sucking on her bottom lip. She knew something.

'Judith, please. Time is of the essence here.'

She looked up at him, shook her head slightly. 'It's stupid,' she declared. 'I've already shown my quota of stupid for the day.'

Samuel quickly and unnecessarily explained about the scarf. Piper figured that if she could be embarrassed, she'd survive the experience.

'It's surprising how often it's the stupid things people say that help the police, so please, what were you thinking?'

She took a breath. 'It's just that the gang's one short. They're missing Mr Blonde.' She looked between Piper and Samuel. 'What? I like *Reservoir Dogs*. Y'know, the film.'

Okay, sometimes people just say stupid things. There again, there was the getaway driver, maybe he was Mr Blonde. Piper offered Judith a smile. 'Well, thanks for your time.'

As he turned, Piper saw Sheldrake taking a printed sheet from one of the Press Liaison Officers. She was right, he didn't envy her getting in front of the cameras on this one. Checking around, he couldn't see Dowling. He moved away from the ambulance and headed directly to Sheldrake's side. 'I don't see Dowling any more.'

'I made a phone call. She'll be working the agricultural shows for a few weeks at least.'

Piper only barely controlled his smile. 'Shame.'

'Isn't it?' Sheldrake's smile was wider but like Piper's it quickly dropped away. 'The real shame is, I had to promise her replacement the first question in the next piece to camera.' She lifted the paper and headed towards the lion's den.

'Where are we?' Piper asked as he went back into the surveillance van.

'Shit Creek.'

'Deepest, darkest—'

Andrews held up a hand, listening intently to whatever was being fed through his earpiece. As Andrews listened, the loss of not just Carlisle but their ears inside the bank sank in. If things escalated inside, they'd have no quick warning, no ability to put a call in pre-emptively.

'The van's in place to be reversed in at any time,' Andrews said. 'Our snipers are in position.'

It was tempting, but Piper shook his head. 'Can't use them while they still have hostages.'

'If they take a hostage it'll be Ari, and even she knows they'll kill her given the chance.'

'That's only one possibility.' And a depressing one. 'We'll wait and see. When that van goes down the service road, I want one of your guys on open mike, full commentary. I need to know what's happening as it happens.'

Chapter 23

'Here.'

Teddington looked at Presswick, feeling sick, not sure why. She'd left the fallen chair on its side, and sat beside him in the seat Judith had vacated. Her head was throbbing, her anger had dissipated and only cold dread remained. She looked at the pristine cotton fold he offered. Handkerchief. From his top pocket. His eyes moved to the gash on her forehead. It was still bleeding, but less so now. She felt another trickle down the side of her face.

She didn't take the handkerchief. 'So now you choose to be human?'

'What do you mean?' His hand dropped.

'She means,' Zanti grated, 'that you are a grade A imbecile.'

'Unless you want to lose your job—'

'My job!' Zanti surprised everyone with the snap. 'In case you haven't noticed, you egotistical buffoon, there's more on the line here than jobs. You took a seat and never once considered letting Miss Arden or me sit because heaven forbid you have to sit on the floor, but it's okay for your staff and your customers to do so. Mr Presswick,' Zanti's voice was clear and strong, 'you can take your job and shove it up your arse.'

Teddington felt an odd burst of pride, but she couldn't figure out why. Her head hurt, her vision was swimming. In an effort to keep what little equilibrium she had, she concentrated on a spot on the floor, on that piece of white thread she'd seen hours ago, when the raid started.

Now her ears were ringing.

Presswick nudged her so hard she nearly fell off the seat. She turned slowly to glare at the man, but she didn't want to pull at the cut so didn't frown.

'The phone,' his hiss was urgent.

What phone?

She looked at it.

Oh dear Lord, it was vibrating. She accepted the call and concentrated on the floor.

'Hello?'

'Ari, it's Matt. We have the van, it's ready to pull into the service yard behind the bank. Is everyone in there ready to accept that?'

The temptation to close her eyes and sleep was nearly overwhelming, but she had a job to do. She looked up, then grabbed the edge of the seat as the world tilted under her.

Someone swore.

'Mr White?'

'Ari?'

Another man spoke. A face swam in front of her. She didn't recognise the dark skin or heavy brow.

'Ari? How many fingers am I holding up?'

She blinked and frowned. Neanderthal. Mr Brown. 'One's traditional.' She looked at the hand. She tried to focus, to think. *Not Brown. Charlie. Charlie Brown.*

The giggle escaped with a bitter edge. She clamped her hand over her mouth and blinked, focused. Brown eyes were looking back at her. Charlie had blue eyes. Contacts. *Think!* He was worried. She had to focus.

'Two,' she huffed this time, 'shouldn't they be spread and the other way round?'

She felt the world shift again. A big hand held her shoulder, steadied her. She looked at the man who owned the hand. *Charlie, my Charlie.* Only he wasn't hers. He'd saved her once; would he save her again? She closed her eyes. *Sod that, wake up and save yourself.*

'What's wrong with her?'

What is *wrong with me?*

'I think she's concussed.'

'Oh,' she agreed with the voice, 'that makes sense.' She tried to think straight. 'Wasn't there a question? Beside the finger thing. Van. That's it.' She looked up. 'Mr White, they have a van ready. Are you okay for them to bring the van round the back?'

She frowned, then turned to the man beside her. 'Did he nod?'

'Yeah,' Charlie said, his tone oddly gentle and surprisingly reassuring.

She brought the phone up. 'Yes, Matt,' she enunciated, 'you can bring the van in.'

'You tell the driver to leave the engine running and go.' Mr White stepped up. 'Any fire from the sniper opposite and I kill a hostage. Understood?'

'Understood.'

Matt sounded very decisive, clear. Teddington envied him. She needed clarity and she wasn't getting any. It was like thinking through treacle, hearing through cotton-wool.

Someone called for Orange. *I could use a drink. Put a vodka in mine.*

Mr Blue was moving. *Must be moving fast, he's all blurry.* A single silly giggle escaped her. *Maybe he's the Flash, moves superfast.* He was kneeling behind Zanti. For a moment Teddington thought he'd sprouted whiskers, then realised he had a bunch of zip ties clamped between his teeth. He was securing Zanti to the chair.

She blinked and tried to focus. Her head hurt, her forehead was throbbing, she could feel the thick warmth of blood slowly moving down her face. Thinking was painful, but it hardly mattered.

'Not long now,' Charlie muttered.

Was that supposed to be reassuring?

Mr Orange re-joined the pack. He was at Presswick's feet, using two zip ties to secure his ankles to the chair supports. For once the bank manager didn't complain.

Her eyes fell to the phone. That was the last conversation necessary. Since she had no reachable pockets, she put the slim device in the only safe place she had—under the left strap of the corset. It was slightly awkward, but her right shoulder was aching and she didn't want the cold metal making it worse. She shivered as it touched the top of her breast.

'Ari?'

For a moment she looked at Charlie, now kneeling before her. His concern was touching, but out of place.

'I'm okay.' She tried to smile, but it pulled at the cut on her forehead. 'You tie us down, you go. The police will come in, free us. I'll get treated for…' why couldn't she remember the word?

'Concussion.' Charlie pushed her back so she was sitting straight, safe. She knew he left because she felt colder and her eyelids were too heavy. *Sleep, I'll sleep soon. Sleep forever. No, sleep can come later.*

It was mind over matter, but she made her body function. She opened her eyes. *Focus, woman!*

Mr Blue and Mr White were near the counter. Each took a bag, crossing them over their shoulders. She figured they should have 'swag' written on the side instead of 'Nike'. *Oh, concentrate.* The man who'd kicked her, Mr Pink, took a bag and another was passed to Mr Brown.

Mr Pink got the handle twisted, couldn't sort it out. 'Oh, fuck a duck.'

Fragments in her mind fell into place as the bag fell over the man's shoulder. Over eight months ago, petty crime, didn't adjust well, strip search, fuck a duck.

'Lester Grimshaw.'

She hadn't meant to say it out loud and only realised she had when everything went preternaturally still and quiet.

Mr Blue and Mr White were looking at her, seeming a little startled. Then Mr Blue raised an arm. Teddington hadn't seen that particular pistol silenced before, it made an odd puff sound, then a nothingness happened, going on for what felt like forever.

Lester stood, suspended. Behind him the colour of the carpet changed. A tiny trickle of blood crept down his forehead. Surprise relaxed to slackness as he fell to his knees, then lay quiet.

'Jesus!' Mr Brown swore.

'She named him,' Mr Blue said, his weapon now levelled at Mr Brown.

Oh God forgive her, she'd inadvertently killed a man.

'Get his bag.'

Teddington watched Charlie move over to Mr Pink's—Lester's—body. She figured Charlie didn't have much choice but to do what he was told, but she wished he'd shown slightly more reluctance to do it. Removing the bag from where it had been slung across the man's chest wasn't easy, and it left blood on the bag handle, but Charlie did it. Somehow knowing he had no other option didn't help her rationalise the action, yet at the same time she tried not to notice that he looked worried about her as he glanced between her and Mr Blue.

Something was wrong. Very wrong. Something other than the dead man on the floor.

Why haven't I been tied up?

She watched Mr Orange. He'd moved on from Presswick and was securing Megan, who was busy telling Lucy it would all soon be over. The girl was clinging to her mother. Mr Orange forced Megan's arms from around the girl to secure them to the support rail of the bench. Lucy's sobs turned to screams as Mr Orange viciously yanked her from her mother's lap and handed her to Mr Blue. For a moment all Teddington could see were wide brown eyes full of fears and tears.

The moment was broken when Mr Orange grabbed Miss Arden with his left hand, his right pointing a pistol at her, dragging her to the back.

Mr Blue paused in his harassment of Lucy to catch Teddington's eye.

Oh my God, he's going to kill me now. That's why I'm not tied up. Dead people can't run anywhere.

Mr Blue's grin was malicious as he pulled the kid towards him, keeping her uncomfortably close, taking her with him as he too turned and headed towards the back, ignoring Megan's screams for her daughter.

Zanti, Presswick and Megan were tied down. Teddington still wasn't. Suddenly Mr White was standing over her. He grabbed her wrist. She was yanked to her feet, held in front of him. More cold metal was pressed against her flesh. Muzzle to temple this time. She was made to walk behind Mr Blue, Mr White's gun pressed against her back. She sensed more than saw that Mr Brown was following them, though she was sure that she heard his footfalls pause, guessed she'd never know why.

Three hostages on the move. Not good odds. If it were only her, she could risk anything, but now she had to think about Miss Arden and Lucy. She couldn't jeopardise their safety. She looked around as they were marched through the hidden part of the bank, which was even grottier than the front. They congregated in the hall to the back door. From the smell, the place clearly had a damp problem.

It was all Teddington could do to stand upright; she was distantly aware that she was rocking back and forth.

She'd faced worse odds, but in that moment she couldn't remember when. The bigger issue was, she wasn't sure how to get out of this.

Chapter 24

Standing in the dim back room, as he followed orders and pulled on new gloves, Charlie struggled with every thought and feeling to make sense of what was happening.

He had retrieved the brown wallet Mr Blue had added to the pile of customer wallets on his way past. The wallet he'd mugged a guy for. One of Lincoln's controls. So that was, possibly, one less piece of evidence against him, but only if he got it and himself right away from here. Given what a total fuck-up this day had turned out to be, that was looking questionable.

He could just see Beamish's head behind the others. That Beamish was the man who'd watched him so intently in the pub the night he'd 'killed' Lexi, had been obvious from the moment of their introduction. Neither had offered spoken greeting nor a handshake. Neither had spoken of the night in the pub nor what Charlie had had to do. Beamish, however, had carried a superior look in his eye. A challenge. Beamish wanted to be top dog. Charlie held the gaze long enough and with sufficient disinterest to make it clear he wasn't impressed. Then he turned to Lincoln and asked how many others were involved.

Beamish soon got the message and went to play with more interesting toys. The way Beamish had treated Grimshaw always reminded Charlie of a child with an insect: cruel and capricious.

They'd spent three weeks constantly rehearsing how this raid was going to go down. And from the second it had started, things had gone differently. Through their preparations, Charlie had constantly asked for backup plans, and the response had been "no need". But standing now at the end of the line, Charlie knew that there were definitely contingency plans in place, and that he hadn't been told about them. He turned back to look at the open door, leading to the front of the branch. He was pretty sure Lester hadn't known about the contingency plans either.

And look what had happened to him.

'Did you hear me, Brown?'

Charlie snapped back to the here and now. He blinked and thought about it. 'Knock three times on the back of the cab when we're in and ready to go. Got it.'

Mr White's expression reminded him of a teacher displeased at not finding fault. 'Good.'

* * *

'What the hell?' Piper couldn't believe it. Surveillance clearly showed one of the robbers had been shot, and without Carlisle's mike, he had no idea what was happening inside. He hit redial. Teddington's phone rang all the way to answer phone. 'Fuck.' He met Andrews' eye and answered the unvoiced question. 'Either she can't or won't pick up.'

'Can't,' Andrews declared, 'but let's hope it's because she's under orders, not because she's already dead.'

Piper's stomach acid rose at the thought.

Andrews looked deadly calm. 'Give my men release to fire.'

'No.' One thing Piper was sure of was that he didn't want a shootout. This wasn't the wild west, after all. 'Not while they still have hostages. Are your guys on open mike?'

Andrews reached out and flicked a switch. 'Spader, you're on open mike. What's happening out there?'

A burst of static preceded the deep, disembodied voice. 'Not a lot, sir.'

Why Piper found that sardonically amusing, he didn't know.

'The van is in position, the driver is away clean. The gunman at the rear window watched the driver retreat but has now moved out of sight. We no longer have a visual on anyone in the bank.'

'Rear door?' Andrews asked.

'Solid, sir.'

'Of course.' Piper nodded. Not only solid, but probably metal-cased, a security door to avoid break ins. 'Keep a running commentary, Spader. Anything you see, report.'

'Yes, sir.'

Even the air inside the van seemed tense as they waited. On the digital clock, mounted above the monitor, the large green numbers seemed to take a year to change. As they crawled through the seconds, Piper worried. He worried about Carlisle—would he survive surgery? He worried about Teddington. She seemed resigned to the fact she wasn't going to survive at all, but he couldn't reach that same point. He refused to. He worried about Charlie—he wasn't the gang member already dead on the bank floor but if they were turning on themselves, he was probably the next in line. But while he was alive, could he protect Teddington? He worried, a little, about his own career. Broughton had said Charlie's fuck-up was his fuck-up, and whatever way you cut it, even though Broughton had said nothing, this whole thing was fucked up.

Andrews and Piper jumped as the van door opened; Sheldrake stepping in didn't lighten the mood.

'Situation?'

Piper appreciated that she both shut the door and took the stool at the front of the ops area, out of their way. With Carlisle out of the picture, Wymark had been redeployed.

'Van's in place, ma'am,' Andrews supplied. 'Driver's out, no visual on any of the gang.'

'Hostages?'

'Three in view inside the bank, three not.'

'Our contact?'

'Not.'

'And the van is tagged?'

'Yes, ma'am. Under the driver's seat. They won't find it unless they remove the driver's seat.'

'Range?'

'Ten-miles.'

'And we have a driver in place to follow?'

'Yes, ma'am. A two-car tag team, in fact.'

Sheldrake took a deep measured breath as she considered. Her only response was a single nod.

For a few more everlasting seconds they waited. Another static burst, and Spader reported.

'The rear door's opening.'

Piper switched his gaze from the floor to Andrews then the speaker.

'First to exit is a woman.'

Teddington?

'Ah, a hostage. Has a Glock to her temple.'

'Description?' Piper demanded.

'Blonde.'

Not Teddington.

'Red dress and coat, crying.'

'Must be Miss Arden.'

'Man holding her is average height, brown hair, grey suit, he's wearing purple latex gloves. There's one bag over his shoulder. It's a Nike holdall, looks fully stuffed.'

Purple. Not latex gloves; nitrile. Odd choice.

'They're in holding position by the door.'

'I have a shot,' a second voice announced.

'No.' Piper was emphatic. With a mumbled apology he looked back at Sheldrake. 'Ma'am?'

'Not while the other hostages are still at risk.'

'Hold your fire,' Andrews commanded. 'Spader, return to commentary.'

'First man has disappeared behind the van. Don't know if you just heard that, but he shouted for the next guy. Door is opening again. A second man has appeared. Shit.'

'Spader?'

'This one's holding a kid, she looks terrified, cry—'

'Describe the man,' Andrews cut across the stream.

'Dark hair and mid-brown skin, trimmed beard. Tan leather jacket. He has another bag over his shoulder, strap across the torso.'

All their ill-gotten gains, Piper presumed.

'Now there's another one coming out. Woman this time. Her hands are up, contusion across her forehead, it's bled badly. She has long dark hair and a sexy burgundy corset.'

Teddington.

'Spader,' Andrews warned.

'She's a lot calmer than the previous two.'

'Resignation?' Andrews suggested to those inside the van.

Piper's expression stressed his uncertainty. 'It's not the first time someone's threatened her life.' *Not even the first time today.*

'Concentrate on the men, Spader,' Andrews ordered. 'They're the ones we're interested in.'

'Next is another male. White, conventionally-cut blond hair. Black suit. Another bag. Another man has stepped out. Very tall, with an overhanging brow. Thick sweater, the kind you get from military surplus stores. No hostage and two bags this time.'

'Do you have line of sight on all?' Andrews asked.

'No,' a different voice came back. 'First four are behind the van.'

Andrews cursed softly.

'I see a man in the driver's seat, wait a second, the first hostage must have gone into the van. Second adult hostage approaching—Whoa! She's tripped, is down, man in black has grabbed her—Jesus!'

'Spader!'

'Have line of sight.' Another voice.

'Not while the other hostages are in danger.' Sheldrake had moved up behind Piper as he radioed the tail car to put them on standby. 'What was the expletive for, Spader?'

'Way he grabbed her, looked like he was going to rip her arm off. She looked like she was ready to rip his head off too but stopped herself. They're glaring. All I can hear is the kid crying. Brunette breaks glare to look into the van. Man in black has a gun to brunette's chin. Now is our best chance.'

'Hold your fire,' Andrews insisted.

Piper found himself gripping his stool and holding his breath. He didn't want Teddington killed on his watch. He'd rather she wasn't killed on any watch.

'Brunette's put her hands up. She's turning to the van, getting in. Man in black and the one in the sweater are now in van. Rear door closing. Van is pulling away.' The man's tone reflected a certain amount of deflation at not being able to take the shot.

Andrews stepped from the van door, caught the eye of one sergeant and, as pre-agreed, gave the nod. Then he left the squad to go in the front of the bank.

Piper couldn't move.

Confirmation came over the radio that the van was out and moving. As agreed, no marked vehicles gave chase, but the blue Astra was in pursuit, hanging back and following the tracker more than the van. Everything was in place. Now all they could do was wait.

Chapter 25

Pushed forward, Teddington first nearly tripped over the bags, and then over Miss Arden. The blonde was vaguely central along the inside of the van.

Behind the cab was the only place Teddington could go, so she did. Her jellified knees made her grateful she could sit back down. There was nothing inside the van for her to cling on to, so she wasn't sure what was going to happen when they moved off, or went around a corner. Charlie dumped his bags with the others in the middle of the van, then moved closer to her, his back against the van wall, his long legs reaching across the width of the vehicle so he could brace himself. And her, hopefully.

At the rear of the van, Mr Blue still had hold of the crying Lucy. It seemed an odd position for him to take up, but Teddington was willing to bet the choice had something to do with tormenting Lucy with the proximity of freedom. Mr White pulled the back door shut behind him and sat opposite Mr Blue. Each of those men had a wheel arch to brace themselves against.

Mr White nodded at Charlie.

Even knowing that it was Charlie under the Neanderthal brow wasn't making Teddington feel any safer. Especially when he leaned across her to knock three times on the dividing wall between the cab and the haulage space. As they started to move, the break in inertia pushed her towards Charlie, but she managed to scoot back. The men had thrown the bags of loot into the middle of the van, and then, like Teddington, they moved around the floor.

She looked down the van towards Lucy. There was nothing she could do with Charlie and Mr Blue between them. Lucy was crying and wriggling, starting to get bolder in her fighting of Mr Blue, using her heels to kick.

'Why don't you let Lucy come up here with me,' Teddington suggested. 'She'll be quieter with me, but just as trapped.'

Lucy was thrashing now, but Mr Blue had brought her onto his lap, his arm trapping her there as she wriggled and squirmed. Mr Blue held the girl tight as he smiled at Teddington.

'She's fine just where she is.' Lucy continued moving over his lap and Mr Blue's smile grew creepier. 'She's doing a grand job.'

'She's just a kid,' Miss Arden muttered.

Too sick to her stomach to say anything, Teddington was glad the blonde had finally found her courage and her voice.

Mr Blue just looked at Lucy and pushed his hips up. Teddington realised that either Lucy was too innocent to realise what was going on, or nothing was going on and Mr Blue was just trying to put them even more on edge. She hoped for the latter and suspected the former. Whatever the case, the best reaction in this situation was no reaction. Teddington looked away. It took a moment to realise that the chattering teeth were her own. This was shock, in part at least.

Bowing her head, she closed her eyes and pulled in a deep breath, a breath that caught when the inflation of her lungs shifted the bruising on her side. She had to get a grip. Her head was banging, her wits felt slow. That was part of the concussion. Her body was quaking. Given that her coat was still in the bank and she was wearing a sleeveless corset, was it any surprise she was cold?

Good. That was good. Fear wasn't taking over, though she would admit that when Mr White had grabbed her after her trip, she was ready to tear his head off. That flash of rage could have been a fatal mistake, probably not just for her.

The reality was that her chances of survival were low, but they weren't non-existent. All she had to do was—

* * *

'Ah!'

Charlie knew enough about Teddington to know she wouldn't have meant to cry out, but the sound was forced out of her as they rounded a sudden bend and she was thrown to the side. He was taking the press of inertia on his right hand, using the thin lip of the sliding door to hold himself. Thankfully only her shoulder hit the sliding door, not her forehead. It still looked bad, but was at least scabbing over nicely.

Her eyes had been closed. She was probably trying to get her reactions under control. That was good, he needed her calm, it was one less thing for him to worry about. And now she was looking up him, centrifugal force keeping her pushed against the van's side door.

'You okay?'

She nodded but as she moved to sit, he raised his arm and pulled her against him. Securing her to his side. It felt foolishly good. He wanted to bend down and kiss her.

Now you really are being foolish.

'Are we being followed?'

Mr White was talking into a short-range radio. Charlie held Teddington close, hoping that she'd warm up. He was torn between what he wanted to do and what he had to do. Static interrupted his thoughts, then Mr Orange's voice came back, barely audible. Charlie strained to hear.

'No tail that I can see.'

Mr White looked back at him. Simon Lincoln had penetrating eyes, but they didn't scare Charlie anywhere near as much as a single glance from Broughton used to.

'If they are following, it's likely to be two or three cars back.' He had to speak loud above the engine noise. He had to ignore the fact that Teddington had laid her head on his shoulder, her hair tickling his ear. That apple scent shouldn't get to him, but it did. 'More likely to be a tracker on the van or an eye in the sky. Tell—' He'd been about to use Stubbs' real name, but if he did that, he was condemning Teddington. 'Tell him to look up, look for a helicopter.'

Mr White did. There appeared to be no aerial tail.

'And this takes care of any on-board device.'

Mr White was brandishing a small black plastic box. Charlie recognised it as a jammer. They didn't cost much and were readily available if you knew where to go. He hadn't thought about it, but clearly Lincoln had. Just like he'd come up with contingency plans that he hadn't shared. And what were all those whispers between Lincoln and Andrew Beamish, the man under the Blue banner? What things did they say? What plans did they make? Plans like dragging Lucy into this? A kid had never been part of the plan. On a school day, there shouldn't even have been one in the bank.

Teddington pressed into him as they went around another corner. She hadn't been part of the plan either, but Lincoln hadn't hesitated to use her. If Charlie put a foot wrong, she would pay for it with her life.

'No tail,' Mr Blue said looking at Lucy, who had finally settled down. 'Do you know that means?'

All wide-eyed and innocent, Lucy looked at the man and shook her head.

'It means we don't need you any more.'

'You're going t-to lez me go?' Hope sprang in her voice despite the brace-induced lisp.

'Yeah.'

At the last second Charlie realised what was happening.

'No!' Shoving Teddington away, he lunged, but Lincoln had the door open. As Charlie reached for Lucy, the girl was sent tumbling and screaming through the open rear. Breaks squealed behind them, cars snaked to avoid the prone girl. Mr White pulled the door shut. All Charlie could do was stare in horror at what they'd done.

'Just throwing out the trash.'

Charlie saw red. He pounced but Beamish was quicker. A boot to the shoulder pushed him off balance, the van turning sharply forced him back.

'You bastard!'

'There was no need for that,' Beamish snarled.

'What about this?'

A sudden cry of pain snapped his attention to Teddington, her jaw tight against obvious pain as her head was pushed down by Carol. The blonde bitch had managed to twist and pin Teddington to the floor where he'd pushed her. Now the spiked heel she had worn was being pressed into Teddington's ear. In prison, Charlie had seen a man deafened by such an act; as a young police officer he'd arrested a girl for affray in a drunken brawl, but the way she'd twisted her heel in a boy's head had increased the charge up to murder.

That girl had been unwitting—Carol wasn't. For a moment, he saw only Teddington, knowing how much danger she was in. He'd always known Beamish was a psycho, but throwing a kid from a moving vehicle? How could anyone do that? Still, it had been done and he couldn't change it. He could do something for Teddington though.

Charlie shifted, moved to his previous spot. 'No,' he said carefully, 'there's no need for that either.'

Only when he'd backed away from the other two men did Carol release Ari, going over to sit with Beamish. Her boyfriend.

As they settled down together, Teddington was sitting up. She looked dazed, confused. Charlie didn't have to move far to simply invite her back to him. Even if his arm screamed in protest. She was more important. With one eye on the others, Teddington carefully eased herself against him. As she nestled under his arm, her head on his shoulder, he was worried. The battlefield had shifted. Beamish was grinning at him. Not a good sign. As Beamish pulled Carol to him, he pointed his gun at Charlie—no, at Teddington. He mimed the action of taking a shot. Charlie felt Teddington shudder. Beamish laughed.

Chapter 26

As soon as they had the all-clear from the rear of the building that the bank robbers were gone, Andrews' men went in the front.

Piper scraped his hands over his face. The gang still had three hostages, at least one of whom, Teddington, had been injured, and another was a child. Carlisle was still in theatre with a bullet in his back. And one member of the gang was dead on the floor.

Hiding in the observation van wouldn't help and while he still had a job, he'd better go and do it. As Piper walked towards the bank, a tall man in a double-breasted suit was being escorted out. Mallory Presswick. Piper didn't care that the man was rubbing his wrists and complaining. If that was all he had to complain about, he had no complaints. The guys from uniform could deal with him, take his statement, though right now they were handing him over to the paramedics. Next out was a short woman with a Middle Eastern look, Zanti Bashir.

'Where's Sam?' Piper heard her say. 'Samuel Frankfort? He came out with that man who got shot? Where is he?'

'It's alright,' Piper said stepping closer. 'Sam went to the hospital to get checked out.'

'Is he hurt?'

'No, don't worry, he's fine. It's just routine to check everyone for shock.' Trying a reassuring smile, Piper wasn't sure he managed it. 'You'll probably see him at the hospital.'

Piper was expecting the final hostage to be out, but there was no sign. He could hear a woman sobbing inside. Checking with the man stationed at the door, Piper went in to find her in floods of tears, pushing away the female officer trying to calm her. One man was stationed by the body of the shot gang member. They couldn't take him outside while the press and public were still out there. The SOCOs would need to do their bit, too. Piper stopped a single step inside the building, standing shoulder to shoulder with Andrews.

'I figured it was best to keep her in here, let the rabble outside disperse a bit. Keep her upset private.'

Piper nodded. The woman had a right to be hysterical, and no one needed that on public news broadcasts.

'Good call.'

Piper blinked in surprise and turned to see Sheldrake behind him. 'How was it out there?'

Her look was sardonic. 'How do you think?'

'Sorry, ma'am.'

She shrugged. 'It's part of my job.'

'Don't give me that twaddle!' Megan shouted, again pushing away the female officer as she stood up. 'My daughter is still with those monsters!'

'She's also,' Piper said, stepping up to Megan, who turned to him with an eye ready to burn him to cinders, 'with Ariadne Teddington. Ari will do everything she can to keep your daughter safe.'

'Ari tried but she couldn't keep herself safe.'

'And she did that to keep you safe. Look, I understand—' He held up a hand and stopped Megan before she ranted at him. 'How it feels to have your child in danger. I know you're going through hell right this moment, just as I would if it were my daughter who'd been taken. But you have to trust me when I say that we are doing everything we can to ensure we bring your daughter home alive and well.'

He watched the anger drain out of Megan and all that was left was devastation. Her shoulders slumped and her eyes pleaded.

'I just want my little girl back.'

Piper put a comforting hand on her shoulder. 'I know.' Then as Megan bowed her head and started to cry, he looked at the PC behind her, a reliable-looking woman who had silently watched all, empathy clear, without being so intense that it would compromise the PC. The PC took up the blanket that Megan had thrown off and placed it around her, leading the now quiet mother from the bank.

Piper watched her leave. He really did understand the terrible position any parent would be in at this point. His own daughter had once gone missing, albeit only for four hours, but they were the worst four hours of his entire life. She'd been eight, much the same age as Lucy was now. He'd hated Charlie for making him stay home, to wait and be useless, while Charlie had searched, but in the end, it had been the right call. Charlie had carried home his little girl, Shauna, safe and sound. Though Charlie had never said what he'd had to do to get her back, Shauna had hinted, and ever since she had seen Charlie as some kind of superhero.

Ten years had passed but the pain of those four hours was something he would never forget. He saw the same thing in Megan Barton. He suspected that Mrs Whittaker, Teddington's mother, was going through just as much anguish and with just as a debilitating sense of helplessness.

'You have a daughter?' Sheldrake asked as she stepped closer to Piper.

For a moment Piper just looked at the woman. Her unexpected bursts of humanity kept surprising him. 'I have two. Twins. And a son.'

'One of each myself.' Sheldrake was nodding. 'Poor woman.'

Piper wasn't sure how to take this softer side of Sheldrake. Thankfully, she seemed to realise her error and the professional shell clicked back into place. She pointed to the dead man on the floor. 'What about this one?'

They stopped behind the first SOCO, who was putting out evidence cards, not that there was much to mark. Just the body. Piper looked down at the man; there was a neat little hole in his forehead, and a congealing pool of blood made an uneven halo round his head.

'That certainly isn't a face from the pictures you showed me,' Sheldrake said.

'No, ma'am, nor is it a face I recognise.'

'Chief Inspector!'

Piper and Sheldrake turned swiftly to see Siddig at the door. She was breathing hard and looked worried.

'You're needed in the field office.'

Their short acquaintance was enough for Piper to know that Siddig wasn't wasting his time. She moved back as Piper strode towards her and they marched shoulder to shoulder from the bank, Sheldrake bringing up the rear.

'What's going on?'

Siddig looked worried. 'I think it's best we talk inside.'

This can't be good.

Once they were inside the hairdresser's, the chemical smells finally muffled by cop sweat and coffee, Siddig turned to Piper and Sheldrake. 'Three facts and none of them good.'

Piper's mouth went dry.

'Firstly, the gang don't have Lucy any more.'

'Thank God,' Sheldrake breathed.

'Not so much, ma'am,' Siddig said. 'They threw her out of the back of the van into on-coming traffic. The civilian driver between the van and pursuit car two had to brake hard and swerve to avoid running the poor girl over. He went into another car and, well… it's rush hour. All but gridlock behind them. The team in car one got to the girl, and got her to the hospital. Hardly standard procedure, but it seemed more efficient than making an ambulance struggle through traffic. She's got some broken bones but considering the bank robbers were holding her at gun point, it could have been a lot worse.'

'Injured girl, grid lock, and…' Piper almost didn't want to know. 'What's the third thing?'

'Well car two is stuck behind the collision and car one is heading to the hospital.'

'So we've got no immediate pursuit,' Sheldrake acknowledged. 'We can still get another car on their tail with the tracker.'

'That's actually the last problem, ma'am,' Siddig said. 'The pursuit cars reported that before they lost the van after the accident, they'd already lost the signal.'

Sheldrake looked to Piper.

Ice washed through his veins. He met her accusatory glance. 'Jammers are available for open purchase, they aren't even expensive. But it means they must have planned ahead.' *Which was really bad news because that wasn't part of the plan that Charlie knew anything about.* 'Right,' Piper said, deciding it was time to take charge again, 'Siddig, get to the hospital. I want you with Mrs Barton. You tell her, you take her to her daughter, and while you're there…' He pulled his ringing personal phone from his pocket as he spoke. 'Get me a status check on Carlisle.'

* * *

Charlie wrapped his hand around Teddington's cold arm. Normally he'd have rubbed it to try to warm her up, but the pain from Beamish's kick prevented that. Now he stared at the van wall and tried to think.

They could bail through the sliding door, but that would be dangerous and given the beating Teddington had already taken, it probably wasn't a great idea. There again, better some broken bones than a bullet in the brain. There was also the fact that he didn't know where they were heading now. The plan he knew about had pretty much gone out the window from the second Beamish fired at Grimshaw. Logically then, he couldn't rely on the post-op plans he knew about. Lincoln and Beamish had been whispering on and off all day—it was clear that he had been kept out of the picture for a reason. When had that started?

It wasn't because of Teddington. Lincoln might have openly distrusted him after the closeness of their connection had been revealed, but it hadn't signalled a major change.

Closeness of our connection. Who are you kidding?

Charlie glanced at the mass of chestnut hair leaning against his chest. Their connection was nowhere near as close as he wanted it to be. He couldn't believe he'd missed her invitation. Well he could, he had, but he'd honestly believed she had no interest in him. He could have checked it out. Piper would have been able to give him her phone number, probably her address. There again, he could have looked through the phone book. There couldn't be that many people called Teddington in the area. Only he'd been a coward, he'd stayed away. Convinced himself that he wasn't worthy of her. He probably wasn't, but he wanted her and the fear that she didn't want him was more than he could face.

He bowed his head over her hair. He could smell apples, but also the scent of *her*. It was a scent he wanted to know better.

That was a prospect for the future; right now, he had to worry about getting the pair of them out of the present alive. He had to think. Looking back now, in all probability, Lincoln had never trusted him. There was the wallet to think about. He had thought it was a test of loyalty, but clearly it was just a prop for blackmail. Thankfully he had logged with CHIS the recording of Lincoln threatening him with being set up as a fall guy, so he should be able to wriggle free of that one.

There was still the matter of the heart. He didn't know what had happened to that, and even though no one actually got killed, the repercussions wouldn't be good. The years of being in the Force should have made it clear to him that there was no honour amongst thieves, no trust. He was just a pawn and he should have seen it sooner. At last he realised the simple truth… he'd just been out of the game too long. But he had to get back into it and damn quick.

Fears for poor little Lucy were a waste of time now. As were fears for himself. It was clear that if they were tried for this, they'd be convicted and they would serve for a very long time. He feared for Teddington. He had to get her out of this. He worried that she'd fallen asleep against him, which with a concussion wasn't a good thing.

Whatever else he did, he swore he would stop Beamish, even if he had to serve time for murder. Again.

Assuming that everything he'd been told up till now was a lie, if he wanted Piper to catch these guys, then he had to stick with the team for now. Teddington was a complication, but she'd understand. He breathed in fresh apples. She would understand—eventually.

Chapter 27

He didn't have to do this, but Piper made himself do it all the same. He tried telling himself that he wasn't doing this to avoid having to face Broughton, but he wasn't that good a liar. There were plenty of parts of being a police officer that weren't pleasant, but they still had to be done. Knocking on Mrs Whittaker's door was just one of those parts.

A weary-looking man answered. The olive skin spoke of the man's Mediterranean ancestry. And this was the first time in many months that Piper had seen him.

'Prison Officer Sanchez.'

The man rolled his eyes. 'Call me Enzo.' He stepped back to let Piper into the house. 'I'm not on duty. I take it you are?'

'Afraid so.' He kept his voice low. 'How is Mrs Whittaker?'

'Frightened.' Enzo was equally careful not to let his voice carry. 'Any news on Ari?'

Piper knew from previous encounters that Sanchez was the same age as Teddington, that they had been friends since the age of eleven. Sanchez lived across the road and it was him who'd helped Teddington get the job as a prison officer. The Sanchez family were close friends with the Whittakers. 'I need to see Mrs Whittaker.'

Enzo pointed to the living room and Piper went through, nodding to the Family Liaison Officer who stood on his arrival and offered a welcome cup of tea. The room was neat and tidy, in some ways too tidy. There was a box of paper tissues next to Mrs Whittaker, a bin full of crumpled white ones nearby. On the carpet were a couple of very small white flakes that seemed to have been torn off by hands that even now were twisting and tearing at another tissue.

'Inspector Piper.' The older woman looked up at him. Her eyes were red from crying, and her skin was pale. She looked tired and stressed, and much older than she had nine months ago when he had been visiting Teddington after her shooting. Innocent people always paid for the misdeeds of others, and here was the evidence right in front of his eyes.

'Mrs Whittaker, I'm sorry to see you under these circumstances.'

She waved the apology away and invited him to sit. 'The news says the siege is over. So what's happening to Addy? Where's my baby girl?'

The pet name surprised Piper, but his surprise was irrelevant, he knew who she was talking about. Piper could see the tears welling up in Mrs Whittaker's eyes and felt his throat going dry. This case was getting to him far more than cases usually did. Even the idea of someone as tough as Ariadne Teddington being called a 'baby girl' didn't raise a smile. His youngest, his son, at just 15, was already several inches taller than him and much stronger, but the man he was growing into would always be that same bundle of incredible squealing life placed in his arms after one of the most emotional days of his life.

'At the moment, two hostages remain in the power of the gunmen. We're tracing them and hope to get them back soon.' He felt like a party political broadcast.

'This is worse than when she was kidnapped before.' Mrs Whittaker looked at the blank screen of the switched-off television set. 'Not that she lets me refer to it as a kidnapping. At least back then you could assure me that… that… that man who took her was unlikely to hurt her.'

Piper swallowed. Oddly glad she couldn't remember Charlie's name, he knew he could tell her the same again now, except that there was more than Charlie to consider and at least one of the other men was happy to leave corpses behind him.

'Mrs Whittaker, I can't give you any guarantees. I can, however, tell you we're doing everything we can to get them back safe.' Which wasn't amounting to a whole lot at that precise second.

'We both know that Ariadne is a very capable woman. It was her actions that secured the release of the first hostage. She was instrumental in getting two additional hostages released when another was shot.'

The noise the older woman made when he mentioned the shooting told him he'd made a mistake. He apologised as the Family Liaison Officer distributed mugs of tea and Enzo reached from the sofa to the chair, taking Mrs Whittaker's hand and offering soft soothing words in support. There wasn't anything Piper could really do. He took a sip of the tea—too hot—but it was something to occupy his time. He looked between Enzo and Mrs Whittaker, caught the words "Aunty Susan". They really had known each other a long time. Enzo had a place here; Piper really didn't. But he needed to be somewhere. Somewhere other than the station.

'I can't lose her,' Mrs Whittaker was pleading with Enzo. 'I can't lose her like Terry.'

'Terry?' Piper asked.

Enzo looked to him, then to the cardboard box at the side of the chair. Piper looked down to see it was full of knickknacks. He looked up again and saw there was nothing on any of the shelves. He frowned.

'Redecorating.' Enzo supplied.

'Addy was going to start painting tonight.'

Mrs Whittaker's voice was distant, her expression lost. Not knowing what else to do, Piper reached down and took the top photo frame from the box. Silver, attractive without being fussy. The picture showed a boy, probably eight or nine years old. Very young, fresh-faced. He was in school uniform, a white shirt, green tie and jumper with a school crest on the chest. That wasn't a local uniform. Over the top of the tie was a silver St Christopher. He saw a cute kid, and Piper could see some echo of Ariadne in the face.

'That's Terrence,' Enzo explained softly. 'Ari's younger brother.'

Piper frowned as he looked at the picture. A quick glance down and he saw another school picture, same boy and a girl who had to be Ariadne. There was also a more recent picture of Ariadne, one of her beaming as she presented her baby daughter to the world. So that had to be about six years ago, before she'd come back to the county. 'What happened?'

'He disa—disappear…'

'He disappeared,' Enzo took up the story when Mrs Whittaker couldn't. 'Vanished a couple of months after the family moved in. There's never been any trace found.'

'The police said he'd run away. But he wouldn't have. I know my boy, he wouldn't have just left. Something happened to him, but the police weren't interested.'

The lump in his throat felt too large to swallow, but Piper had to. 'I'm sor—' His mobile demanded his attention, he placed the picture back in the box, '—sorry.' He glanced at the screen. A text, from Broughton.

Station, now.

'Mrs Whittaker, I'm sorry about what happened with Terry, but I can assure you that I will not stop until we have Ariadne back. But right now, I have to go.'

'What's happened?' Mrs Whittaker was on her feet, her expression pure fear.

'I've been asked to return to the station, no reason given.' He stepped forward, put his hand lightly on the older woman's upper arm. 'I'm sure it's nothing to worry about. If there had been a major development I would have had a call, not a text. This is probably something procedural. The Senior Investigating Officer may want a conference about the way forward.' He offered a tight smile, and no indication that he was in fact the SIO in this case. Then he left.

* * *

Waves of exhaustion were trying to drown Teddington. She had to fight to keep her senses, her eyes were drifting closed.

It was good to be with Charlie but even that wasn't comfortable. After everything that had happened to and around them, it was clear they were in a doomed relationship, however much she wanted him. He was the first man to touch her heart since her divorce. *Always had lousy taste in men.*

Focus!

Jumping from the van was a possibility, but they were leaning against the sliding door. Opening it would take enough movement that Mr White or Mr Blue would shoot them before they could get out. She didn't want to get shot again.

Charlie was staying calm, she'd have to do the same thing. He had a better understanding of what was going on than she did. He'd have a plan.

She hoped.

She looked at the bags piled in the middle of the van. Money. And probably quite a lot of it. However much it was, was it worth all this? Worth shooting a police officer? Worth throwing a kid under a bus? God, she hoped Lucy was okay. She'd hate to think how Megan would be if the kid had been killed in the fall.

Thank God there hadn't been a bus.

Focus.

She couldn't help Lucy any more, she had to help herself. And only herself. Evidently Miss Arden was as fake as her name. Thinking it through, Teddington guessed Arden's appointment was to ensure that Presswick was in the building to open the safe, or safes. That was why she'd been so quiet through it all; she'd had nothing to fear. The van was cold and the frequent sharp turns had calmed down. The singing of the tyres had changed. They weren't on tarmac roads any more, but concrete. There were a few places around the area where that change occurred. The song changed again, became less rhythmic, and much bumpier. A damaged concrete road. She was no expert but she suspected that these were too common to give an exact location. The van was slowing, now moving too slowly to be on a main road. Even a B-road. Was this a farm track? Were they reaching their destination?

She looked up at Charlie. Under all that make-up she could see worry in his eyes. Was he as much out of the loop as she was?

At the back of the vehicle, Mr White, Mr Blue and Miss Arden were tensing, moving, grabbing bags. The vehicle stopped, the rear door was opened from outside. Teddington saw a big guy, tall and blocky. He had black hair and almond-shaped eyes. Definitely some oriental blood in his lineage. He scowled when he saw her. Mr White and Mr Blue were straight out.

She sat up and Charlie shifted to kneel, sliding the door behind them open. The others were pulling the bags out. Mr Blue offered Miss Arden his hand; Charlie reached in for Teddington. She took his hand and shifted awkwardly. As her feet went to the concrete floor, she realised they were in some empty storage facility. Their van and a blue Caravelle were parked within a few metres of each other and they were the only things in the place. She didn't mean to but she swayed on her feet.

Charlie steadied her with both hands. 'Look at me.'

She did but she didn't feel well. 'Everything's blurry.'

'Good.'

It took her a second to realise that Charlie hadn't spoken. Tilting her head was a mistake that nearly knocked her off her feet; she put one hand up, leant on the edge of the van and looked at Mr White. Behind him, figures were loading the Caravelle, getting in. The oriental man was throwing something into the Transit. Something splashed on her. Petrol.

Charlie had turned to face Mr White. 'She's concussed and needs medical care. I know a doctor, struck off, so no danger of him ratting on us. She's no use to you. You can keep my share of the money, but let me take her out of here.'

Mr White smiled. 'Oh, I'm keeping your share all right.'

Teddington couldn't figure out how to warn Charlie as Mr White raised his gun. Charlie's own gun was up. He fired.

Nothing happened.

'Well, you said you wanted to use blanks.'

Charlie's hand tightened on her arm for a fraction of a second then was ripped away. Teddington saw him fall back, the force of the bullet pushing him along the floor. The gun in Mr White's hand was smoking, Teddington screamed. Petrol woomphed its ignition. Heat washed up one side as Teddington's world turned to ice. Another hand gripped her arm. She was dragged backwards, reaching for Charlie, but being pulled away from him and the burning van. Mr White's hands were way too familiar around her rump as she was bundled into the other van.

The rear windows of the people carrier were tinted, so as Teddington looked out at the unmoving corpse, her whole world seemed blacker. Charlie had never been hers, and now he never would be.

Hands were moving over her.

She looked down, Mr White was pulling the seatbelt across her as the vehicle pulled away. She took another sorrowful look back at her dead dream. As they moved away from the scene, Teddington was overly aware of Mr White's closeness.

'Why is she still with us?' Miss Arden demanded.

'Until we're clear, she could still be of use.'

'You're Mr Blonde,' Teddington said to the woman. 'The missing Reservoir Dog.'

The woman laughed and pulled the blond wig from her head. 'Not exactly.'

Ari's swell of grief at seeing Charlie dead flooded her with hate of all these people for their part in that. 'Oh, I'd say dog is exactly what you are.'

The kick was sharp. She almost wondered if it broke her shin, yet painful as it was, it was a million miles away. She ignored the pain, didn't even flinch. Just sneered at the other woman. Teddington looked over the lank brown hair in a sharp and unflattering bob.

'Should've kept the wig.' Teddington turned to stare unseeing out of the window. 'You looked better as a blonde.'

Chapter 28

'A complete fuck-up.'

Piper stood before Broughton's desk, overly aware of the man's earlier declaration. *His fuck-up is your fuck-up.* He was actually a little sick of it repeating in his head. He was even more aware of Sheldrake's presence in the room. Over the last few hours he'd had cause to utterly switch his opinion of the woman. But he still wasn't entirely sure he trusted her. Broughton had been right about Sheldrake, she was media savvy. She was also intelligently political—she'd offered a lift to save him from bothering one of the uniform patrols, whose mopping up job was just beginning.

He'd managed to put her off, saying that she must have more important things to do than drive him to Mrs Whittaker's, so he'd left on his own. Somehow, he wasn't overly surprised to find her waiting for him in Broughton's office. Here to watch his downfall. It was his call, his watch, his fuck-up. One perpetrator was dead, a hostage shot, another being stitched and plastered back together—worse yet, a child—and two more still captive. And that was before they started thinking about the money and property stolen. The other thing they'd taken with them was his career.

So even this was all over, bar the shouting. He had nothing left to lose. Telling Sheila wouldn't be fun. His wife was understanding, but he wasn't sure she'd understand this.

'What have you got to say about your informant now?'

Piper swallowed. That was the easiest question to answer. 'That he gave us all the information he had, though clearly it wasn't all the information there was to be had.'

'He told you there would be a raid. He said a six-man team. There were only five in that bank and none of them the fuckers he named!'

Piper could have contradicted his superior officer, but he held back. 'No, sir.'

'The sixth man,' Sheldrake said softly, 'was the driver.' She made no comment when both men ignored her.

'In fact.' Broughton was deceptively calm all of a sudden. 'It seems that while we were fucking ourselves over in Glenister Street, the whole fucking bunch of them were off God knows fucking where. And what about your fucking informant? He's suspiciously quiet.'

'Dead men tell no tales,' Sheldrake mused.

That stopped Broughton in his tracks and Piper's heart hammered at the prospect. Both men turned to Sheldrake.

'I admit, gentlemen, that it's not a pleasant prospect, but at this point it's one we need to consider.'

She spoke so calmly, Piper knew it could only be said by someone who had no personal connection to the man, who could afford to be so detached.

'Even if we don't want to,' she persisted gently.

'Charlie's not dead.' Piper had to say it: the sound made the denial more tangible. Besides, Charlie wasn't the robber corpse on the back floor. He was under that overhanging brow and Piper didn't think he was dead. Yet.

'Look,' he said when Broughton went to speak, 'Constable Siddig called, said that while they were plastering Lucy's leg, the girl told her that the four others were all alive as were the two hostages. Yes, this lot have demonstrated a willingness to kill, but I don't believe Charlie is just another victim. If he's still alive and he's still involved, he'll do his damnedest to get Teddington and Arden out of there alive.'

Broughton looked at him like he didn't know, or believe, what Piper was saying. 'How can you continue to defend that fucking man?'

Easy. 'I trust him.'

The DCS surged to his feet. 'How the—'

'Broughton.' Sheldrake stepped forward, her tone so calm that it seemed out of place. 'I appreciate that this is your office, but would you mind moderating your language just a little?'

The older man looked to the elected official and took a moment to control the rebellion in his eyes before obeying her mute indication and sinking back into his chair.

'Chief Inspector,' she redirected her attention. 'Why do you trust Charlie Bell?'

'He's a good man.'

'He's a murderer.'

Ignoring Broughton's grumble, Piper kept his attention on Sheldrake. 'Bell always does the right thing.'

'Even when the "right thing" is against the law?'

He swallowed. Bell certainly waded into grey areas deeper than Piper was usually prepared to dip his toes. 'Apparently.'

'So, to summarise,' Sheldrake said, 'we have a bank heist gone wrong, a dead robber, an officer with a bullet in his lung, an injured child, and two hostages, one of whom may well be concussed, gone God knows where. Oh, and an informant we're going to choose to believe is alive, but is currently off radar.'

'Yes, ma'am.'

'You can see how this could be construed as a set-up, by Charlie Bell, to make us all look like idiots?'

'I don't believe that to be the case,' Piper said, 'but yes, ma'am, I can see your point.'

'Good.'

They all turned when Broughton's desk phone rang. As he answered, Sheldrake spoke in lowered tones to Piper.

'Right now, the two remaining hostages must be our priority.'

As Piper agreed, Broughton was signing off.

'The pursuit team got lucky. Car two managed to get out from behind the crash and cruised around looking for the van.

They managed to pick up the tracker,' he announced. 'Clearly their jammer wasn't up to much.'

'Good.'

'Not really,' Broughton told them. 'Apparently, the team followed the tracker and found the van in a derelict farm building thirty miles away. They figure the gang had a second getaway vehicle there, but it's gone now. They're away clean.'

The phone rang again.

Chapter 29

It didn't matter what she looked at. Whether her eyes were open or shut, all Teddington could see was that horrific moment when Charlie fell back from a bullet to the chest.

Something special inside her was gone. She didn't quite know what, but she suspected it might be the last vestige of hope. She thought she'd given up in the bank, but like the man walking while leading a horse, she'd had a backup. She knew now she had been hoping Charlie would get her out safe.

No hope of that now.

A face landed on the floor in front of her.

Her stomach rebelled, but she hadn't eaten since breakfast so it had nothing to throw up. She blinked and realised she was looking as a prosthetic mask, a latex face.

'Easy,' Blue grumbled. 'That's strong stuff.'

Looking up, Teddington saw the non-blonde removing the last vestige of make-up from Mr Blue's clean-shaven face as he removed the gloves, then started picking a thin layer of something from his fingertips. When done, the other woman picked up the mask and dropped it into a wire mesh bin she pulled from under seat. No wonder they hadn't bothered to hide their faces. She hadn't recognised Charlie under the contacts and caveman brow, but she was only now beginning to see the implications. Apparently her brain hadn't been functioning even before she'd cracked her skull on the chair arm. Mr Blue looked like a completely different man and clearly, he hadn't left any fingerprints behind. She thought about Charlie—when he'd touched her face, it hadn't felt unusual. No, he'd been wearing latex gloves when they'd walked in. He'd taken them off because they were making his hands itch. It didn't make sense. It didn't matter anyway, he was dead and beyond the reach of the law.

As she watched, Mr White pulled back his light wig to reveal a much darker head of lightly greying hair beneath. The wig went into the mesh bin along with the face. A thin veneer of even white teeth followed.

Mr White ran a wet wipe over his hands and face, revealing skin darker than in his disguise. As he finished with the third wipe and took another, she realised that the olive tone suggested either a really good tan, or Mediterranean blood in his family tree. There was no way any of the witnesses in the bank would pick these men out in a line-up. But she could. Which meant she was too dangerous for them to leave alive.

Shit.

'You missed a bit,' she said as Mr White threw the wipe down and didn't move to take another.

He glared at her.

'No, really, your ear is whiter than the rest.'

He looked to the other woman for confirmation. She nodded and he grabbed another wipe. Teddington turned to the window. She didn't notice their location as she watched Charlie fall again. And again.

The van came to a halt. Mr Blue and the woman opened a side door and started unloading their bags of swag. The other side door was opened by the driver. As Teddington stared forward, she remotely registered the man and his bulk as he reached in and dragged out the full wire bin. A small movement caught her eye. The keys still hung in the ignition. If there was any chance of her escaping this, that might just be her best hope. Driving with concussion wasn't a good plan, but it was a better plan than dying.

The van shifted as Mr White stepped down. She heard some fluid being poured, then that distinctive whoosh of ignition. It took her back to that warehouse again, Charlie falling. They were burning the evidence and Charlie was dead on the floor beside it.

'Ari!'

At the sharp repeat of her name, Teddington refocused on Mr White. It occurred to her that she should call him Mr Olive now. It occurred to her that something was wrong—very wrong—with her.

'Get out!'

'Oh, just lock the bitch in there.'

The voice was female and it only dimly registered that she'd obviously pissed the non-blonde off. Knowing that gave her, however oddly, a glimmer of hope. She might not survive this, but this lot had been pissing her off all afternoon. If she had a chance to get a little of her own back, so much the better. Galvanised, she stepped out grabbed the car for support and found herself almost at eye level with Mr White. She was wearing three-inch heels so he must be five ten.

Mr Blue handed the woman one of the bags. The driver was taking the others, and the three headed away together. The Caravelle was parked near a wall, but the sound suggested to Teddington that there was open space behind them in the rest of the garage. She didn't see the point in looking around to see if anything was there. Instead she just looked at Mr White. He was easily as emotionless as she felt.

'Are you going to kill me?'

He didn't even blink. 'Yes.'

'Now?'

He paused. She guessed he was considering it.

'No.'

'Then can I use a bathroom?'

No change of expression.

'I didn't get the bathroom trip the others did.'

He still didn't respond.

She huffed, a bitter smile twisted one side of her mouth up. 'You must be a hell of a poker player.'

Without a word, he moved the gun and pointed for her to follow the others. She did, a little unsteadily, but she was finding her sea legs. The large garage opened into a house, a working corridor into the 'servants' area. This was a dark, cold space, lit by a flickering fluorescent bulb about halfway down. Doorless storage rooms opened off the corridor. Ten yards down, she saw two doors, one directly ahead, another to her left.

'In there.' Mr White indicated to the left-hand door.

Teddington opened it to find a cold, damp wet room, where there was still enough ambient light to see, but only just. The shower and drain, the gritty surface of an insufficiently cleaned floor, suggested this was where they came in and cleaned before going into the house proper. She stepped through and turned to close the door, only to find Mr White in the way.

He met her eye and then meaningfully looked behind her. She frowned, then turned. There was a big unlockable window above the toilet.

'Oh.'

She moved over to the pan, turned, already tugging at the top of her leggings. She paused, looking up at Mr White.

'Any chance you could actually turn your back?'

'Nope.'

For a moment, she didn't move. *Oh well.* The guy was going to kill her at some point and her bladder was pressing. As long as he didn't shoot her on the throne.

'I don't want to die like Elvis,' she muttered as she pulled the jersey fabric and panties down in one. It was embarrassing peeing while being watched, but the relief was too great to dwell on it.

As she realised there was no way to avoid twisted panties pulling her clothes back up, she decided quickest was the best option. That was a mistake. Her head swam as she tried to stand and she went heavily back down. Her left hand on the mildewed wall, she took a moment to steady herself. She was safe sat down, but she had to get back up. She wanted to minimise exposure, so she pulled her leggings and panties as high as she could, and yanked both up in one as she stood. When she'd finished wriggling, Mr White came to stand before her. She was effectively blocked from moving away from the toilet. He maintained eye contact. Teddington wasn't sure what was going on and frowned in mute question.

'I need to go, too.' A small movement of gun and head pointed her attention downward.

Teddington felt her brows rise then she looked meaningfully down at his crotch, then back to his face.

'You're going to kill me,' she said. 'Why the hell wouldn't I hurt you while I was down there?'

She was somewhat surprised when he actually smiled.

'I see why Bell liked you.'

Apparently it had been a test. When he grabbed her arm and took her out, she wasn't sure if she'd passed whatever test it was.

Chapter 30

'Sir!'

Piper turned at the call, surprised to see Constable Siddig rushing down the corridor towards him. She'd removed the utility hi-vis and bulky stab vest to show a good, sturdy figure beneath. She also had a worried expression on her face and a piece of paper in her hand.

'Sir, have you got a minute?'

Heading for his office, Piper wasn't sure he did have a minute, he was half surprised he still had a job. Though his continuing assignment on the current case owed as much to Sheldrake's intervention as to his own capability. *Who else is going to be so motivated to sort it all out?* she'd asked Broughton. Piper wasn't sure if that was a compliment or a condemnation. He didn't want to spend time working it out, right now—that would be demotivating. 'Sure.' He was at his office door. 'Come in.'

Siddig followed him into the small office where he could at least get some privacy. Siddig closed the door on her way in, apparently that privacy was needed now. She stopped in front of his desk as he slumped to sit on the edge of it. She wasn't exactly to attention, but she was close to it, her hands behind her back, and he wondered if they were clasped loosely or tight.

'What can I do for you, Constable?'

'I thought you'd want to know that Dominic came through his surgery well, though he's likely to stay in an intensive care unit for at least a couple of nights, then he'll have to spend a while in the high-dependency unit.'

For a moment Piper had to stop and think. He didn't know anyone who called Carlisle by his first name and it was a long time since he'd heard it. No, wait, it had been earlier than afternoon, he just continued to think of the man as Carlisle not Dominic. 'That's good news. Are you and he…' Not wanting to put a name on it, he let the question trail off.

'No, sir.' She looked momentarily away. 'Not any more, I mean we were just… you know.'

He nodded. Station romances weren't uncommon; sometimes they were just the result of long hours or tense situations. They happened, they didn't necessarily mean anything. He'd never indulged himself, being married. That was the one aspect of police life his wife wouldn't understand and he'd never risk losing her.

'And the Bartons are happily reunited. I feel a little sorry for Lucy, though. Not sure her mother will ever let the girl out of her sight ever again.'

He nodded. 'Typical parental reaction. She might ease off in a year or so. Whatever, that's not our problem.'

'No, sir.' She brought her hands forward and held out a piece of paper. 'I thought this might be of interest.'

As he took the folded paper he saw the crush creases, so her hands had been tightly clasped after all. He opened the sheet. It was a photocopy of her original notes, plus a grainy CCTV picture and a couple of additional handwritten notes. The picture wasn't very clear, but it was clear enough to know that the face Siddig had circled in red might be said to belong to Neil Grey, but as far as Piper was concerned, that face belonged to the man he knew as Andrew Beamish.

The whole operation had been kept quiet. Only he, Carlisle and Broughton knew all the details. CHIS had various bits of logged evidence—Charlie Bell was one informant, an operation that Piper had wanted to keep very close to his chest.

He turned back to the young woman, Neil Grey's arresting officer.

'What significance do you assign this?'

'I saw the suspect profile in the incident room. His was on the top of the clipboard.' Her lips were a tight straight line, and her eyes held a sudden note of caution. 'The guy was a suspect, albeit one that wasn't actually at the robbery as expected. But you have one name, I have another, which means he's hiding more than we know about.'

Piper didn't react.

'When I got off shift, I checked the records. I thought it might give us the opportunity to find out something about him. The address details on the report are what he gave on arrest, but I checked it this evening. The address exists, but the house was condemned seven years ago.'

Which would let it pass the cursory checks undertaken on arrest.

'He couldn't have lived there, not even as a squat. It's a dead end.'

It was. 'So why bring this to me?'

She swallowed. 'I thought you should know.' This time she licked her lips, gave an almost imperceptible shrug. 'All information helps. Even if just to illustrate a subject's personality, or eliminate a line of enquiry.'

'Who else have you showed this to?'

Now she looked worried. 'No one.'

Observant, intelligent, discreet. Just what he needed. 'You're off shift?'

She nodded.

'I can't authorise overtime, and you can't tell anyone else what I'm about to ask you to do.'

The door burst opened and Broughton stormed in. He didn't look happy.

'I just had a call from Doctor Harding. Apparently, when they went to move the body of the dead gang member from the bag into the mortuary, he noticed something odd. Then he realised that the hair was a wig and the skin tone was make-up.'

Siddig looked from Broughton to Piper. Her eyes were wide and she looked a little surprised. 'He'd effectively hidden his true identity.'

'That's why they weren't wearing masks,' Piper surmised. 'All the men in the mugshots we've got… could've been in the bank this morning.'

'Which,' Broughton was a bit too happy to point out, 'puts your mate Charlie right back in the frame.'

'Charlie?' Siddig asked.

'Charlie Bell.'

'What's Charlie Bell got to do with this?'

* * *

Mr White took Teddington out of the wet room, through a kitchen and to a large room that might once have been a proper dining room, but now held some beaten sofas and a rather scrappy dining table with no chairs. The table was lit by an unshaded standing light with an old style iridescent bulb. The day outside was quickly fading to night, though a bright moon still gave some illumination.

The remaining gang members were at the table, the five bags open, the contents spilled across the table top.

Mr White pushed her towards the nearest sofa. It sat opposite another one, a large hearth to her right, the table to her left. Teddington sat where she was told to and watched as the spoils were divided. The number five rang with all the other bells in her head. Her eyes rested on the gun Mr White had left so casually by his right hand. There was her future, just there, hidden in a little slug of lead. Though in all honesty, she wasn't sure if bullets did in fact contain lead. Not that it mattered: she wasn't afraid she was going to die of lead poisoning.

Looking to the rest of the group, she had a limited view of what they had and what they were doing, but it was clear that more than just money had been taken. In fact, Mr Blue seemed more interested in the stuff that wasn't cash. When Mr White looked up, she had to ask the question weighing on her mind.

'Why kill Charlie?'

'He made himself a liability.'

'How?'

Mr White pinned her with a hard glare. 'He tried to shoot me.'

'With what you knew were blanks.' Teddington watched Mr White closely. He wasn't as in control as he wanted people to think.

'It's your fault.' The answer came from Mr Blue. 'He wanted to get away with you, but no money. Nothing to link him to the robbery and both of you free to turn Queen's evidence. That wasn't happening.'

'What if I swore to keep my mouth shut?'

Mr Blue laughed.

Mr White answered, 'I wouldn't trust that or you. Too many people know who you are and that you were in that bank.'

'We can't have a prison officer blabbing to the law.'

She turned to the man who'd added that. Mr Orange. 'Oh, like you'd have a say in anything. What is the point of you anyway? What did you do to earn your share of the pot?'

His nostrils flared as he twisted to level a gun at her head.

'Put it down,' Mr Blue muttered.

She watched Mr Orange's chin move, compressing his lips, the breathing through his nose audible.

'Martin!'

Orange put the gun down and turned to Mr Blue.

'She's still with us because she's the most dangerous to us, which is what makes her potentially the most useful. But she's not going to live long enough to draw another breath outside this house. Once we're done here, when we're ready to leave and there are no cops to get past, I'll kill her.'

'There you go,' the woman sneered across, 'you're next.'

'Oh just get on with it, then.' Even Teddington was surprised by her snap. 'Cut all this crappy foreplay and kill me.'

Chapter 31

Siddig's question ran around Piper's head. *What's Charlie Bell got to do with this?*

'Everything,' he answered after Broughton closed the door on his way out. 'How well do you remember Bell?'

'Hardly at all,' Siddig answered honestly. 'He was already on remand when I started. I do remember that plenty of people here refused to believe that he killed Phillip Mansel-Jones. At first, they praised him to the skies, saying what a great officer he was, then when he testified that he had killed the man in self-defence, there were still a lot of questions about why he'd been in Mansel-Jones's house anyway.'

Questions that Piper knew the answer to, but which had never been answered satisfactorily as far as the official records were concerned. As Siddig discussed her observations, the doubts crept into Piper's mind again, that hated voice in the back of his mind that questioned what kind of copper withheld evidence and knowingly allowed an accused man to lie under oath.

The kind that knows the difference between right and justice.

'Thank you, Constable. One last question. Did you encounter either Bell or Mrs Teddington when they were here last year?'

She shook her head. 'I was on duty, but had no contact.'

Good. Piper leaned forward. 'Did you see either of them?'

A slight frown on her forehead, Siddig leant towards her senior officer. 'No. Nor did they see me.'

Piper nodded, contemplating the woman before him.

'Why do it, though?'

It was impossible to form an answer to that question as there were so many different possibilities. He focused on Siddig. 'Can you clarify the question?'

'Why hit the bank today? Was there a significance in the timing?'

Piper smiled. He had known the significance, but Siddig was the first to actually ask the question out right. 'Presswick, the bank manager, reported that an unusually large amount of cash was being run through the bank today.'

Siddig frowned. 'How unusually large?'

'Apparently it's not unusual for the branch to hold one hundred thousand.'

'Really?' Siddig blushed at her own interruption. 'Sorry, sir, but that seems like an awful lot of cash for what's a fairly small branch.'

Piper shrugged. 'Perhaps it is, but that's what Presswick said, so I have to take it at face value.'

'So having a hundred thousand is reason enough to hit the bank today.'

'Possibly it would be,' Piper interrupted her, 'but that's what usually goes through. Today, it was half a million.'

For a moment Siddig stared at him, loose-jawed. 'That's a better reason.'

Piper huffed a laugh. 'Five times better. And it may not be the only reason. The money was for one of the many businesses owned by Rhys Mansel-Jones. Also, a number of personal security boxes were opened up and emptied.'

'Let me guess,' Siddig said, 'One of the boxes was held by Mansel-Jones.'

'Two of them, actually.'

For a moment she starred at the wall over Piper's head. He knew there was nothing much there but an old policy poster and last season's football league chart. He waited, interested to know what Siddig came up with.

'Why wasn't there more security today for that much money?'

'Again, according to Presswick, the money wasn't supposed to be there long enough to bother. It's sad to say half a million isn't as much bulk as you might think. As those men demonstrated, it could easily be carried in five holdalls, with plenty of space for whatever was in those security boxes. So, it was delivered from their normal armoured vehicle this morning and it was supposed to be collected this afternoon. All done quietly and without fuss. Extra security would have led to unwanted questions and attention.'

'Do you know the time of the delivery and planned collection?'

'Eleven and two respectively.'

Siddig frowned. 'That's a tight window of opportunity. So someone had to know what the arrangements were, because the raid happened just after one.'

'Five past, to be exact.' Piper like to be exact. He liked that Siddig was thinking through the possibilities.

'So was the organiser someone from the bank, or someone from Mansel-Jones' own team?'

'Good question.'

Siddig had her arms crossed, her index finger tapping on her arm. 'What about the bank employees? The ones off-duty as well as the three inside?'

Piper nodded. 'Checks on all employees and ex-employees were kicked off as soon as the raid started.' He'd had to wait until then to avoid tipping the gang off. Charlie knew Lincoln was planning the raid, but he didn't know where Lincoln was getting his information.

'Your file said Simon Lincoln was in import-export. I did a little digging and he had a lot of dealings with Mansel-Jones' companies.'

Taking the initiative. Piper liked that; Siddig reminded him of Charlie when he started. He smiled at her. 'True, but dig a little more and you'll find even Sheldrake's been known to take a photo op with Mansel-Jones, and she's not guilty of anything.' That he could see. 'Rhys Mansel-Jones is a legitimately successful businessman. He's even been chairman of the local Chamber of Commerce. A lot of people in the area have a lot of dealings with him and his companies.'

'What about the client Presswick was seeing?'

'What about her?'

'Well, her appointment ensured Presswick's presence. Could there be a link?'

'Presswick would have been there anyway.'

'Oh.' Siddig looked suddenly deflated.

'But you show good instincts.' He noticed that that finger was tapping faster again.

'She was one of the hostages taken, wasn't she?'

'She was.'

'What if she's not a hostage?'

Smart girl. 'It is beginning to look that way. The name we were given was Beth Arden. The only Beth Arden in a fifteen-mile radius is sixty-seven and a resident of the St Mary's Hospice Care facility. Not surprisingly, she was in the home all day.'

Siddig sighed. 'Another dead end.'

'Not necessarily,' Piper advised. 'One of the lines of enquiry to follow in the aftermath of all this, is who got hold of her identity? It could be a relative of hers or of someone else in the facility. It could be one of the staff or one of the various therapists that come in to give palliative care.'

Siddig shoved her hands into her trouser pockets. 'Technically, Mansel-Jones hadn't come for the cash so it's still the bank's liability, but the raid's still going to inconvenience Mansel-Jones. After all, he wanted that cash for something.'

Was she going to the same conclusion he had? 'So?'

'So, if the focus was Mansel-Jones, that fits rather neatly with Bell's apparent hate for that family.'

Not the conclusion he was looking for.

'But isn't it just a little too neat?'

Piper tried not to react. 'Go on.'

Her dark eyes swivelled up to his—no disguising the intelligence there. 'We know that at least one of the men in that bank was hiding his identity, and you said earlier that Lincoln had threatened to implicate Bell if he refused to help them. Maybe this is all just a little too convenient. We've missed something. Misdirection.'

His lips may have twitched, but Piper controlled the smile. He liked her way of thinking. 'Siddig, I'm going to risk trusting you.'

She looked a little uncertain. 'Thank you, sir, but I'd like to think that's not a risk.'

'So would I. Which is why I'm doing it. There's one possibility you didn't mention, probably because not many people knew about it. There's one more potential source of information for when that money would be in the bank.'

'Who?'

'Us.'

For a moment Siddig just stared. 'Why would we know?'

'Normally we wouldn't, but because it was an unusual amount of cash, and because there wasn't to be any extra security at the branch, Presswick reported that it would be there to our Major Crimes Team "just in case".'

'Doesn't that put us in a tricky situation, given that we knew there was going to be a raid?'

Damn it, she had to notice that, didn't she? 'We didn't know about the money until the end of last week. We didn't know where the raid would be until today. If it comes out that we had surveillance on the bank before the raid started, I'll claim it was part of the preventative measures we planned after the notification.'

She nodded, and licked her lips before she spoke again. 'Okay, but are you really saying what I think you're saying?'

Again, Piper nodded. 'I believe someone in this station is a turncoat.'

Chapter 32

Piper shivered in the open warehouse with the evening wind cutting through him. The light was fading, so the SOCOs had erected harsh temporary lamps to spotlight areas of interest. The generator sound was already grating on Piper's nerves as he looked at the shell of the van they'd supplied to the bank robbers. They'd torched the bloody thing, so DNA was going to be hard to get. Some latent prints might have survived, but it was unlikely. The blaggers had all worn nitrile gloves, except the two hostages. Possibly one. Didn't stop the SOCOs crawling all over the van like albino bugs.

On the other side of the warehouse, the floor had been swept and tape-marked with the dimensions of a building. He'd been over and recognised the layout of the Invicta Bank: the measurements were an exact match. So this was where the gang had rehearsed.

DS Harker was acting as scene manager. She stepped up beside Piper. 'It's a mess, sir.'

'Yeah,' he agreed with the understatement. It had been a miracle the burning van hadn't brought the whole warehouse down with it. Piper frowned over the various marks in the dirt covering the floor. 'What do you reckon that is?'

Harker looked. 'Tyre tracks.'

'No.' Piper pointed this time. 'That scuff there.' He moved off, Harker in tow until he reached the yellow and black tape keeping them back. The tape surrounded an area of disturbance separate from the tyre marks. 'Has all this been photographed?' It had yellow tags and a long rule beside a handprint.

As Harker checked her notes, Piper wondered whether she really looked too young to be doing this job or whether he was just getting too old.

'Yes, sir,' she said with certainty, 'images twenty-seven through thirty-nine. We think either one of them fell down or was knocked off his feet. The handprint and the boot marks suggest he got back up.'

'A fight?'

Harker considered the floor. 'Single blow,' she stated. 'Insufficient scuffs in alternate directions to indicate a multi-body altercation.'

God, has she swallowed a bloody dictionary?

Piper held in check the myriad reactions to the image. 'So someone took his lumps then just got back up.'

'Pretty much,' Harker agreed.

'Must have been a hell of a punch, the body seems to have skidded a few inches.'

'Somewhere between four to eight inches, depending how tall the man was.'

'How tall do you think he was?'

Harker puffed out her cheeks. 'Difficult to say. The only thing we know about him is large hands and size eleven boots. But the two footprints we found suggest a narrow stride, so we can't be certain, but I'd say "tall". And yes, that is about as scientific as I'm prepared to get.'

Piper nodded. A tall man got knocked down, someone separate or separating from the group. A single punch. If it was a punch. Piper felt his breath juddering. What if he'd been shot? There was no blood and no body, but that wasn't a guarantee. Charlie was an ornery bugger: what if he'd got up, staggered away. He could be seriously hurt, dying in a ditch for all Piper knew. Only he didn't dare show that. For a moment Piper stared up at the blank tin roof and asked any God that might be above him to give him the strength to sort this mess out. He turned to Harker. 'You find anything else, let me know.'

Chapter 33

Staring up at a corrugated sky, Charlie had heard the van disappear into the distance, taking Ari away from him. He hadn't wanted to move. Ever. He hadn't even wanted to breathe. It hurt. All the same, he was extremely grateful for the pain. Pain meant he was alive and he was overly aware that he very nearly hadn't been.

When Lincoln had pointed that gun at him, he'd believed he was a dead man. Thank God Piper'd had the presence of mind to insist he wear a bulletproof vest throughout the operation. Of course, the vest wasn't quite the protection the public thought it was. Yes, the breastplate had stopped the bullet, but not before the force of it had deformed the plate, punching his sternum with enough force to knock him off his feet. Then again, if Lincoln had gone for a head shot, it wouldn't have been any use at all.

As he'd fallen, the sound of the fire in the van had drowned out all else.

Knowing the white van would be tracked, Charlie lay still only as long as it took the others to drive away. The instant that the sound of the engine disappeared, he groaned as he forced himself to his feet. As quickly as he could, he grabbed the pistol he'd dropped, and threw it into the van, into the fire, before staggering away. He was lucky he moved when he did—the heat reached the fuel tank and turned it into a fireball, setting off the blanks. Pausing at the edge of the building, he released the side straps of the vest, unable to control his groans. The pressure eased but the pain remained, restricting his breathing. He remembered Ari saying that her corset acted like binding on the ribs, actually protecting her from any severe damage Grimshaw might have inflicted. Perhaps he should have left the vest done up. Too late now.

He staggered in pain along the edge of the building then walked, slowly and carefully to the nearest bus stop. He had just enough cash to pay for the two buses home, though he had to get off two stops earlier than he would have liked, because that was where his money ran out. Every bump in the road was a jolt of pain, every breath was torture, but he made it home, using the key he'd hidden in the nearby graveyard to get in.

Getting the key had been the trickiest part. He'd slipped it under the flower holder on one of the graves. He'd picked one where the flowers were wilting rather than dead, in hope that whoever cared enough to leave flowers wouldn't be back too soon. The movement of kneeling and picking the key up forced air from his lungs. He'd had to stay there for a few minutes to get his breath back and control his racing heart before he could get to his feet again.

Back in the flat, the temptation was simply to crash on the bed, but he couldn't. Sweat from his exertions had warred against the glue used to stick the latex to his forehead. In places, the prosthesis was beginning to separate from his skin. In the bathroom mirror, he saw the top edge had largely peeled away. Given the dark make-up, he looked like Frankenstein's Asian Monster.

He used scissors to remove his jumper and cried out in blessed relief when he released the weight of Kevlar from his shoulders and chest. He looked at the deformation of the breast plate and shuddered.

What he saw in the mirror was no more reassuring. A purple bloom of bruising flowering on his upper and mid-chest. There was an area of dense trauma on the inside edge of his left pectoral—directly above his heart. Either Lincoln had got extremely lucky or was a better shot than he'd given the man credit for. He knew that area would muscle-scar—when the swelling disappeared, he would have a permanent dent in that spot.

Breathing carefully, he reached up to pull at the latex mask. He wasn't sure what hurt most, the reluctant glue or the effort of holding his arms up. He needed a solvent. The only thing he had was a superglue remover that had come with the glue.

It irritated his skin a little and he had to be very careful not to let it drip in his eyes, but it slowly helped part the latex from his face.

He stripped. As he threw the jeans over the back of the chair, something clattered to the floor. He hadn't taken his own wallet out of the flat that morning, and he'd ditched the brown one on the way home. There shouldn't have been anything else. He went over and picked the thing up, looked at it. Oh yeah, the watch Lincoln had given him. That seemed like a million years ago, now. It was old-fashioned, the face was simple and clean. The strap was good leather, the stitching even and precise. This was quality without flash. This was the 'something extra' Lincoln had promised him.

It was a good watch, but that was all it was. Charlie turned it over in his hand. Engraving.

R Best Brother P.

Why was that something special? He put it to the side, and was about to go wash when he realised it wasn't the only thing he'd picked up during the raid. Reaching into the back pocket, he retrieved Ari's picture. A smiling baby, a girl in pink.

Sasha.

He recalled the catch in Ari's voice when she'd spoken of her daughter. He'd have to keep this safe, so he slipped it into his own wallet then he headed to the shower room.

Standing under the spray, he washed off any remnants of mask and make-up, horrified by the colour of the water from the dye used on his hair. Afterward, Charlie looked in the small mirror, studied himself. Covered the bruises, and the only obvious sign of trouble was the redness across his forehead and darker-than-normal hair. Hopefully the redness would fade soon, and no one would comment on the hair.

He looked in the bin and figured that he'd need to burn the latex to hide it properly. He really needed to speak to Piper, but after making the call to advise the target bank this morning, he'd taken the SIM card from the phone and pitched it into the river. The phone had been supplied by CHIS for contact purposes. He hadn't yet got around to getting a personal mobile.

Glancing down, he saw the watch again.

R and P. Brothers. Rhys and Phillip Mansel-Jones. He frowned. Couldn't be, could it? He picked the thing up. It was possible. But not urgent. Right now he had more pressing matters to consider. He shoved the watch in his pocket. He gingerly pulled on a thick plaid shirt, buttoned up and headed out.

With his hand still on the door, he stopped dead in his tracks to see Piper, hand raised ready to knock on the other side. He stepped back. 'Come in.'

Leaving Piper to close up, Charlie moved across the room, carefully lowering himself to sit on the only chair. Normally he'd have taken the bed, but he wasn't sure he could move so low and get back up again any more.

Piper, for the first time ever, seemed to tower over him. 'Where would they have gone?'

Cold washed through Charlie. For Piper to ask that question meant that the tail had lost the van after the change. They didn't know where the gang had gone, so there was no one rushing to Ariadne's aid. Charlie gave him the address where they'd met that morning.

'You're sure?'

'No, but it's all I have. We did the walk-throughs in the same warehouse where they swapped the vans.'

Waiting as patiently as he could, he listened to Piper call the information in. Whatever he was told didn't improve Piper's mood.

'Any news?'

Piper's Adam's apple bobbed as he shook his head. 'All we know is that neither hostage has turned up, alive or dead. So, the driver was the sixth man? The missing Reservoir Dog.'

'No.' Charlie frowned up at Piper. 'That was Carlos De Silva. There's only one hostage—Ari.'

Piper wasn't as surprised as Charlie expected. 'The blonde?'

'Part of the gang.' Charlie nodded.

'Yeah, we were wondering. When the names were released, we struggled to find her. I did wonder if I got it wrong. That little girl was so nervous she wasn't exactly speaking clearly. The only Beth Arden we found was in a cancer care hospice.'

A rough huff of a laugh escaped Charlie, which was a mistake. The movement hurt his chest. 'She said something this morning about the make-up job she was doing on us being better than dealing with God's waiting room. Maybe she works at the hospice sometimes. Hair and make-up as palliative care.'

All he got for his reasoning was a small brow movement. Piper never was big on congratulations.

'It's a possibility I'll get checked out. So, who is she? What's her connection?'

'Carol Freeman. She's Beamish's girlfriend,' Charlie supplied. 'Had a job in the make-up department at the local TV studio until they moved production to South Wales.'

'Shit.' Piper dragged his hands back through his hair. 'Why didn't you answer your phone?'

'Ditched the SIM after the last call to you.'

'Why are you separated from them now?'

'They shot me.' He displayed his bruised chest. 'Well, Lincoln did.'

'So Teddington's really out there on her own right now?'

'Yeah, and she probably thinks I'm dead.' Which didn't make either of them feel any better.

'I've got to go.' Piper turned towards the door, the chair creaking caught his attention. 'You stay put.'

'No way.' Grimacing and grunting in pain, Charlie pushed himself up from the chair.

'What do you think you're up to?'

'Going with you,' Charlie declared. 'To get Ari.'

'Like fuck.'

'Now you sound like Broughton.'

Chapter 34

'An-dy….'

Teddington found the other woman's little-girl-lost tone grating on every taut nerve. When not simpering, the other woman was giving one sexual pout after another. She glowered over to see the woman leaning towards Mr Blue. Andy. She filed that for later. The ex-Miss Arden had removed her red coat and was leaning on her forearms, purposely squashing her breasts together and giving Andy the best view possible.

'Can't you just kill her now and be done with it? Please?' She gave Andy what was supposedly a sexy come-hither body shake. 'For me?'

'Car-ooool,' he returned in a fair imitation as he leaned towards her, their noses less than an inch apart. 'Don't,' he snapped, making her jump, 'use my name.'

Names, she should try to remember the names, just in case. Mr White—still unknown. Mr Orange—Martin. Mr Blue—Andy. *Pandy.* Teddington shouldn't have laughed, it was a silly giggle and completely uncontrollable. And it drew too much attention to her.

'Shut up,' Mr White told her.

She met his gaze and didn't care. 'Like it matters what *you* say. I just realised, you had it all worked out,' Teddington said looking across, keeping her head still to stop her vision swimming. 'Five bags, five of you. You didn't shoot Grimshaw because I recognised him, you killed him because you always intended to. Mr Brown, too. You didn't need them any more.'

Neither had stood a chance. Any guilt she felt for getting Grimshaw killed disappeared. Nothing was going to change how she felt about seeing Charlie die. Nothing was ever going to blank that from her memory.

'What was the plan? You get the money and freedom while the others get the blame?'

'Just remember how limited your usefulness is, too.' Mr White's voice was calm, chilling her to the core. 'And now we know exactly who you are. Finding and hurting your family won't take too long either.'

The heat of her headache washed clean with icy fear. She hadn't thought about that, about her family. There was only her mother left now. She had never considered that her involvement might lead her mother to harm.

A different sickness churned in her stomach and dizzied her brain as she turned her head to push the gang into the periphery of her vision. She had to think. Think her way out of this. Dissension in the ranks was good. Andy Blue's willingness to kill, less so. She cursed her luck that she'd asked to go to the loo earlier. She couldn't now use that excuse to get out of here.

I'm going to die here.

The thought was surprisingly peaceful as it echoed around Teddington's head. She was through with fear, there was only blank acceptance.

She was going to die here, where no one knew where she was. She could be dead here for days or weeks or even years before anyone found her. If they ever did. And there would be no one to protect her mother.

Stop it!

The unbidden thought was a wake-up call, just as she was ready to sink into oblivion. She was not going to give up. Survivors never gave up and she wasn't ready to die. She wanted to be with Charlie, but she wasn't prepared to cross the veil to join him.

Okay, concussion, check. Bruised ribs, check. Fighting spirit, not so much but could be drummed up. One against five wasn't such great odds. *You've had worse.*

Which was true, but only when she'd also had backup.

If she could get her hands on a gun, she might have a chance. And Mr White might just have left his within easy reach. All she had to do was rattle them enough to break them apart before they were ready.

'Hey, Mr White,' she called his attention, noticed that when he turned his head to look at her, he didn't reach for the gun. 'How long did it take you to realise you weren't top dog?'

His lips thinned and paled.

'Took me ages. You know. Back in the bank I thought you were calling the shots, probably because you were firing them. But Mr Blue, Andy over there, he kept on whispering in your ear, didn't he? A snippet here, and sentence there. He's the one that's really in control, isn't he? He's the master, you're nothing more than a puppet.'

The last sneered word had the desired effect. Mr White reached for his gun. But Andy slapped his own hand down, stopped Mr White.

Teddington watched the two men. She was right, she was sure of it. Just like they'd never planned for Grimshaw or Charlie to live, she was sure that Andy was really the one pulling all the strings. Even Miss Arden—real name Carol apparently—didn't have the hold over him that she thought she did. They were cracking apart and Teddington would have to take advantage of those cracks. She also had to be careful. Push too much, and they could just close ranks on her. For the moment the best she could do was stay shtum.

Sitting still, she stared ahead and kept quiet. Looking away was one thing, but she couldn't stop tuning into what was being said around her. Their exchanges told her that these men weren't a gang any more. It was nothing overt, just a new tension in the air, the shortness with which they spoke to one another. Everyone seemed to be backing off from Mr White.

Teddington looked across, discreetly. Mr White, Mr Orange and the driver were distinctly separate from Andy and Carol, who was fiddling with what appeared to be a diamond necklace.

'I want this.'

Teddington was surprised to hear a tone of awe rather than greed. She focused on the necklace Carol was holding up. It was beautiful, but with the sparkles along the whole length and three large drops at the centre, it was way too flashy for Teddington's tastes.

'Then take it,' Andy said before picking up some books and turning to the driver. 'Make sure she doesn't get greedy with any of the rest of it.'

'Hey!'

Only Andy wasn't listening to Carol, or Mr White's objection to him taking the books. Mr White's demand to know what happened to their plan fell on deaf ears. As Mr White made to follow Andy, Mr Orange stepped into his path. No words were spoken. None were needed. The menace was obvious enough.

Andy simply walked out of the room.

Carol grumbled but the driver told her to be quiet, reinforcing the instruction with a raised gun. Not quite a Mexican standoff, but not quite right either.

'So who's in charge now?' *So much for staying shtum.* Teddington berated herself once the words were out of her mouth.

'We're a team.'

Teddington focused her attention on Mr Orange, blinked. She wanted to blow a raspberry. 'Really?'

'I'm in charge,' Mr White declared

'You might want to check that with Andy.'

Mr White stormed over. She saw it coming, but didn't care. The slap of hand on cheek cracked loud across the nearly empty room. Her head snapped to the side, her lip split. Knowing the stupidity of goading him, Teddington simply looked back. It didn't matter that Mr White was just a blur, he wasn't to know that. Her calm was making him boil with rage.

'Andy said to leave her alone,' Martin said.

'See?' Teddington taunted, Mr White's face flowing in and out of focus. 'Andy left orders. He stopped you coming at me before. He's the big man here. Not you.'

Mr White snarled. 'I don't take orders from him.'

Teddington had no idea what demon was driving her on, but she wanted to hurt this man for hurting Charlie. 'Yeah, you do.'

This time the crack reverberated through her face as well as the room. The punch broke her nose. The force pushed her to the side and she didn't have the will to push herself back up, so she half laid on the sofa and let her blood soak into the fabric. It smelt old and dusty beneath the copper flow.

Charlie was dead. She'd soon join him. She wished she hadn't wasted the last six months, but wishing couldn't change the past.

Mr White stalked away, back to the table, then he was standing over her again. Teddington looked up at Charlie's killer, the gun being levelled at her head. The others were shouting at him. Warning him. Mr White wasn't listening.

A gunshot cracked.

Everything was silent.

Mr White gurgled, blood bubbled from his slackened jaw, his arms dropped, the gun slipped from his fingers, his knees buckled. He landed on his knees and fell forward for a suspended moment, then his chin caught on the edge of the sofa and the two of them were face-to-face. One dead, one soon to be. He slid to the floor. Mr White turned grey as the bare floorboards dyed red.

Chapter 35

'What the hell?'

Piper faced Broughton and noted the use of 'hell'. That meant Broughton was in a better mood. He noticed how Broughton's eyes slid to Charlie, or more precisely to the bracelets he wore. Early on a Tuesday evening, the station was still buzzing from the events in Glenister Street. With Charlie following, Piper was aware of more than one harsh look and muttered comment when he didn't dump Bell in either a cell or an interview room.

'I said he's not under arrest.' The handcuffs were to reduce the aggravation that Bell's appearance in the station was bound to, indeed had, caused.

Broughton was rather red-faced. 'Would you care to explain why?'

Piper recognised the dangerously low, deceptively calm tone. So he didn't explain that to arrest Charlie so was to violate the terms of Charlie's parole, thus ensuring he went back inside when he was more useful where he was. Piper was similarly aware that the thin ice had been cracking under his feet for a long time now. Time for him to break through, or break out.

'Because we got good visuals and descriptions of the bank robbers, and none of them match Bell. The only man even near tall enough was the one who stepped out with Mrs Teddington, and that wasn't Charlie. You saw that with your own eyes.' If his lies weren't just destroying his tenuous chances of career continuity, they were definitely paving his road to an ulcer. But it was the right thing to do. Besides, he owed Charlie.

'We also now know expert prosthetics make eyewitness reports unreli—'

'Look.' Charlie stepped in. He'd promised to hold his temper, but it sounded like it was a losing battle. 'I appreciate, sir, that you have a whole shed load of issues with various parts of this investigation, particularly my part in it, but I'm here because Ariadne isn't. You know I've given Piper all the information I have, so I assume you know that the address I gave for this morning's meet is empty?'

Broughton glowered at him. 'So?'

'So you—'

Piper put his hand on Charlie's arm. It wasn't much of a restraint, but it was enough. Charlie snapped his head to Piper, glares clashed with warning. If anything, the tension in Charlie increased, his eyes squeezed shut and his hands balled into fists.

'Sorry,' he muttered. He sighed as he looked at Broughton. 'Sorry, sir.'

Broughton's brows shot up. 'Well, that's more respect than I ever got when you worked here.'

'Sir,' said Piper, to head off the storm he knew was building up inside Charlie, 'we think we've figured out a way to find them.'

'How?'

'Her mobile,' Charlie said.

Piper could see Charlie was struggling with his emotions. He hadn't seen this much turmoil in the younger man since he'd had to struggle with access rights to his son. 'We think.' Piper took up the thought process. 'That she must still be carrying it.'

'According to the list Piper had,' Charlie said, 'there were fewer phones recovered than hostages. There's a chance she still has her phone on her.'

'A slim chance.'

Broughton wasn't enthusiastic, but he wasn't throwing the idea out. Piper took that as a good sign.

'I checked with her phone company for what model she has on contract, and there wasn't one like hers recovered from the bank or the burned-out van, so unless it's been taken, she still has it. As long as it's switched on, we can trace it. But I need your authority to do that.'

Broughton simply regarded him. No response. No display of emotion. Piper could see Charlie clenching his fists, the way his shoulders were up, he was shifting from foot to foot. *For God's sake keep it controlled.* Broughton picked up his phone, dialled a number and calmly gave the order.

Closing his eyes, Piper released the breath he hadn't realised he was holding.

Chapter 36

'You really are a danger to everyone around you.' Andy walked into the room and stood in front of Teddington, pointing the gun at her.

Her gaze slid to the corpse on the floor, then to the gun sitting only a few inches from her. Sighing, she pushed herself back into a sitting position to face the man standing over her. Her head swam from the concussion and broken nose, but oddly, sitting upright soon made that feel better. The outpouring of blood was lessening the pressure in her head. She didn't try to stem the flow, just let it happen. As she looked up at the man over her, she hoped the blood didn't stain the picture of Sasha stashed in her corset. Only it wasn't stashed there any more. It was in a dead man's pocket. Someone else she'd never see again.

'You're the one with the gun.' Though right now, even though he wasn't even pointing that gun at her, she was all too aware of it being at his side. 'So, I'm wondering, why not just shoot me and fuck off with your woman over there?' He didn't move, just looked down on her. A new idea occurred to her. She sat forward, well aware that would allow him to see right down her corset. If it worked for Carol, she could use the same tactics. 'Oh Andy.' She smiled, made her voice as sultry as she could. 'Hw about a turn around? Shoot her and fuck off with me.'

She watched his eyes, they darkened. *Oh, dear God, he's actually thinking about it.*

Then he smiled. 'It's always a possibility, but then again, maybe I'll shoot you then fuck you.'

Teddington couldn't quite hide her revulsion at that idea. She leaned back and looked up at him. 'So what's stopping you?'

He shrugged. 'Depends how much Charlie told the police.'

'What?' She didn't understand that. 'Charlie's dead, you've already made him pay for anything he might have done. What makes you think that he said anything to the police anyway?'

'The van.'

Teddington frowned. 'I must have been hit one too many times. What's the van got to do with anything? You torched it.'

'Not the van they gave us. The one Grimshaw saw in the street. He might not have noticed it straight off, but I did. It was there before we arrived. That means the police knew we were coming. Ergo, Bell grassed.'

'Could've been Grimshaw,' she pointed out.

'Nah, he didn't have the nous to make that kind of deal. He'd have fucked himself over at the bank, given it away that he knew what was going on. Had to be Bell.'

'If you noticed that before you went into the job, why go through with it?'

'Because I could.'

Could it really be that simple? Why take the risk? *Because some people like risks.* That was it.

'You're an adrenalin junkie.'

'Yes I am.' Andy laughed. 'But I'm not an idiot. I always have an out.' Stepping over Mr White's legs, he squatted down beside Teddington. He reached to wipe some of the blood from her face. 'You're really not bad. Even banged about. I think—' His hands went to her knees, and pushed up towards her crotch. She grabbed his wrists, glaring at him. He stopped but they both knew it was because he stopped. She hadn't stopped him.

'Hey!' Carol objected.

He didn't even bother looking at her.

'I think you're really quite resilient. You get knocked about but you bounce back.'

Teddington saw the cold, hard calculation in his eyes. Felt the way his fingers gripped, his thumbs pressing into her inner thighs. Her stomach churned. She'd met men like him before, men in jail.

Men who'd thought they could control any woman just because of the gender difference. They liked to hurt a woman, got a sexual thrill from it. They liked to force themselves on women and make them beg for what they really wanted. They turned her stomach. But none of them had left her as cold as this man did.

'You could be fun.'

Finding some last vestige of strength, she pushed Andy's hands away. 'I'll never be your fun.'

* * *

'This is ridiculous!'

Piper completely understood, but his phone was ringing and he needed to answer it. 'Tough. Now sit down and wait.' Giving Charlie no choice, he closed the interview room door and answered. 'Give me some good news.'

'Sorry.'

Not as sorry as Piper was when he heard what Siddig had to say. 'Nothing?' he repeated, blankly.

'No, sir. There obviously had been something there but the place was spotless. I could smell the bleach.'

Piper thanked her. If she could smell bleach at the address they had for Andrew Beamish, then it had to be a recent clean up. As hollow a victory as it was, that meant they were getting closer, narrowing the gap. 'Well there's nothing more you can do there tonight.'

'Not here no,' Siddig agreed with him, 'but I'll start looking into that other matter when I get home. See what I can unearth about Teddington's missing brother, Terrence Whittaker. I want to make a first run at it without using police resources.'

'That can wait. Get some rest and have a life.'

He was surprised how easy her laugh was. 'Maybe you don't get it, sir, but I want the Force to be my life.'

After they ended the call, Piper looked at his phone. He wasn't sure how he felt about a young woman thinking that way. *Oh, you're just getting old, you wouldn't even turn a hair if a man had said that.* Hoping that didn't make him a complete sexist pig, he headed over to see if the incident room had any news on Carlisle.

* * *

Teddington was quaking inside.

The way Andy had looked at her put a collection of personal horrors in her head that she wanted to ditch, but couldn't. To distance herself from that, she was having to distance herself from everything else.

Ignore the way Carol was trying to monopolise Andy.

Ignore the way Carol was glaring at her.

Ignore the way her heart was vibrating.

Vibrating?

You said vibrating.

There were times when she just wished the voice in her head would go away.

Vibrating!

It was annoying as the screaming of a phone.

Exactly.

Teddington tensed and blinked. She leant forward, resting her elbows on her knees she rested her head in her hands, starring at the floor. She'd put her phone on vibrate. Now someone was phoning her.

Please be Piper. Please be Piper. Please trace the call.

Find me.

* * *

Forcing his jaw to relax, Piper headed into the interview room. Broughton was bad enough, he didn't need the dirty looks from everyone else. As he walked into the room, he saw Charlie straighten from his slouch.

'What's happening?' Charlie demanded.

'Wheels are in motion to trace the phone,' Piper said as he sat opposite.

'Is this really necessary?' Charlie asked as he put his hands on the table. The cuffs clinked on the table top.

'Surprisingly enough, yes.' Charlie was the one wearing handcuffs, but Piper had run the gauntlet of resentment as he'd passed through the station. Several people wanted to know why such a traitor wasn't back in jail. 'Just be glad you're here voluntarily. Broughton wanted you arrested and there are a lot of people in this station who'd be happy to comply. You aren't exactly popular around here.' Piper sighed. 'So, okay, what is with you and Teddington?'

Charlie looked down at his hands. 'I love her.'

Piper had figured as much, but he wasn't letting Charlie off the hook that easily. 'You barely know her. You haven't even seen her in six months.'

'Nearer to eight months,' Charlie corrected. Then he sighed and shrugged. 'Not that it seems to make any difference.'

No, Piper thought, *probably wouldn't.* Three and a half years inside wouldn't teach either that much about the other, but it had been enough. They had worked well together before, the common ground, the shared experience bringing them closer together. Piper had seen the synchronicity between the two of them. There were similarities between them and enough differences to make it interesting. If Piper was in the matchmaking game, putting this pair together would be a no-brainer. Just look how well they'd worked together in that bank.

In that bank.

His most recent conversation with Broughton had not been a pleasant one. Driving to the station, Piper and Charlie had agreed their story. Charlie had told Broughton he'd passed the data to Piper in a phone call this morning, had re-joined the rest, only to be shot and left for dead. Charlie had even offered to stand in a line-up if Broughton wanted him to. That hadn't been part of the agreement, and Piper knew why he'd offered. Of course, Broughton did too, or at least he'd be able to surmise. When

Broughton insisted Charlie be arrested right then and there, he'd had to talk fast to prevent it.

'Does Teddington know how you feel about her?'

'Nope.'

Of course not. You idiot. 'Has she said or done anything to indicate her own feelings?'

'She said screws and cons shouldn't mix.'

Piper considered that. 'You're a free man now.'

'She said that too. She also said she wasn't sure if she'd be able to forgive me for today.'

Equally understandable. It was an impossible situation. Well, near impossible. 'Grovel,' Piper suggested. 'And then some.'

The unspoken fact that Charlie could only grovel if they found her alive stood over their shoulders like a spectre at the feast.

The door opened and Broughton strode in. He didn't greet either of them, but barked out his question. 'Were you in the Invicta Bank in Glenister Street this afternoon?'

'No.'

'Then we won't find any contradictory evidence to that fact,' Broughton said tightly, 'when we search your flat.'

'No.' Again there was no pause and Charlie had no problem returning Broughton's angry gaze.

Piper couldn't fault Charlie's confidence. There was nothing left in Charlie's flat—it was all sitting in two black bags in the back of his car.

'You'll need a search warrant first,' Piper pointed out. 'We don't really have time for such distractions.'

'Got one.'

'Here.' Charlie winced as he stood. Had to take a moment to push down the pain.

'You should be in hospital,' Piper said. The amount of bruising he'd seen could cover something worse. 'Your sternum could be fractured.'

'If it was, the way Doc Moore pressed it, he'd have broken it into pieces.'

Moving awkwardly because of the damage to his chest and the cuffs on his wrists, Charlie reached into his jeans pocket. 'Take my keys.' He threw them on the table. 'You want to waste your time, feel free, but for God's sake stop screwing with me and go save Teddington's life!'

Chapter 37

The phone wasn't ringing any more. But if the police knew it was on, they could still trace it. Or at least they could if all the conspiracy theories were even half right. She was in the middle of nowhere, so if the police could get any kind of signal, they'd be able to find the right building at least. Deciding to take that as a sign of hope—the cavalry was on its way—Teddington had to figure out how to survive in the meantime. Her ploy of winding the gang up against themselves was suddenly backfiring nicely. She should just have kept quiet and hoped they'd forget her. If her head wasn't already in her hands she'd have slapped herself. If she could affect her own escape, so much the better. Her eyes again slid to the pistol Mr White had dropped when he died.

For a moment she wondered who he'd been. Did he have someone who'd mourn his loss? She didn't—couldn't—know and didn't really care. She had someone who would mourn her, several someones, hopefully. But it was her mother who weighed most heavily on her mind. Her mother had lost a husband and a son; a daughter was all her mother had left. Teddington knew all too well what it was like to lose a daughter and she wouldn't wish that on anyone. And she wasn't going to cry over a dead scumbag.

She refocused her attention on the gun. She knew it wasn't firing blanks. Were there any bullets left?

How many had Mr White fired?

Two into the bank's ceiling and the one that shot Charlie. Three. She had no idea what type of gun it was, or what a standard magazine held. Old revolver guns like in Westerns held six bullets, so she'd guess more than that. How many more? Couldn't be that many, the grip wasn't that big. Maybe seven or eight. For caution, she'd assume seven and hope for more. That meant a minimum of four more bullets. Four bullets, four of them. She'd never fired a gun in her life, she was unlikely to be even vaguely accurate, but she couldn't miss from a few inches. Hopefully. There was still the matter of four of them and one of her. Outnumbered and outgunned. Her chances were slim, but slim was better than zero.

Looking across, she saw Carol still admiring the diamond necklace. No. Teddington looked closer—this was a different necklace, no pendants on this one.

'Why?' The question was spoken before Teddington had a chance to think about it.

'Why what?' Andy asked.

'I was wondering why your girlfriend likes diamond necklaces so much.'

'Why not?' Carol asked, coming around to stand closer. Holding the necklace in front of her. 'They're pretty. They're rich.'

Carol was focused on the necklace; the men behind her on the money. Clearly the spoils had been divided. It was now or never.

Teddington slid off the sofa, grabbed the gun. It felt cold and heavy. Awkward. She moved it into her grip. Carol was shouting, the men were moving. Teddington squeezed the trigger. Carol hit the floor.

Teddington stared, felt sick. *Oh God I've killed someone!*

The moment didn't last.

The men were shouting at her, Carol was screaming at them to shoot the bitch, Teddington was shouting for them to stay back. On her feet now, she held the gun two-handed away from her, neither her elbows nor her shoulders locked. Like she'd seen in the movies. Carol was holding her arm, the necklace still clasped between her fingers. She'd been winged. Some of the diamonds now looked like rubies.

The three men remained standing by the table, Andy to one side, Martin and the oriental man to the other. They were all pointing guns at her. Carol was on the floor, shouting.

'Shut up!' Andy screamed. 'All of you be quiet!'

Teddington was half surprised they obeyed, but they did. She moved carefully backwards. Once she'd got past the sofa, there was nothing in her way. All she'd have to do was head for the door, so long as she could keep them pinned down. She could make for the Caravelle. The keys were still in the ignition. She could get away.

'Nice move, Teddy-girl,' Andy spoke as she inched away. 'Smart, too. I should have got the gun out of your way.'

'Always have an out,' Teddington threw back at him. 'That's what you said. Well now I have one. Stay put.'

He'd started to move forward, but stopped. 'Or what?'

Teddington was struggling to believe that she was looking at a man over the sights of two guns—down hers, and up his. Not that either was particularly clear in her vision. How the hell had life come to this? 'Or I'll shoot.'

Andy smiled. 'You could barely hit Carol from less than a metre away. I doubt I'm in that much danger.'

'But you know I could get lucky, and if I do…' Teddington smiled, her peripheral vision telling her she was at the end of the sofa, she could start moving across soon, 'You're dead and you don't strike me as the wanting-to-be-dead type.'

Suddenly Andy stood straighter with his gun to his side. He made an odd movement with his hand. Teddington saw the other two men as she stepped to her left. Martin was moving towards her; she swung her aim. Something hit her thighs. She squeezed the trigger as she was forced back, tipping over the arm of the sofa. Her head punched into the dusty cushions. The gun skittered away, dropping from her surprised hands as she found her head and chest pinned to the sofa.

Shit. She should have seen it coming, Andy deliberately distracted her and pushed the sofa against her. Effectively trapping her. *Shit, shit, shit.*

Andy bunched his hand in her hair, pulling her more upright. She leaned up to avoid being scalped. The phone had slid uncomfortably down her corset, pressing her breast against her ribs. Andy pressing his gun up under her chin was more of a concern.

As she was brought to her feet, pushed against the wall, she focused on his eyes, expecting fury. The amusement she saw was more frightening.

'Did you really think that was going to work?'

She had, but obviously she'd fucked up. 'I live in hope.'

'Not for much longer.'

Teddington ignored Carol's grumble as the woman was helped to her feet.

'Andy, just kill her and let's get out of here.'

'You going to let her boss you about like that?' Teddington asked softly. 'Who's really in control here?'

The gun inched her chin higher.

'Not you.' Andy's words were growled before he turned his head to look at the men behind him. 'Go.'

Teddington looked past Andy's head to watch Martin and the other man grab bags from the table and head out towards the garage.

Shit, shit, shit!

Andy and Carol were obviously a couple, they'd be leaving together. She was just a loose end now. The cavalry wouldn't be arriving in time.

* * *

Charlie rubbed his wrists. He daren't rub his aching chest, it was too painful. He'd been checked out by the police doctor, but there was nothing worse than what he'd diagnosed himself. The guy had recommended painkillers, but stopped short of providing any.

Broughton had finally agreed to the cuffs being removed, but only if Charlie was escorted out of the station. Kicked out would have been a better phrase. He'd tried to reason with Piper, but even he'd pulled rank, as far as he could these days. Piper had also put Charlie in a panda car and told the PC not to stop till she reached Charlie's flat.

Now all Charlie could do was pace and worry.

Had they traced the phone?

Had they located it?

Did Teddington still have the phone on her when they left the bank?

He couldn't remember for the life of him. *The life of her*. His heart was doing twenty to the dozen. He ignored the fact that his flat had effectively been tossed by the search team. At least he'd got his keys back. Out of curiosity, he opened the drawer. The two hundred quid had gone. Too much temptation, apparently. Still, he hadn't been able to spend stolen money, anyway. If someone else could, he didn't care. He should tell Piper, just to highlight one scumbag in the service, but he didn't even a have a phone to call him any more. He slammed the drawer shut with too much force.

The bed in the next apartment groaned. It wasn't unusual. The next apartment was owned by a spaced-out woman making the rent by scoring any punter desperate enough to pay her. He heard the fake moaning and the headboard started to bounce against the wall.

Great.

So he was trapped here listening to the fake ecstasy of a prostitute, with no contact to the outside world. No way of knowing if Teddington was alive. His world was hanging in the balance and there was nothing he could do. This was worse than being in a prison cell. This was purgatory.

Chapter 38

'Will you just have done and kill her?'

Teddington ignored Carol as she looked at Andy. He was looking back at her, but all she could see in his eyes was her own reflection. She wasn't looking good. She wasn't feeling good either. Everything hurt, from the shin Carol had kicked, past the broken nose to the top of her head, which felt like it wanted to explode it was under so much pressure. That was definitely concussion. She knew she'd feel bad for a few days, if she lived that long.

The other two men were gone, along with two of the bags. The sound of an engine echoed down the stone corridor from the garage. Two engines, she counted. Probably the Caravelle and something a bit throatier than a car. That was a motorbike, she realised. Sounded like quite a powerful one too.

'Carol, get the bags.' Though he wasn't talking to her, he never looked away from Teddington.

'But there are thr—'

'Get the bags.'

Teddington could see his patience was running out. Carol on the other hand…

'My arm—'

'Just get the bloody bags!'

Carol was grumbling, but Andy's focus was back on Teddington.

'You sure you want her tagging along?' she asked softly as Carol, grumbling, did what she had been told.

'You offering better?'

'Could be.'

The pressure of the gun lowered, but she could still feel it at her neck. She wouldn't survive if that trigger was pulled now. 'Always had a thing for powerful men.' She licked her lips, tasted the blood on them.

They all heard the screech of tearing metal. Andy turned around, his fist still bunched in Teddington's hair. Through the unadorned windows they heard and saw a motorbike screaming past, a second and third was close behind, blue lights flashing.

Andy and Carol both swore.

'Kill her and let's get out of here.'

Andy was already forcing Teddington before him. 'No. We need her now more than ever.'

Teddington calculated the risks. One false move and her head was getting blown off. She could try a surprise attack, kick Andy off his feet, but right now, that was most likely to get her shot. The police were just outside. It was time to let them do their job. Andy said she was his shield, so for now that's just what she'd be.

'I really can't manage all the bags.'

Teddington turned her eyes towards Carol. The woman looked pale and her arm, which she held awkwardly, was still bleeding. The force of Andy's hold steered Teddington toward the table.

'If you want to keep your head, show me what a clever girl you are.'

'You won our last fight,' Teddington said carefully. 'I'm not rushing into another.'

She was forced to walk backwards as Andy told Carol to put a bag over his shoulder. The gun moved away from her neck. If there was a time to move it was now, but Teddington stayed compliant, still. Andy had her hair so tight, all she could do was stare at the ceiling. There was every sort of moulding up there, mildew too. This had once been a great house, but all things decayed, especially bodies once there's a bullet in them.

Finally, the tension at her scalp was released. She was able to tip her head forward more, see where she was going. She was made to lead the way back down to the garage.

'How the fuck did they find us?' Carol demanded.

'I don't know.'

Teddington did, but she wasn't about to say. It might not have been Piper but it had been the police. They had traced her phone. Andy was steering her through the house, back to the garage. She was surprised to see the Caravelle still where it had been left.

They didn't stop at the blue people carrier as she'd expected, but Andy took her past that to a classic car. Teddington didn't know what type of car it was—cars weren't her thing—but it was a sports convertible, top already down, which she thought was just patently stupid at this time of year. Carol scuttled around, plucked some keys off a hook and unlocked the car, opening the boot to stow all three bags.

'You're driving,' Andy told Teddington.

'I can't.'

'You can't drive?' Andy seemed surprised.

'Yes, I drive, but—'

'Then get in the bloody car!'

Fear shook through her. 'Concussion, remember?'

Fetid breath hissed close to her ear. 'Adrenalin junkie, remember?'

She held her hands up and away from her. 'Okay, but you'll need to let go of my hair so I can see what I'm doing.'

The grip tightened and Andy's face appeared at her ear. 'Just remember this gun'll be on you at all times.'

'Yes, Andy.' She hoped she sounded more submissive than she felt. 'I'll only do what you tell me.'

This time she felt his small laugh over her skin. 'You really are something, Ari.'

She forced herself not to judder when she felt his tongue on her ear.

'You could have been the best thing I ever stole.'

Taking it slowly, Teddington eased herself into the low driver's seat as Andy helped Carol into the cramped back seat, then got himself into the front passenger seat. Teddington wasn't in the least bit surprised when the pistol came up and pressed coldly into her temple.

Carol passed her the keys.

'Start the car.'

Teddington's hand was shaking, so it took two stabs to get the key in the ignition, but the car started first attempt. It purred as it idled. Andy opened the garage door remotely.

As the barrier went up, it revealed that the driveway ahead of them was being illuminated. Though from this angle it was impossible to see what with.

'Drive forward slowly, turning left,' Andy instructed.

Finding first was easy enough. She carefully depressed the accelerator and eased off the clutch. She didn't want to gun the engine, didn't want to spook anyone into firing at them. The clutch was smooth and bit gently. The car crept out of the garage to face the amassed lights of the police.

For a moment, Teddington blinked. Night had settled in but there were lights out there, headlights that blazed like suns. She shook her head and focused; it wasn't as easy as it should have been.

The driveway ahead of them had been choked with police vehicles. Even in the haze of her condition, she could see that there were various vehicles, some marked, some not. Some were cars, two vans and two more motorbikes blocked their exit. One car faced the way out—she saw it had been crumpled into a marked police car. The airbags had activated. That was the tearing they'd heard from inside. Both damaged vehicles were to one side of the driveway. She assumed the driver had been taken away. Whether it was Martin or the oriental man, she neither knew nor cared.

The sound of the opening garage door had caught their attention, now the police and the firearms team rifles were focused on them.

Teddington allowed the car to roll forward until they were within shouting distance of the line. She knew that the dashboard light would show up the gun at her head. Then one man stepped forward.

Piper.

Teddington focused on him. He wasn't the hero she wanted, but he was the only one she had. His suit was rumpled, his tie knot loose. He looked grim, drawn and tired from the day.

She knew how he felt.

If this was to be her last day on earth, she wanted it to be remembered. She wanted to be remembered, not just to fade away into the abyss of the unknown. It was bad enough her mother didn't know what happened to Terry; she didn't want to be another millstone.

Chapter 39

Charlie paced. The headboard was banging the wall again. But this was a different session, another punter. It made him sick to have to live next door to that. He'd looked through yesterday's paper again. Even spotted and circled an ad for a lodger. Anything had to be better than this.

He stuffed in hands in his pockets, his fingers encountering that watch again.

R and P.

Brothers.

He didn't know how that felt, being an only child. His only child was dead. His parents hadn't contacted him since before the trial. Not since he'd told them he was guilty and they had to stay away.

The only person he wanted in his life right now was in danger and he couldn't do anything about it. It was torture.

All relationships were a minefield.

'Fuck me, big daddy.'

Charlie glared at the wall through which he'd heard those words. Some families were worse than others. He thought about the watch. He thought about his inability to help Teddington. Things he could, things he couldn't do.

If this watch was something to do with the Mansel-Joneses then he had a potential in. If he had an in, he could do something. He wasn't sure what, but he had to do something.

Grabbing his coat, he headed for the door.

The one thing he knew about minefields—they could be blown apart.

Chapter 40

Piper stood before the massed force and looked at the silver three Series.

Charlie was out in the cold. Teddington had a gun to her head. He didn't want to think about how much worse today could get. All he had to lose was his career, and the way the rules were tying his hands these days, that might not be such a great loss.

Beamish shouted at them. 'Clear the way!'

Piper peered into the gloom. This time, Beamish's face matched that in their data, his make-up long gone. The brunette in the back was clearly Carol Freeman, but she looked quite different from the blonde in the bank.

'Mr Beam—'

'Now!' Beamish shouted. 'Or she dies.'

It wasn't that much of a threat. If he killed his driver, he wasn't going anywhere. On the other hand, Piper would have let a civilian die. He watched as Beamish pushed the pistol harder against Teddington's head, but she wasn't giving way. Her head was still upright. The other side of her forehead was raw, scabbed and swollen. That, he knew, she'd suffered when Carlisle saved her life. Even though she'd only hit her head on the arm of a chair, indications were that she was concussed. Concussion and driving didn't mix. He looked at her. The bruise on her left cheek was new, as was the dried blood on her top lip from her nose. He looked nowhere but at her. She looked directly back at him. She was calm. This wasn't a woman in fear, she'd gone way, way past fear. She blinked, then something changed. He saw her hands on the steering wheel flex.

Piper returned his gaze to the man with the gun. 'I can't do that.'

'Try harder!' Teddington yelled suddenly.

Piper looked at her. She was going to pull that one on him? Now? Her eyes didn't look right. With the amount of light on her, she should have been shielding her eyes, squinting at least. Beamish was, but she wasn't. Was this a result of concussion? It seemed likely. Everything about her appearance shouted beaten. But her eyes told of determination.

They had the guy from the van; they had the guy from the bike. He had Andrews in his ear asking for permission to fire. There were two risks if Andrews fired: Teddington could be hit in error, or Beamish could reflexively shoot Teddington.

Piper concentrated on Teddington. She wasn't beaten. She had a plan.

'No,' he muttered so Andrews could hear, 'move your men to look outside the wall. If they get out, take out the car tyres.' As he turned he moved his mike aside, and shouted the order. 'Clear the drive!'

It was obvious his colleagues didn't understand, but he wasn't worried about them. He was worried about Teddington. He didn't know what she was going to do, but she had a plan and he trusted her.

The vehicles were being started, moved aside. As one van reversed, the lights highlighted the solid stone wall and the column that flanked the open gateway.

Now there was only one thing in the way of the car and the exit. Him. Piper turned to face the car. The engine was revving, but the car was stationary. He had a momentary vision of American on-street drag racing. That car was going to speed past him.

He moved aside.

Teddington gunned it.

For a second the wheels spun, then she was shooting past, she was speeding down the drive. He realised that at that speed, she was never going to make the ninety-degree turn through the gate.

Dear God, she has no intention of turning outside the gates.

Twenty metres to go and she was doing maybe fifty, sixty.

At the last moment she swerved.

The impact reverberated through the ground and the air. He was drowned in a tsunami of sound, grinding tyres, buckling metal. Screams, and not all from the occupants of the car.

Crashing silence.

Even nature was stunned into holding its breath. No wind blew, no bird cried. No one moved.

Not from the car.

Piper was running. It was like a nightmare, the car never seemed to get any closer. Other people were there before him, checking out the passengers. Beamish was immobile, probably dead. Carol was groaning. Teddington had hit the stone wall about half and half. Her side was more protected, but still damaged and she was slumped over the wheel—not moving, and trapped in the wreck.

Chapter 41

Charlie had got only a few metres down the road when he heard someone call his name. At first, he didn't answer, he was determined to confront Mansel-Jones, offer him the watch, find a way to blow that bloody family apart.

The call was repeated. He turned around and saw the kind of top-end Mercedes that really didn't belong around here. He looked through the window that slid further down as the car reached him and saw Russell Towers. Charlie frowned. What was his barrister doing here?

'Mr Bell, would you get in the car please?'

'Why?'

'Well, mostly because I don't want to be on this street too long.'

The honesty and self-awareness of the man's smile echoed something in Charlie—his own wish to get out of the area, probably. What he had been planning to do had waited four years; it could wait a few minutes more. He reached out and opened the door. The soft leather seat felt like it was cuddling him as he sat. The car was beautifully warm as he shut the door and they moved away.

'No offence, Towers, but you don't make social visits to men like me. What's going on?'

Towers actually laughed. 'You might be surprised who I socialise with, but you're right, I'm not just dropping by. Detective Chief Inspector Piper called me. He said I was to take you back to the station.'

'Did he say why?'

'Superintendent Broughton wants to question you. He also said that Broughton was sending uniforms, so it would be better if you arrived voluntarily.'

There was sense to that. He just hoped it worked out.

'You know I can't afford so much as an hour of your time, don't you?'

Towers laughed genteelly. 'You know I have plenty of clients who can and do. Between them all, they cover your bills.'

Now Charlie nearly laughed. 'Is that legal?'

'I won't tell if you don't.' The man smiled as he drove. 'Besides, what you lack in financial rewards, you more than make up for in making-my-life-interesting rewards. Something that is usually, sadly, rather lacking in my other clients.'

'I'll take that as a compliment.'

Towers laughed again. 'You should.'

For a few minutes, they were silent. Charlie considered the man beside him. He always got the impression the barrister was actually a lot older than he looked. He also supposed that as a barrister, rather than a solicitor, Towers didn't actually get to spend a lot of time at the sharp end in the interrogation room.

'Did they tell you anything about Teddington?'

Towers glanced across to Bell. 'Teddington? Are you referring to Prison Officer Ariadne Teddington? What's she got to do with this?'

On the journey Charlie told him, surprised to find out that Towers hadn't heard about the raid because he'd been in court all afternoon and hadn't seen the news.

Now Charlie sat across from Broughton, Towers at his side. The DCS looked as happy as a bulldog chewing a nest of hornets. They'd gone through the motions of what was said to be a voluntary interview, even though it was being taped.

'Do you know the Invicta Bank on Glenister Street?'

Charlie frowned. 'Of course I do.'

'When were you last in the Invicta Bank?'

'Never, I'm with Santander.'

'So you weren't in the Invicta Bank today.'

'No.'

'Glenister Street?'

'No.' Charlie scowled across the table. 'We've been through this, why go through it again?'

'Let's go back to November 18th last year,' Broughton said far too evenly.

'Why? What's this about?'

Broughton ignored the question. Instead he went through all the details of Charlie being listed as an informant, and through details he'd given of the intended raid today.

'But you know all of this,' Charlie asserted. 'Why have you dragged me back to go over old ground?'

'What time did you leave Glenister Street?'

'Superintendent, I really must protest,' Towers cut across Broughton's continuance. 'You cannot keep pressing my client in this way. He's here voluntarily and has shown an obvious willingness to help you in any way he can, but he cannot give you details he does not have. However many times you ask the same question, the answer remains the same: Charlie Bell was not in the Invicta Bank on Glenister Street today. And you don't have a single shred of evidence to suggest he was.'

'Is that what the rest of the gang will say when I ask them?'

'You'll have to catch them first, Superintendent Broughton,' Towers pointed out. 'And even then, you have voice recordings where my client is threatened with being set up if he does not comply. Until you have actual evidence of any wrong-doing on my client's part, may I respectfully suggest you back off?'

Charlie watched Towers. He was totally reasonable and clear and level, but for the last moment, his voice had deepened and for a second the steel and the danger of his edge was clear. Charlie was oddly proud of the man.

'And perhaps you can also explain why there is, since your officers searched my client's home, two hundred pounds missing from his personal possessions?'

It was a first for Charlie to see Broughton look as if he was actually internally squirming.

'We only have his word the two hundred is missing.'

'At this point, that's enough.'

Broughton's eyes narrowed. 'Two hundred is a lot of money to keep lying around.'

'It's really not.'

It struck Charlie that this really could only have been said by the best paid man in the room.

'In fact, if I open my wallet now,' Towers went on, 'I suspect I'm carrying nearly that much in cash, just to have that much in cash on me.'

Broughton offered a tight smile. 'You having that much cash, I can understand. But him? In his job? Perhaps your client can explain why there was two hundred pounds in cash in his home to, allegedly, have been taken.'

Towers and Broughton turned to him.

'Emergency stash.'

'What for?'

Huffing out a sigh, Charlie tipped his head, hardly able to believe they were wasting time with this nonsense. 'Emergencies.'

'What emergency,' Broughton snarled, 'were you expecting?'

'I don't know.' Charlie's response dripped with sarcasm. 'That's why they're called emergencies.'

He received a warning look from Towers. He was pushing it a bit with the attitude. He almost wished he hadn't mentioned the money to Towers now. 'Look, I just kept back a little cash when I could to make sure I had a fallback in case something unexpected and expensive turned up. It's not like I've got good credit any more. I can't just whack a charge on a card and pay it off on payday any more. So I was building up a stash of—'

He cut himself off as DCI Piper walked into the room.

'Did you find Teddington?' Broughton asked.

Charlie was a little surprised. The DCS wasn't renowned for caring that much for people he didn't know. It was particularly peculiar when it was known that he wasn't impressed with anyone involved in last year's prison riot and its fallout.

'We did.'

'I'll let Sheldrake—'

Piper put his hand on Broughton's shoulder, kept him in the chair. Charlie's heart sank. Broughton's concern was about the rungs above him, but not Piper's. Piper's move didn't bode well. Looking tired and near his limit, Piper sat down next to Broughton and quietly told the other three men what had happened.

Charlie felt like the blood had washed out of him. He struggled to believe what he was hearing.

'She deliberately crashed the car?'

'Yes.'

A car crash that had killed Beamish and seen both Carol and Teddington rushed to hospital. According to Piper, it wasn't clear how they were at this point.

'That's either extremely brave or extremely stupid.' Towers' even, rational voice brought Charlie back to the present.

A present that he found was over twenty minutes later, when Piper's voice chimed into his consciousness, announcing the termination of the interview. He had obviously sat there like an idiot as the others had carried on talking.

'But aside from the established emotional connection between my client and Mrs Teddington, I have to point out that you have no reliable evidence to continue to hold my client, let alone accuse him of anything.'

Though he hadn't been arrested on returning to the station, Charlie was very glad of Towers' continuing efforts to ensure that he wasn't. Breaking the conditions of his parole was not in Charlie's interests. Charlie knew Towers, Piper and Broughton were still talking, but he wasn't listening. Teddington was hurt and it was his fault. Guilt hit like a sledge hammer. She'd said she wasn't sure she could forgive him and he realised he didn't deserve her forgiveness. He wasn't sure he could forgive himself. Every time their paths crossed, she got hurt. He had to stay away from her.

'Are you even listening?'

Broughton's sharp demand pulled Charlie's attention to him. 'Sorry, sir, I was thinking about Teddington.'

'And I was telling you to stay away from her. Understand?'

He swallowed. It wasn't what he wanted, but it was probably what Teddington needed. 'I understand.'

Chapter 42

Despite his exhaustion, Piper wasn't sleeping well, much to his wife's discontent. Every time he closed his eyes he saw Teddington driving into that wall, and the way she looked when she was brought out of that wreck. He'd made a call just before midnight to find out how everyone at the hospital was. It wasn't a great result. Lincoln, Beamish and Grimshaw dead; Freeman, Carlisle and Teddington severely injured, all in high-dependency care. Then there was Bell, who was probably in need of hospital treatment and not getting any. On the positive side, they had Carlos De Silva, the driver, and Martin Stubbs in custody, Bell had walked free, and Piper still had his job. He doubted his prospects had survived, but he could live with that. He was happy to be a DCI for the rest of his working life.

Walking into the observation room, Piper found Siddig reviewing the interview videos of De Silva and Stubbs. Neither had been overly helpful. They hadn't said much, but they'd each reacted to different pieces of data. Stubbs had spat feathers when he'd heard that Beamish had at least one other identity. De Silva had reacted, which was to say that the tension in his musculature increased, when he heard that the money had been intended for Mansel-Jones.

'He knows something.'

Piper looked at the image on the screen. The recording of De Silva's interview.

'But what does he know?'

'More than we do.'

'That wouldn't be difficult.'

Siddig nodded. 'The problem is with everyone else dead, and Bell having to stay quiet, we've got next to nothing on them.'

'We've got enough.'

'True,' Siddig allowed, 'but it doesn't solve our biggest problem.'

Piper dragged a breath in. No, it didn't, and he was beginning to think nothing would.

'I spoke to the forensic team when I first got in,' Siddig said after a moment. 'They're going to run Beamish's prints and DNA as a priority.'

'So we'll get the ID on a dead man.'

'Hopefully.' Siddig slowly turned to him. 'And that might lead us somewhere.'

'Or it might not.'

'Do we give up trying then, sir?'

He considered it. 'No.' He looked at her. 'That's just the bad news. Here's some good news. Carlisle has come round, the doctors are very positive for his recovery.' He watched her smile—it was good to see hope in anyone's eyes at the moment. 'And then there's this.' He held up a trifold of paper. 'I've got a warrant for Simon Lincoln's residence. Hold on.' Piper stopped her when she moved to stand. 'I want your help on this, but it has to stay under the radar. I need to log all this evidence back in and you need to get back to your day job. I'll brief you when I get back.'

* * *

The rules required that Piper waited while the TAC team went into Lincoln's house first and did the initial sweep to ensure it was empty. They'd given any occupant a chance to answer the door, but with no response after a full minute, they were cleared to break in.

Five minutes later, Andrews came back out. His usually expressionless face was twisted into a glower.

'Nothing.'

Piper frowned. 'Nothing? How can there be nothing?'

'It's been swept clean,' Andrews said on a sigh. 'There's some personal stuff, bank accounts, bills, the usual. But nothing that's not the usual stuff. At least not yet.'

'All being bagged and tagged?'

'All being bagged and tagged. But I wouldn't hold your breath.' Andrews looked back at the house. 'Whatever secrets Simon Lincoln was keeping, he took them to his grave.'

Chapter 43

'I don't understand.'

Piper wasn't overly surprised. He sat at Teddington's bedside. It was Friday. Teddington had regained consciousness the evening before, and at police request, she'd been placed in a single side room. He'd claimed consideration for her health and her mother's need to take care of her daughter as an excuse for telling the team not to interview her. The truth was he'd wanted to be the first to talk to her for very different reasons. She had suffered a broken leg, arm and two broken ribs—caused by the crash, not Grimshaw. The doctors said the only way to know if the skull fracture was caused by the knock against the chair or the way she head-butted the steering wheel in the crash was under autopsy, so they were all happy to leave that mystery unsolved.

What was clear was that the concussion was very real, and the reason she was still being kept in hospital. Now she had a surprisingly small scab on her forehead and facial skin in a variety of interesting colours.

'You want me to lie?'

Piper was uncomfortable with the word, but glad Teddington had kept her voice down even though the door was closed. He took a breath and tried again. 'I want you to say you didn't *see* Charlie in the bank.'

She looked down at her pale hands as they gripped and twisted together on top of the thin blankets. There was still a saline drip in her hand. She was chewing on her bottom lip and controlling her breathing carefully. Finally, she looked up at him. 'Mum said you visited her on Tuesday.'

Piper nodded.

'Thanks for doing that, taking care of her. She's been through enough.'

'You mean your brother?'

Now she nodded.

'That picture wasn't in the front room the last time I visited.'

'No.' She carefully exhaled. 'It used to sit upstairs on the landing, but because the frame is silver, it was taken by the lodger we made the mistake of letting into the house. She stole it and a load of other stuff. Now we have it back, Mum keeps it downstairs so she can't easily lose it again. That frame's so distinctive that when I saw it in the pawnbrokers I knew it was ours. I showed the guy inside a picture of Terry that I keep in my purse, and he held the frame back while I brought your lot in. When they finally decided to listen to me.'

As she spoke Piper felt his frown deepen. 'Finally?'

She nodded. 'I made several complaints about that bitch of a lodger, but they weren't that interested. I guess I didn't make friends last year.'

'I'm sorry about that. They shouldn't have treated you any differently than they'd have treated anyone else.' And he was going to chew the ear of whoever hadn't helped.

'I'm not sure they did,' she told him. 'I'm sorry, but…' she sighed and shook her head. 'It doesn't matter, it's sorted now. Anyway, how's Carlisle?'

The switch surprised him. 'He's okay,' Piper reported. 'He's still in a great deal of pain—he lost sections of his lung after all. But he's alive and getting stronger.'

'And he's agreed to this?'

'His statement has been that he didn't recognise any of the armed men that invaded the bank that day.'

She was frowning at him. 'So what's the official version of events?'

'Charlie provided all the details but was double-crossed and shot before anything started. Had he not been wearing a bulletproof vest, he wouldn't have survived.'

'Well at least that's true.'

He understood her cynicism. What he didn't understand was why she wasn't happier to know Charlie was alive. 'The story is that the bank job was done by five men who were heavily disguised and a sixth getaway driver. While visual identification of the perpetrators is impossible, their proximity to you, and now their own testimony puts them in the bank, except Carlos De Silva, the driver. We have evidence of Lincoln saying he'd set Charlie up, and that's what he did.'

'What about Mr Orange, Martin something?'

'Martin Stubbs? He was on the motorbike and sustained minor injuries when he was stopped, but nothing significant. Unfortunately.' He saw her slight smile at the unprofessional comment. 'Both him and Mr De Silva are swearing blind that Charlie was there.'

'Have to ask, I'm still not clear what he was doing there.'

'Charlie?'

'No, Martin Stubbs. He wasn't much use.'

Piper smiled. 'Not in your view perhaps, but if Presswick hadn't opened the safes, Stubbs would have cracked them.'

'Ah, that makes sense. Andrew Beamish said he always had an out. What about Carol? I suppose that bitch survived?'

'She did,' Piper said on a sigh. 'Actually, there's a bit of twist. Things are going back and forth like a bit of a tennis match with her. She originally claimed that she was nothing to do with the heist. Charlie states that she was the make-up artist that changed their appearances. Then she says she was forced into doing the make-up because she was afraid of Andrew Beamish. They were in an abusive relationship and she had to do what he told her.'

Teddington gave an odd look as she stared at her hands.

'What is it?'

'It probably was an abusive relationship. Andy said some things to me about liking beaten women.'

'Yeah, well,' Piper allowed, 'there's one of the major difficulties of abusive relationships, they're often too easily and too well covered up. There again, there's no evidence of Andrew Beamish actually existing.'

Teddington blinked at him, frowned briefly before putting her hand to her forehead; apparently the move pulled at her injury. 'Can you run that by me again?'

'Andrew Beamish was a false name. No one seems to know him, or have heard of him, except Carol and that's the only name she has for him. We've come up blank on fingerprints, and the DNA is being checked, but since the guy is dead, it's not high on anyone's agenda.'

'And that's it? That's all the information you have on the man?'

Piper nodded. 'Pretty much. We have an incident record that records his name as Neil Grey, but that's all at the moment.'

'Well he said he always had an out, I suppose not existing is the best out of them all.'

Piper had to agree with that.

'So you've got eyewitness reports that can't be trusted because we know make-up was used. The testimony of two surviving men which can be countered by recorded evidence that Lincoln was going to set Charlie up anyway. And you have a convicted murderer who says he was shot in a warehouse in the morning, while the others say that happened in the afternoon. The evidence can support the shooting; what about the timing? What about the testimony from the doctor who examined Charlie's chest?'

'Charlie hasn't exactly got many friends on the Force, and that includes the particular medic who checked him over. That's why the guy wouldn't prescribe painkillers even though he could, and why he didn't take a timestamp of the bruising. He was just happy to know Charlie was in pain.'

'Jesus, I get that cops don't like the idea of a rotten one, but that seems over the top.'

'Charlie was a bright star in his time. People respected him. Possibly hero-worshipped him. His betrayal was bad enough, but after Sheldrake's campaign, and what happened last year…'

'Rubbed salt into the wound?'

'For most, yeah. For others he ripped it open and bundled a load of nettles in.' He was relieved that she understood at least a little of what was going on.

She was nodding and biting her lower lip. 'I might just have a bit of seasoning to add to that.'

Now Piper was worried, the pain in his stomach burning again. 'Why?'

'It's one of the things Beamish said, before I got concussed, he mentioned me wearing a wire during the prison riot. As far as I was aware, that little snippet is known only to the police.'

Piper took a breath. *Have to tell Siddig that.* 'I'll look into it.'

'So what do you need me to lie for?' she asked. 'Is it Charlie's identity and the timing of the shooting?'

Piper tilted his head. 'That and the time you were pulled into the manager's room.'

'Of course.'

'I'll need to take an official statement, but that can wait.'

'You can take it now if you like,' she offered. 'I didn't see Charlie Bell inside the bank, and in that office nothing much happened. I was just kept separate, I don't know why. Maybe it was a plot to set someone up.'

Piper nodded, but she wasn't looking at him any more. 'Thank you. So, what happened to the last man?'

She looked from her hands to the man sitting beside her. 'I don't know.'

'Ari—'

'Chief Inspector,' she cut him off and she looked more like the Officer Teddington he had first met when he walked into HMP Blackmarch—strong, honest and dependable. In many ways, formidable. 'I suffered a head injury during the raid and I sustained a concussion. I even fell before I reached the van, though I'm not sure anyone who survived can testify to that.'

Piper didn't tell her that the snipers had already made statements to that effect.

'By the time I was actually bundled into the van, everything was hazy. I don't actually remember the move from one van to another, I don't know what happened to the other man. I just don't know.'

That was as good as they could hope for. 'You know you will be a key witness at the trial?'

She nodded, though only once; her head was still apparently delicate. 'Naturally, but I can't tell them what I can't remember. In fact, I'll be sure to attend court in a sombre suit with my hair pinned in a tight bun. I've been told I look rather intimidating like that.'

He smiled. 'I suspect you do.'

Her look chastised him.

'In the nicest possible way, of course.'

'Of course.'

Now they were both smiling like laughter wasn't a million miles away.

He took a breath. 'I also have to ask, why did you crash the car?'

She blinked and licked her lips. 'By that point I was physically broken, but my spirit wasn't. Though it had been touch-and-go on that front for a while too. I felt sick and I knew Beamish wasn't averse to a casual kill. Then I thought I'd rather go out with a bang than with a whimper. I wasn't going to fade away to nothing, the way Terry sort of did. I wanted to live, and even if I didn't, I wanted my mother to know I died trying.'

'She'd be proud of you. Well, she is proud of you.' Nothing new had turned up on Terrence Whittaker yet, so he wasn't going to tell her he'd reopened the case.

Teddington smiled. 'She said she'd seen you since. I bet she bent your ear a bit.'

Piper nodded. 'In the nicest possible way of course.'

Watching him, Teddington suddenly lost her smile. 'Am I going to face charges for killing Beamish?'

'No.' He reached out and squeezed her hand. 'Ariadne, you did what you had to, in self-defence. No one in their right mind would prosecute or convict you.' For a moment she squeezed his hand back. 'I'm glad you're okay.' He clocked her odd look. 'That you'll *be* okay.'

'Thanks.' Her smile was wan and short-lived. 'How is Charlie?'

'Bruised, but recovering. He's pissed off to have to live under suspicion again.'

'But he hasn't been arrested, has he?'

He shook his head and sat back. 'Thankfully no.' He got the impression she was as relieved as he was at the news. 'And he managed to keep his job.' Charlie wasn't the only one experiencing that particular relief.

'They didn't have any reason to sack him, did they?'

Piper made a face. 'Well he admits some involvement, and despite his injuries he officially only had the two days off work he'd booked as annual leave. He's back at work, so there's not a lot they can do unless they want to claim he's shirking the heavy-duty stuff.'

'Is that likely?'

Piper shrugged. 'I hope not. He's desperate to get out of his bedsit. He wants to see you, but Broughton has ordered him to stay away, at least until a clear determination can be made as to whether or not he'll be charged with anything.'

'What's that going to take?'

'Your statement and a CPS review.'

She nodded once, but didn't look happy. 'Send someone tomorrow, I'll give a full statement.'

For a moment or two he simply watched her looking at her hands. Again they were twisting in her lap, the same habit her mother had displayed. She seemed a little lost.

'Do you want me to leave?'

She looked up, as if she was going to give a distinct answer, but thought better of it and instead just shrugged. 'I don't want to keep you from your job.'

It wasn't that much of a bother; he still *had* his job, just about, but this was his day off. 'I've nothing urgent to get back to.'

She offered that weak smile again.

'Can I ask you something personal?'

'Can I slap you if it's too personal?'

'You want to be arrested for assaulting a police officer?'

She offered a small laugh. 'Not really. What's the question?'

'Are you in love with Charlie Bell?'

'Wow.' She looked away. 'That is a personal question.'

And one she wasn't answering. Then she dragged a breath in and looked at Piper. 'Yes.'

He smiled. 'Good.'

'No, it's bad. Very bad.' She laughed at herself. 'Loving him isn't the problem. Trusting him and being anywhere near him, that's the problem. I really thought he was dead, Matt. It felt like he was gone. I grieved for him until I heard he was still alive this morning.' She blinked and there were tears on her lashes. 'And it hurt so much. I keep losing people I love and I'm not sure I can go through that again.'

Piper suspected this was just a moment of weakness; she was feeling especially vulnerable, but she'd recover, as would her courage. 'Do you want to see him again? Talk to him?'

She sucked on her bottom lip and took her time to answer. 'No.'

Chapter 44

Two weeks passed before Piper received an odd message.

Reaching the Archive Rooms, he found PC Siddig already there. He moved closer and she indicated that he should sit at one of the thin tables put there for research purposes. She sat opposite. She didn't look happy.

'Have you found something on Terrence Whittaker?'

She swallowed. 'No. I wish I had, sir, this is the about the other matter.'

'Okay, what have you got?'

'I've traced the root of the names Andrew Beamish and Neil Grey. They both died as young children. Beamish was the son of Angela Beamish, she worked in a brothel in Hagar Street, got arrested several times for soliciting. The boy died of an accidental cocaine overdose. Mother had left it lying around while she was with another John, and the boy, not knowing what it was lapped it up. That was twenty-two years ago. Neil Grey was the twin of Jerry Grey. Jerry started out as a pickpocket in his early teens and went on to various petty crimes. He's got a long list of arrests and charges. Jerry claims in several interviews that he wished he had disappeared when he was seven like Neil did. Says that he should have been murdered instead of Neil. Jerry claims that if he had died, his mother might have loved him. He was sure Neil wouldn't have turned out as bad as he, Jerry, did. Neil went missing twenty-one years ago.'

Piper's phone was ringing, he checked the number and answered. 'Whatever this is Charlie, make it quick.' Piper looked at Siddig and apologised silently. 'Good… Okay… Yeah, just stay in touch.' He rang off.

'Something up?'

Piper looked up and smiled. 'Actually no. For the first time since getting out of prison, Charlie actually sounded positive. He's got a new job, and he gets to move in a couple of weeks. He's making a new life for himself.' He frowned. 'And one that doesn't include Ariadne Teddington.'

Now Siddig was frowning. 'That's good isn't it? Teddington doesn't want to see him. He's making a life without her. All good.'

Piper made a non-committal noise.

Siddig inclined her head and scrutinised Piper. A smile spread slowly across her face. 'Oh my God, you're an old romantic. You were hoping for a happy ending.'

Raising his head, he glowered at her. 'Happy endings are for books. Now Jerry Grey and his twaddle. Typical delusional self-pity. How does any of what you said actually help us?'

'Well, I looked into that, and into some of the other cases from a similar time frame till now, particularly the unsolved ones.'

'I'm assuming from this conversation that you found something.'

She swallowed again. 'I believe I have.'

He watched her shift uncomfortably and check the room around them. She was obviously nervous. 'Why am I getting the feeling that I'm not going to like this?'

'Because you're not. These kids died around the same time that Terry Whittaker went missing. But the problem comes much later, in that none of these cases has ever really been thoroughly investigated, never reopened. We never even got a name on Beamish's client. Look, I've checked all the records, spoken to a few of the officers who were involved. It's not there in black and white, but the same thing comes up in all the conversations. The same name.'

This time she licked her lips. His gut was knotting, his hand slipped to the indigestion tablets in his pocket. He was relying on these more and more often, he really had to go see the quack.

'Okay, enough foreplay, give me the name. Who's the mole?'

'Dominic Carlisle.'

THE END

Acknowledgements

While writing is a solitary profession, never, ever think that a writer is alone in their work. And there are a few people I need to thank with this one.

Police procedure is always a tricky one and I have to admit that there were a few times in this book that I played fast and loose with the rules for dramatic effect. That said, I am very glad to have had confirmation of some of the CHIS procedures from Dorian Lloyd of the South Wales Police. For the rest I apologise to all serving officers, the exacting standards and procedures you have to follow are great in real life - not so much fun to read.

I'd like to thank my editors. Thanks Sam, for the reading the first very rough draft and telling me what was and wasn't working so I could do more of one and sort out the other. To Tony, for keeping the structure in place and pointing out the dropped plot. And to Clare for making me polish the manuscript further. Similarly, thanks to Betsy and the cover designer for getting the cover sorted when the first offering didn't fit what was in my head.

And of course, thanks to all the friends and family who have supported me when I faltered, steered me in the right direction when I was going wrong and picked up the slack because I was busy writing.

Lightning Source UK Ltd.
Milton Keynes UK
UKOW01f0126130218
317792UK00001B/113/P

9 781912 175932